A Good Year

A Good Year for the Roses

Amanda J Field

CHAPLIN BOOKS

www.chaplinbooks.co.uk

First published in 2020 by Chaplin Books

Copyright © Amanda J Field

ISBN 978-1-911105-55-8

Printed by Imprint Digital

Chaplin Books
5 Carlton Way
Gosport PO12 1LN
Tel: 023 9252 9020

www.chaplinbooks.co.uk

Chapter One

As the last plaintive notes of the pedal steel guitar died away, Derek lifted the needle off the record and carefully lowered it again at the beginning of the track.

"Not again, Derek!" said Wendy, hands on hips. "How many more times?"

"I've got to learn the words by Friday," he said, reasonably, not looking up from the record player. He fiddled with the volume knob.

"You must surely know them by now. I'm already singing them in my sleep," said Wendy. "Maybe I should get up there and perform it instead of you. I could be the next Tammy Wynette."

She went out to the kitchen, pointedly closing the door behind her, and he heard, above the song's chorus, the sound of the kettle being filled and the wail of the baby. He concentrated on the song, listening to the way the notes were bent, the slight break in the voice at the emotional climax of the chorus.

Immediately the door clicked shut, Bobby – who was wearing only a rather grubby Dallas Cowboys T-shirt and a nappy, lurched over to the door and tried to reach up for the handle. He was scooped up by Sharon and taken back – unprotesting – to the settee, where he resumed repeatedly thumping an Action Man figure against the dralon cushion. It was Georgie's Action Man, but Georgie didn't seem to notice, absorbed as he was in trying to rewind a cassette tape spool by sticking a biro into one of the holes at the centre. Sharon distracted Bobby by pressing the eject button of the portable cassette player so that the tape loader sprang open. As Bobby reached for it, she expertly whisked the

Action Man away and gave it back to Georgie, who sat on it to prevent further theft. Bobby looked bewildered, conscious that he'd been cheated in some way, but unsure how.

Sharon was going through a Little Mother phase and had appointed herself the minder of her three younger brothers and sisters. Sometimes when Derek saw her going off down the road with her friends from school, each with a wicker basket dangling from their elbow, they looked more like a gaggle of middle-aged gossipy housewives than a bunch of ten-year-old girls. It did take a bit of pressure off Wendy, though as soon as Sharon discovered boys, she would doubtless not want to spend her time looking after the little ones any more.

"I can't get this to work, Dad," said Georgie, flicking back the long dark fringe out of his eyes. "The tape's still all twisted up."

Derek reluctantly took the record off the turntable, closed the lid of the player and put the record back into its sleeve. The picture on the front showed George Jones (after whom Georgie had been named) against a black background. A spotlight picked out George and shone on the blond surface of his guitar with its ornate fingerplate and inlaid fretboard. He was looking straight at the camera, smiling slightly, and with a sincere expression in his dark brown eyes. The title of the album was written in red lettering against the dark background. Derek ran his fingers along the title, then put the record back on the shelf alongside his other George Jones albums and turned his attention to his son.

"I think all we can do is to throw that cassette in the bin," he said, looking at the loop of twisted, creased tape.

'Oh, Dad – no!"

"Why? What was on it?"

"T-Rex. I taped it off the radio. It took me ages."

"Well, it's a goner now. What about this one?" He picked up another tape off the table.

"I don't want that. It's that woman."

"Jessie?"

"I don't like her," said Georgie. "If that tape had got ruined, I'd have been pleased."

"She's got a good voice, you know. People come and see the band because of her."

"I still don't like her. Her teeth are too big."

Derek laughed.

"Don't laugh at me, Dad. They frighten me, her teeth."

Derek ruffled Georgie's hair and headed out to the kitchen.

Georgie inserted the tape marked 'Jessie' into the player and pressed the record button, erasing Jessie's voice and replacing it with the sound of Sharon singing a nursery rhyme to Bobby and of his father whistling as he laid the table for tea.

*

The sun was just breaking through a bank of hazy cloud when Chalky dropped Derek at the strawberry stall. He kept the engine of the Morris Oxford running while they unloaded the crates from the boot, stacking them at the back of the layby by the grass verge. Derek took the buckets of cut flowers from the seat-wells. One bucket of tulips had tipped over, soaking the carpet. He tried to mop up the water with his handkerchief.

"There's your float money," said Chalky, handing him a small drawstring bag. "I don't finish until six today, but I should be here well before half past. Do you need a hand wheeling the stall over, nipper? Only I'm a bit pushed for time and this new foreman at the mill is a stickler."

"No, it's fine," said Derek. "You get off."

"Has Alan said anything to you yet about this new bass player?" said Chalky, opening the driver's door.

"Only that he's coming to rehearsal on Thursday."

"Well, I just hope he's better than that nutcase we auditioned last week. A good steady player, that's what we need, not a heavy metal merchant."

He got in the car and drove off. Derek sat down on the curb and lit a cigarette, unwilling to get the working day underway just yet. He was amused that his brother even knew what heavy metal was. Ten years older than Derek, Chalky had old-fashioned ideas about how the band should sound and whenever they suggested that he use sticks rather than brushes on the drums, he reminded them that it had only been five years ago that the Grand Ole Opry had permitted a drum-kit on the stage ... and what was good enough for the Grand Ole Opry was good enough for him. Rumour had it that bands playing the Ryman before that had to hide their drummer behind a curtain – and anyway, only a snare drum was allowed. Chalky still wore his hair slicked back in 1950s style and on stage he wore a red shirt buttoned to the neck, with one of those black bootlace ties topped by a small horse-head emblem. The movements of his arms when he used the brushes made it look like he was stirring a pudding.

Derek stubbed out his cigarette and looked across the road to the edge of the Bere Forest. Only an occasional car passed by, a flash of colour against the dark green of the trees. Once when he'd been standing here in the early morning, a deer had emerged from the trees and had stood stock-still, gazing across at him.

Up the road, the pub was stacking empty barrels on the forecourt, ready for the brewery truck to collect. Derek got up and went over to the stall, removing the chain that locked it to the fence and taking the chocks out from behind the wheels. He got behind the end of the stall, putting his back to it and walking backwards to push it off the grass. It stuck and he wished he'd asked Chalky to help after all. Then suddenly it shot forward and he had to steady it as it ran onto the tarmac.

It only took five minutes for him to position it, open the flap and arrange the strawberries along the counter. The buckets of flowers he placed on the ground at the front. He grabbed the A-frame board and walked with it to the end of the layby, close to the road. The board had a big picture of a strawberry on it - painted by Chalky's late missus – and some writing underneath. Derek didn't know what it said, exactly, but it brought the punters in.

He raised a hand in greeting as the pub landlord shouted 'morning, Derek!' and went back to the stall, stowing the bag of change under the counter. He felt the monotony of the day sinking into him already. Ten hours to go.

*

Gerry finished his coffee from the machine and threw the plastic cup into the bin, grimacing at the foul after-taste.

"See you later at the burger van!" he said to the room in general. "First one there buys the extra mushrooms."

The other cabbies looked up, but no-one said anything. They continued to huddle around the ashtray on the table, staring at it despondently as if it were a religious icon that had failed to work the miracle they had been expecting.

'Miserable buggers,' thought Gerry as he shrugged on his car-coat – the one with the fake sheepskin lining – and pushed at the swing doors. Outside in the lobby, the air was instantly fresher and Gerry congratulated himself, as he did every day, for never having taken up smoking. His dad had favoured cigars – big fat ones that he thought made him look like a swell, but had actually made him look like he really was: a bit of a wide boy. Perhaps that had been what had put Gerry off in the first place. His dad had wanted him to take over the market stall in Charlotte Street and Gerry had helped him out on school holidays but never really liked it. All those pinched-faced people turning over the merchandise, prodding it contemptuously and then behaving like they were doing you a favour when they finally bought something. Besides, Gerry was more interested in cars – it stood to reason that he would become a driver.

Through the windows of the lobby he could see a group of youths clustered around his cab, which was parked on the double yellow line outside.

"Oi!" he shouted as he emerged onto the street, giving a quick thumbs-up to Ginny, the despatcher, on the way. The youths looked up and Gerry realised he knew one of them. They were younger than he'd thought at first glance, and probably just hanging around because they were bored. He

6struggled to remember the lad's name but couldn't bring it to mind.

"All right, kiddo?" he said. "How's your mum?"

A big grin appeared on the boy's face, lighting up his pale, thin features.

"Aw right, Gerry?"

Pleasantries duly exchanged, the lads moved off and Gerry got into the cab. The radio sprang into life immediately with a call for him to pick up in Milton. He could see Ginny through the office window as she was speaking and she gave him a wave. He wouldn't turn Ginny out of his bed, he thought – not for the first time. She was a redhead with a curvy figure and a taste for short skirts. She also had a boyfriend who was an amateur boxer, so Gerry sensibly kept his distance.

The traffic through Fratton was a nightmare, so he cut through to a familiar rat-run and was at the Milton pick-up in less then ten minutes. There was no sign of the customer, so he got out of the cab and knocked on the front door. There was no response, though he could hear a dog barking somewhere at the back of the house. He was just about to get back in the cab, cursing, when the next-door neighbour emerged, a fat party with dyed blonde hair.

"Taxi's been and gone," she said.

"What do you mean?"

"Your lot have already picked her up, five minutes ago."

"Thanks, love," said Gerry, mentally downgrading Ginny from someone he'd like to take to bed to someone who couldn't organise a piss-up in a brewery.

*

Alan counted them in and the band swung into *Wildwood Flower*, Alan's Fender Telecaster sounding clean and crisp. The new bass player, despite his appearance ("He's a HAIRY!" Chalky had exclaimed in horror as he saw Pete arriving for his audition) laid down a nice solid line, turning to smile at Chalky.

Alan moved forward to the microphone:

"Howdy, everyone and welcome to Friday Night is Country Night. We're the Smith & Wesson Band and will be entertaining you right through until eleven o'clock. Will you pleased give a warm Bricklayers' Arms welcome to Miss Jessie Smith and Mr Hank Wesson."

Chalky did as much of a drum roll as is possible with brushes on a snare drum, and Derek – now in his 'Hank' persona – and Jessie strode onto the stage to a burst of applause. They went straight into the George Jones and Tammy Wynette number *We Go Together*. The dance floor filled up immediately, many of the customers wearing Western shirts and boots and a few of the men sporting Stetsons.

Derek usually liked singing *We Go Together* but found it particularly irritating tonight – Jessie had been a real pain from the minute they'd arrived at the gig, so singing about moon-and-june and having to gaze at her lovingly was a bit of an effort. The evening hadn't started well, anyway. Wendy had forgotten to iron his shirt – the black one with the pearl buttons – so Alan and the others had had to wait in the van while she got it ready. Then when they'd got to the Bricklayers', Alan said that – not for the first time – they'd been billed as the 'Smith & Western Band' and he'd railed on about what 'ignorant peasants' the organisers were. Derek couldn't really see the difference. Then for some reason Jessie had made a fuss at the soundcheck, claiming that Derek deliberately asked for her microphone to be at a lower volume than his and that he was always trying to upstage her. The real reason was that Jessie always bawled into the microphone at the top of her voice, so they had to turn down the volume to avoid feedback. Derek went outside for a cigarette while she calmed down. It had been a slow day at the stall and he was feeling edgy – once the gig was underway he'd known he would be fine. He tuned his guitar: just putting the guitar on made him feel better. It was a blond Hofner twin-pickup semi-acoustic – a nice old one that he'd found in a secondhand shop in Southampton; he'd got someone to embellish the wide black leather strap with his name in silver down the front. The action was a bit high

7

and by the end of a gig, his fingers were sore, but he'd never want to part with it.

When Jessie had emerged from the dressing room – which doubled as the pub's storeroom – she had been in an undiminished foul mood. This time, it had appeared that her suede fringed jacket had a small stain on the sleeve, which she had made worse by rubbing it. She'd been frustrated because there had been no-one she could reasonably blame for this, not even Derek. The new bass player, Pete – whose hair stuck out in a frizz around his head and who looked as if he should be playing in Deep Purple rather than a country band – was unused to Jessie's attention-seeking ways, and therefore had fussed around her, trying to help. Derek had wanted to tell Pete that this wasn't a good idea, not least because Jessie's husband – who accompanied her to every gig – was the possessive, jealous sort, but instead he had avoided the commotion by escaping to the gents' toilet, checking his reflection in the mirror, making a minute adjustment to the angle of his Stetson, and adopting an expression that he'd hoped was like the one George Jones had on the album cover, so that he could inhabit the persona of 'Hank' rather than 'Derek'. Unlike Jones, however, Derek's face was thin, his eyes were dark but looked small in his face and his lips were narrow. In fact, he could have passed for Hank Williams, which is why Alan had suggested the name for him in the first place. Jessie, on the other hand, was larger than life: taller than Derek, well-built with a mass of blonde hair. A big voice and, as Georgie had accurately pointed out, big teeth.

At the break, Alan tried to persuade Derek to do the new number – *A Good Year for the Roses* – in the second set, but Derek was anxious about it because he didn't feel ready. When they'd run through it at rehearsal, he'd been distracted by Alan's harmony in the chorus and wandered off the tune.

"OK – let's get back on stage," said Alan, picking up his unfinished pint. "Where's Pete got to?"

He scanned the room, spotting Pete at a corner table surrounded by four giggling girls, one of whom was wearing hot pants and a check shirt and had her hand on Pete's leg.

"I think we're going to have trouble with Pete," said Alan, grinning.

"You know he only drinks whisky?" said Derek. "Neat, no ice."

"Expensive trouble, in that case."

The rest of the gig went well. Derek didn't even mind too much when Jessie sang *The Deepening Snow*, possibly the most maudlin, sentimental claptrap he'd ever come across, about a woman looking out the window at the grave of her husband and praying to the Lord to make the winter pass quickly so her 'darling' wouldn't have to lie there in the deepening snow. Jessie even affected a tear or two at the end of the song. You had to admire her really, he acknowledged.

Outside, by the van, Alan shared out the money – four pounds each – and they headed for home, Derek travelling in the van with Alan and Pete. When they passed the group of girls that he'd been chatting up, Pete wound down the window and banged on the side of the van. Derek and Alan exchanged a look.

As they neared Wickham, Derek felt his Hank persona begin to dissipate. He wondered whether George Jones always felt himself to be 'George Jones' or whether there was another person behind the stage act, a secret person. One thing for sure: Jones didn't have to spend ten hours a day minding a strawberry stall. And he certainly didn't have to go home to a wife and four kids all crammed into a council house that was too small for them and wonder how on earth he'd have enough money to pay the bills.

"Are you still up for cutting this EP?" asked Alan as they drew up outside the house, having dropped off Pete. "If we pooled our money from the next four gigs, we could get the studio at Eastleigh for a day and have an engineer to do the mixing. Then we'd sell the EP at our gigs."

"No money for the next four gigs?"

"It's OK, Derek. I can lend you something to tide you over."

"Thanks, Alan. I appreciate that. You know I'll pay you back as soon as I can."

"Of course," said Alan, knowing that Derek would do no such thing but also knowing that the Smith & Wesson Band would be nothing without him. "I'll fix it up, in that case. We'll have to have a chat with the others about which songs to include."

"That'll be an interesting discussion!"

*

Driving into the car park where the burger van was set up, Gerry noticed another four Double-A cabs had already arrived, and there was a huddle around the van, some drivers already holding steaming cups of tea. Pat, the owner, had the griddle full of burgers and was flipping an egg over when Gerry approached and placed his order.

"Did you hear the one about the naked woman who hailed a cab at 2am?" said Gerry, grinning in anticipation of getting an audience for the joke he'd heard the night before.

"Not now, Gerry," said one of the group. "We've got serious things to discuss here."

"I can tell you now – Pompey are never going to win against Arsenal so there's no point in you discussing it."

"Shut up, Gerry. Why do you have to make a joke of everything?"

"Why? What's going on?"

"Sabotage, that's what."

"Eh?"

"Someone is sabotaging our business."

Each cabbie had a story to tell about how they'd got to a pick-up, only to find another taxi had already collected the customer.

"That happened to me, too," said Gerry, relating the incident of the Milton pick-up and feeling guilty at having immediately blamed Ginny. "Who's behind it, do you think? Not Alf Barnett's lot, surely?"

"No, Alf would never do a thing like that," said Lenny, an older driver who'd been in the business for years. He rubbed at the stubble on his chin. "This'll be some new start-up, wanting to muscle in."

"Anyone given us a name?"

"No – to the punters, it's just a taxi, isn't it? They can't tell one bloody firm from another. It's probably some Paki firm."

"Oh, for goodness sake, Lenny. Grow up!"

"Well it might be," said Lenny, looking a little shamefaced.

"Or it might not. Tell you what - maybe Ginny could tell customers to make sure it's a Double-A cab that shows up before they get into it."

"We could give it a try," said Lenny, "but I don't hold out any hope that it'll work."

*

The next morning, when Gerry ran down the stairs from the flat to start his shift, he found the windscreen of his taxi smashed. Glass was all over the front seat, but nothing had been taken – even the two-way radio and the meter were still there – and there was no sign of what had been used to smash the screen. No other car had been touched. Gerry's bedroom overlooked the parking bays, but he hadn't heard a thing, probably because he'd sat up late watching *Kojak* over a few stiff brandies and then gone to sleep the moment his head touched the pillow.

"Bloody kids!" he said. They were always roaming around the estate, looking for trouble, out and about long after they should have been home in bed. Their dads were mostly absent, and if they were around, they were feckless; and the mothers … well, don't get him started on the mothers …

He used the radio to contact Ginny.

"Hello, gorgeous," he said. "I've decided to spend the day in bed. Want to come and join me?"

"Gerry, you're incorrigible."

"I know. Seriously, though, I can't come in for a while. Some idiot's smashed my windscreen. I'll have to take it to be repaired, so I'm guessing it'll be around eleven o'clock before I can start."

"You too?" said Ginny, sounding disbelieving.

"What do you mean – 'me too'?"

"You're the third driver this morning."

"Tell me you're kidding."

"I wish I was. Harry and Roger – they've both had the same thing. We've had to turn away a dozen customers already this morning. I've told Big Bertha. She's on the case."

Big Bertha was the owner of the Double-A. In an earlier age, they'd have referred to her as a 'Pompey Brute'. Five feet tall in her best shoes, she was built like a wrestler and had a face and voice to match. She was stern with the drivers, and wouldn't stand for any nonsense, but was well respected because she ran a tight ship and was very picky about who she employed. She'd taken over the business when her husband – a meek soul who crept around the place like he was the tea-boy rather than the proprietor – died from a heart-attack. In a sense, she'd always been in charge and the drivers liked it that way. Gerry felt a pang of pity for whoever was targeting the Double-A because Bertha would definitely track them down, and they'd definitely wish they'd never been born.

"She says you're to stay away from it – you and the rest of the drivers. She'll deal with it herself."

Chapter Two

Jessie was adamant. If there were going to be four tracks on the EP, then she would be singing two of them. She said this very emphatically to Derek, who – anxious to avoid an argument – said that it was up to Alan which tracks they would record. Her husband decided he would be the one to tackle Alan about it. He droned on, going over and over the same point, despite the fact that Alan kept nodding sympathetically, agreeing that it was only fair. Expecting an argument, the husband was somewhat nonplussed.

"But what about a duet?" Alan asked. "Does that count as a track by Jessie or a track by Derek?"

This seemed to throw the husband into a further state of confusion and he retreated to consult with Jessie. Eventually, Alan got everyone to agree that they would record *A Good Year for the Roses* and *When the Grass Grows Over Me*, both numbers sung by Derek; and that Jessie would sing *Blanket on the Ground* plus a duet with Derek on *Somethin' to Brag About*. Jessie seemed pleased with the result, even though she'd actually given way on the duet idea.

"He a master of diplomacy," said Chalky the following Saturday, as he assembled the high-hat on his kit. "I don't know how he does it. He gets exactly what he wants and never seems to upset anyone."

"Remember that gig at Titchfield?" said Derek. He moved out of the way to allow Pete to wheel the Marshall amp onto the stage. "It was before Alan joined us – we were using that nipper Jason as a stand-in after the big row with Charlie."

"That was quite a night!" Chalky gave a 'whoop' and Derek laughed.

"What's all this?" asked Pete, walking over with a lead he was uncoiling.

"You should have seen it!" said Chalky. "There we are, in this working-men's club – bit of a dive, really - and the place is packed. Jason has brought some of his family with him, and they're sitting at a table near the front. His wife only looked about fifteen, but she was a pretty girl. Blonde hair. It's all going fine until Jason suddenly takes his guitar off – right in the middle of his solo on Rocky Top – and leapt off the stage. Apparently, some bloke has come up and put his arm round Jason's wife. Jason clobbers him, they both fall to the floor, and before we know it, everyone in the place is fighting. It's like a scene from a Western – people were throwing chairs, the barman was ducking down behind the bar …"

"And we were still playing!" said Derek.

"We didn't know what else to do," said Chalky. "Besides, there was no escape from the stage so we figured we were safest staying there. After about ten minutes, the fighting stops, everyone sits down again and Jason climbs back on stage, his shirt all torn. He just picks up his guitar and carries on."

"Brilliant," said Pete. "Sometimes I look over at Alan when he's playing, and he's so laid-back he might well be asleep. He actually has his eyes shut when he's playing a solo. OK – time for the sound-check, I believe."

He tapped his microphone and adjusted its angle, before giving a few loud experimental riffs on the bass. A couple of punters looked up, their expressions doubtful, at the long-haired spectacle before them, dressed in trousers whose flare was so wide that it entirely covered his shoes. Chalky gave a couple of tentative kicks on the bass-drum pedal and rapped the edge of the snare drum. Jessie appeared, asking – as usual - for her microphone to be turned up, and Pete pretended to make the necessary adjustment.

"I'm glad we got this fill-in gig," he said. "Who was supposed to be on tonight?"

"A band called Silvertown, apparently," said Derek, adjusting his guitar strap. "They called in to say their lead singer had gone sick, so their agent put us in instead. Nice to be able to help out. I've always liked the Docks & Labour Club crowd and we've not played here for ages."

"Where's Alan, anyway?" asked Chalky, scanning the room.

"Gone to see the Big Man. Ah – here he is!"

Alan, with a face like thunder, was marching through the club's double doors towards the stage. He trotted up the steps.

"Council of war, gentlemen!" he said. "And Jessie, of course."

They huddled round.

"I just saw the entertainments secretary to confirm that we'd need cash at the end of the evening, not a cheque, and he queried the amount. I told him that's what we'd been booked at, and he said 'just because you've brought that woman with you this time, you want more money'. I asked him what on earth he was talking about, and he said that last time we played here, we were a four-piece and we'd done it for £30. Now we were asking £40."

"I thought that's what they were going to pay Silvertown anyway?" asked Chalky.

"Exactly. And, no, we didn't have Jessie with us eighteen months ago when we were here, but that's hardly relevant. Jesus Christ – I thought we were doing them a favour, bailing them out like this on a Saturday night!"

"So, did you win the argument?"

"No," said Alan. "He's refusing to budge. Says it's £30 or we can go home."

"Let's go home, in that case," said Pete, unstrapping his bass and putting it back on its stand. He folded his arms and stared out at the crowded club.

"Fighting talk, Pete! What does everyone else think?"

"'That woman'? Is that really what he called me?" asked Jessie. Her husband had come anxiously towards the stage, sensing a problem. "I think I'll go and have a little word with him, in that case."

"Or *you* could go home, Jessie, and we'll do the gig as a four-piece," said Pete, trying to look serious but hardly able to get the words out without laughing.

She cuffed him on the arm. "Less of your cheek, newcomer. Now where do I find this so-called entertainments secretary?"

"Best not, Jessie. If we all agree, then we'll just pack up and go," said Alan.

They all nodded.

"Just one thing before you unplug the PA, though." He strode up to the microphone. "Ladies and gentlemen, we're very sorry that you will be spending your Saturday night without any live music. We stepped in at the last minute when Silvertown were unable to make it, but unfortunately your committee is refusing to pay us the money that Silvertown would have received. So we're going home. Thank you and goodnight."

The punters looked bewildered, as well they might, as Alan joined the rest of the band in packing up all the gear they'd spent the last forty-five minutes assembling.

"Laid back, eh?" said Pete to Derek, sotto voce. "I think our Alan might be a smoldering volcano under his calm exterior."

The entertainments secretary was notably absent as they carried the gear through the lobby and back out to the van.

"Not too early for a take-away curry and chips, is it, lads?" said Chalky.

"Too right it's not!" said Alan. He jumped in the van. "Get a move on!" he shouted out of the driver's window at Derek, who was still smoking a cigarette.

Derek hurriedly stubbed it out and got into the passenger seat next to Pete. Alan shoved the gearstick into reverse and put his foot on the accelerator. There was a sickening crunching noise. He quickly pulled on the handbrake, glanced across at Pete and leapt out.

Hearing Alan's cry of "I don't believe it!", Derek and Pete joined him at the rear of the van.

"What complete idiot left that there?"

All three of them knew the answer to that question.

There, trapped under the rear wheels, was Derek's black guitar case containing what remained of his beloved Hofner.

*

Gerry had no intention of 'staying away from it'. It was his car, his earnings, that were being damaged and he intended to sort it. If he could beat Big Bertha to it, then all the better – maybe then he'd be respected by the other blokes instead of being thought of as the joker in the pack. Gerry didn't know how he'd got this reputation: it was all a front. Deep down, he was solitary and miserable. His ex-wife didn't want to know about getting back together and now had found herself yet another new boyfriend; he never saw his kid; he spent his days and nights driving his scuddy Ford Scorpio for equally scuddy customers; he was developing a paunch; and his flat looked like the typical bachelor pad with telly, sofa, piled-up menus from takeaways, a stack of well-thumbed lads' magazines and not much else. Even having a pint in the evenings had somehow lost its savour.

He felt the loneliness most keenly when he had to do an airport run. In the back of the cab would be a couple full of excitement and anticipation at going on holiday: they'd be keen to tell him where they were going (somewhere warm and sunny), what a great deal they'd got (all-inclusive), and how she (it was always the woman) had gone shopping for a new set of clothes to wear. They'd fuss about the passports and check for the fifteenth time whether they'd got the tickets. He'd drop them off at Gatwick, unload their suitcases, and then head back to grimy Portsmouth where it would either be unseasonably chilly, or so scorching that the metal of the car door was hot enough to burn his arm as he rested it on the open window. He knew that going on holiday was not a glamorous or relaxing business at all; that their flight would probably be delayed; the hotel would be disappointing; the nightly entertainment dire; and that they'd probably be stuck with some boring couple from Scunthorpe for the entire week, with the husband droning on about trains or the state of the economy. It was the idea of the holiday that Gerry craved, not the reality. He supposed he could go on his own, perhaps on one of those 18-30 singles holidays. He might just about pass for thirty when the light was behind him. What was a year or two either way?

A thought struck him about how to find out who was sabotaging the Double-A. He could get someone he knew to book a cab, then they could tell him who turned up first. The difficulty was that whoever was doing this was pretty cunning – they didn't steal every booking; the blokes reckoned it was about one in ten. So his plan might take a while to work, and it might be rather expensive too, because to make it look legitimate, the person would have to actually take the taxi for the booked journey each time. And who could he trust to do it and keep their mouth shut? A picture came into his mind of the young boy who'd been hanging around his taxi with his friends. He still couldn't remember the lad's name, or that of his mother, but he knew where they lived. In the meantime, he'd drop off the car at the repair place, then knock on a few doors around the estate and find out if anyone had seen the windscreen being smashed.

*

It was a busy day on the stall, helped by the fine weather, and by mid-afternoon Derek had almost sold out of strawberries. A number of regulars had dropped by – they liked to chat and it made the hours pass a little quicker. He'd even been able to ask one of them to look after the stall for a few minutes while he ran up the road to the pub to buy a packet of crisps. He'd had a quick half of lager while he was there. The packed lunch that Wendy did for him wouldn't have fed a mouse, to be honest: he'd eaten his sandwiches by eleven o'clock and was still hungry. He could have had some strawberries, of course, but when you spent your life selling the wretched things, you didn't exactly feel like eating any.

When he got back to the stall, Roy and Anne had turned

up. He knew them from the gigs but had never seen them at the stall before. Roy was a big bear of a man who drove a Ford Granada with a Confederate flag draped over the dashboard. They liked to dress up for the C&W nights at the Bricklayers' Arms and were fond of a dance called the 'slosh', an elaborate dance done in lines that took up most of the dance-floor. Derek was faintly embarrassed at being on the stall – and at being 'Derek' instead of 'Hank' – but if Roy and Anne were surprised to see him there, they certainly didn't show it. Roy explained he was on a day off work – he worked for the railway at Eastleigh – and they'd decided to go for a picnic in the Bere Forest. He proudly showed Derek an old wind-up gramophone stowed in the boot of the car.

"No electricity needed – see?" he said, unveiling half-a-dozen 78rpm records. "Take a look at this little vintage collection."

Derek politely leafed through the records, then muttered something about not having his glasses with him.

"No problem, Hank. Let's see - we've got Tennessee Ernie Ford, Hank Williams, Bill Monroe, Patsy Cline, Jimmy Rodgers … I can play one for you now, if you'd like."

"That would be great, Roy."

"What would you like to hear?"

"A bit of Tennessee Ernie would go down well."

"Right you are, then, mush."

Anne leant into the boot of the car and wound up the player, while Derek tried not to stare at her legs and bottom in their tight denim jeans. She put the record on. It was *Sixteen Tons*. 'The story of my life,' thought Derek. 'Another day older and deeper in debt.'

When the record ended, Anne asked Derek if he'd ever been to Nashville.

"No," he said, smiling at the mental image of himself at the airport, trailing Wendy, Sharon, Bobby, Georgie and the baby along behind him.

"Well, we're going in six weeks' time," said Anne, "with the BCMA, the British Country Music Association. We're so excited. You ought to come, Hank. See the Grand Ole Opry and all that. Stand on the stage where George Jones performs."

Derek shook his head. "It's a nice thought, Anne." He felt a bitter stab of jealousy but dispelled it by laughing. "As a matter of fact, I don't even have a passport at the moment." Or ever, he thought.

"Perhaps another year, then. Anyway, we'll bring our photos to show you when we get back, now we know where you work. Besides, we'll see you on Saturday at the Ponderosa, won't we?"

"Yes – see you there. I'm doing a new George Jones number on Saturday, by the way: *Good Year for the Roses*. It's going to be on our new EP too."

"I love that song," she said. "Don't you, Roy? It makes me cry."

"It was written by Jerry Chesnut, wasn't it?" said Roy who was a walking catalogue of artists, composers, studios and dates. "Best thing he's ever done, in my view. Tops *Four in the Morning* by a mile."

They put the records away, folding them into a blanket as if they were tucking up a precious baby, and drove off, waving. Roy tooted the horn and it proved to be one of those musical ones. Derek winced, but gave them a cheery wave anyway.

Nashville. How he longed to go there and how impossible an idea it was.

*

The maisonette where the young lad lived with his mother was in a cul-de-sac just off the main road through Milton. It was in one of those prefabricated blocks that had been all the rage ten years ago, presumably because they were quick and cheap for the council to build, but were now starting to look a bit run-down and neglected. The rain had stained the frontage, the outside staircase was notched and scuffed and there were rust marks under each balcony. The shell of the blocks was concrete and they had been lowered from a crane, one on top of the other, a bit like putting Lego together. Gerry remembered watching the builders.

As he sat there, looking up at the net-curtained window of the top maisonette, the name came to him: Darren. He got out of the car and ran up the stairs to the front door.

*

The scene at the Railway Club had been embarrassing and Derek was ashamed that he hadn't handled it better. They'd set up to play in the function room at The Swan, but wouldn't be needed until after the dinner, so Alan had suggested they could catch the first set by a new band who were playing just down the road. Chalky and Jessie said they would stay behind and look after the gear, so Alan, Pete and Derek headed along the main road to the Railway Club. It was one of their regular venues and the man on the door recognised Alan straight away and shook his hand.

"Listen to that guitar!" said Alan as the sound of a lightning-fast solo drifted through the door of the hall into the lobby. "They say he's made a neck out of a piece of wood and rubber bands, and takes it to work with him every day to practise his fingering for hours and hours."

He quickly signed the visitors' book and rushed through the door into the hall, not waiting for Derek and Pete. Derek began to sweat as Pete moved forward to the desk.

"Just your name and address and signature here, please," said the doorman, handing Pete the pen. "I've not seen you before, have I? You new to the band?"

"Yes, just joined. Bass," said Pete, playing an imaginary guitar as if the man wouldn't know what he meant otherwise. He finished writing and moved aside for Derek, setting the pen down on the visitors' book.

Derek couldn't think of any way out of the situation and found himself saying: "Well, I'm not new. You knows me – why on earth would I need to sign in?"

"It's just CIU rules, Derek – I've got to do it by the book."

"Well, I'm not doing it. You can stuff your stupid club

rules and your stupid club too. I'm out of here."

He turned and pushed his way past four people who were queuing behind him and went back out into the street, leaving the doorman open-mouthed. Pete stood for a moment, irresolute, then followed Derek outside, muttering an apology.

Derek was hurrying away along the pavement, hands shoved in his pockets, and Pete trotted to catch up with him. He put a hand on Derek's arm.

"Derek, mate – don't rush off."

"Bloody jobsworths. I hates them," he said viciously, pulling out his cigarettes and dropping one on the pavement.

"It's the poxy club's rules, that's all. Come on back – let's find Alan. We can still catch half an hour of the first set. You know you were keen to hear them."

"Well, I'm not keen now. You go back if you want. I don't know why Alan didn't wait for us in the lobby – rushing off like that like some bloody teenage groupie."

Behind Derek were the lighted windows of a Rumbelow's shop. About twenty televisions were on display, all showing David Frost interviewing someone Pete didn't recognise, some in colour, others in black-and-white, all giving off a flickering light. Pete looked closely at Derek as he lit his cigarette, his hand shaking slightly.

"You can't read or write, can you, Derek?" he said softly, turning to gaze into the window so that Derek wouldn't need to meet his eye.

Derek was silent for a moment, debating how to reply. He barely knew Pete and had no idea whether he could be trusted.

"I never did learn," he said, eventually, and as he spoke he could feel his rage ebbing away. "Truth is, I never really went to school." He risked a glance at Pete, but Pete was looking in the shop window and all Derek could see was his hair and the tip of his nose. "Most of the time it's not a problem. Alan looks after me – Chalky too, of course."

"But not tonight," said Pete.

"No."

Pete scuffed the toe of his shoe against the front step of

the shop, waiting for Derek to continue but he said nothing more.

"Does Jessie know?" asked Pete.

"No. Just Alan and Chalky – and now you. You won't tell Jessie, will you?"

"Of course not."

Two young girls with long blonde hair and short skirts walked past them on the pavement and Pete wolf-whistled. They giggled and hurried away.

"Know why I learned to play guitar?"

"Tell me," said Pete, looking directly at Derek now.

"Remember that song about Johnny B Goode? How he never learned to read and write so well, but he could play guitar just like a ringing bell? That's how I seen myself. Except I never could play like that, like Alan do – just rhythm, that's all."

"Rhythm guitar is the backbone of a band, so don't run yourself down. What about reading? You could still learn."

"No, I'm too stupid to learn it now." He stubbed out his cigarette.

Pete laughed. "Stupid? So says the man who learns all his song words from the record, and who can sing like George Jones? Who can make grown men cry when they hear his voice? I don't think so."

Derek tried to laugh but it turned into a cough.

"We ought to get back to The Swan," he said. "We're on in twenty minutes."

They started to walk. "I could teach you if you wanted," said Pete.

"Nah, I tried that. My sister tried a few years ago. I know she meant well, but all she had was some Janet & John books. Kids' books. It made me so angry, a man having to read kids' books." He thought that might have sounded ungracious, so he added: "Thanks for offering though."

"I was thinking that we might start to read that new Johnny Cash book."

"Johnny Cash?" said Derek. He stopped walking. "Now there's an interesting man."

"It's his life story. Looks a pretty easy read to me."

"You read a lot?"

"All the time."

"I suppose you went to grammar school and all that."

"Boarding school, actually."

"Your parents posh, then?"

"No – my father taught there, so they didn't have to pay the full whack. I hated it, to be honest. How come you never went to school?"

"We was travelling all the time when I was growing up."

"But Chalky learned to read?"

"Yeah – me dad had a small-holding when Chalky was a nipper. They lived on the site. Time I came along, they was back on the road."

In the distance, they could see Alan hurrying along towards them, looking at his watch and speeding up in a clumsy trot.

"So?" said Pete. "What do you think?"

"OK, then. But you've got to promise not to tell no-one."

"I promise."

Chapter Three

Darren was just the age that Gerry had been when he started getting into trouble. Except that Gerry had had a mother and a father at home, and Darren only had his mum. Plus he was thin and pinched-looking and he had a couple of big gaps in his mouth where teeth had fallen out, probably from existing on a diet of beefburgers, chips and sweets, whereas Gerry had been solidly built and even as a thirteen-year-old, had been able to see off kids older than himself. It had started with the usual stuff – stealing from shops, the odd bit of vandalism when they were bored. And they were always bored. Throwing stones at windows of abandoned houses, tearing down the fence panels that bordered the park, or running off with a 'diversion' sign that the road-menders had put up. Then, when they were bored with that, it seemed a natural progression to gang up on the old man who lived in the next street. He was probably only in his thirties, looking back on it, but everyone over about seventeen seemed old to them. The man was a big, shambling figure with wild hair who lived with his sister. He'd had a stroke and was unable to speak, so he uttered what – to Gerry and his mates – were frightening, animal-like noises in an attempt to communicate. They'd lie in wait for him when he shuffled to the corner shop to buy tobacco and would taunt him, pretending to be apes, scratching their armpits with both hands and making 'hoo-hoo' sounds. The first time they did it, the man wept and Gerry was ashamed, but as leader of their gang, he didn't feel he could back down, so they did it again and again. They even knocked his stick away once.

It got worse. By the time he was fifteen, he'd been in court three times – first for theft, then for criminal damage, and finally for assault. The last charge (the judge had called him a 'delinquent' and Gerry hadn't known whether to feel proud or guilty) brought a spell in juvenile detention. Suddenly, he wasn't the biggest boy, the strongest leader, but just the new kid who was there for one reason only: to be exploited by the 'old lags' of sixteen. The pecking order was already firmly established and the new kid was always at the bottom. It was three hellish months, the only slight relief coming when another boy became the 'new kid' and Gerry moved one rung up the bullying ladder.

His parents had been furious with him and refused to visit, though they'd taken little notice of Gerry for years before that, his dad and mum always busy with the market stall. They never had time to enquire where Gerry was going after school or who his friends were. After he'd got out from detention, vowing never to go back ('that's what they all say,' said his dad, cynically) Gerry spent every spare moment working on the stall, saving every penny and hating every moment. What changed his life was leaving school and getting his first car on his seventeenth birthday. His dad might not have been talking to him any more, but he did grudgingly say that if Gerry saved up his money, he'd match it. The reward had been an old Ford Anglia. You could see the road through the rust in the chassis, but Gerry had got a mate to spray it bright orange – and he'd loved the angle of that back window. Cars would be his future: it was crystal clear to him the moment he was handed the car-keys.

What would life be like for Darren, he wondered. He just couldn't picture a future for the lad any more than he could picture his own boy's future, a boy he barely knew any more and whose role as father had been replaced first by an ever-changing series of 'uncles' and now by a salesman in a suit who thought money bought you class.

At that point, the door opened and there was Darren's mum. She was wearing denim jeans and a red T-shirt with holes in it. Her feet were bare. She looked tired; the kind of tiredness that even a month's sleep would be inadequate to fix. She frowned as she saw Gerry.

"What're you doing here? I never ordered a taxi."

"No, I know – I just wanted to ask you something. You and Darren."

She passed her hand through her hair as if suddenly conscious that it was greasy and needed washing. Still blocking the entrance to the hall she yelled over her shoulder. "Darren! Get here!"

Gerry suddenly felt a bit nervous about what he'd come to ask, but Darren bounced out of a room at the rear, and his face lit up when he saw Gerry. He pushed his way under his mum's arm so that he was standing on the doormat.

"Give me five!" said Gerry, raising his hand. Darren high-fived him and laughed.

"Ain't you gonna ask Gerry in, mum?"

"Sorry – yes. Come in," she said. "Sorry about the mess – I was just about to clean up when you knocked."

Gerry accepted this for the lie it was. They crammed into the tiny kitchen, which had a view over the bins at the back of the maisonettes. Two kids were kicking a football around the yard, shouting and swearing in a way they'd clearly copied from footballers they'd seen on the telly. The kitchen sink was full of dirty dishes and there were crumbs all over the work surface.

"Cup of tea, Gerry?"

"That would be great – thanks."

Darren's mum put the kettle on and opened the fridge. It was empty apart from a bottle of Coke and a half-empty bottle of milk.

"So what's this all about?"

"I've got a bit of a problem at work, and I need Darren's help to sort it."

His mum made a scoffing sound. "Darren? What use could he possibly be?"

"Well, I need your help too, but for Darren it's kind of a detective job."

"A detective job!" said Darren excitedly. "You mean like Sherlock Holmes?"

"Well, sort of," said Gerry. He explained the problem

with the taxi firm that was stealing their bookings. "It would be a case of you phoning us to book a taxi every couple of days for a short journey – say, down to Commercial Road. You could give a different name each time so they don't twig. I'd reimburse you for the fare, and Darren can be the eyes and ears. If a firm turns up that's not the Double-A, then you take the taxi as normal – except Darren writes down the registration number and a description of the driver and passes it to me. As soon as we've got that, you're off the hook."

"No, I don't think we can help you with that, Gerry," said Darren's mum. "I've got enough on my plate as it is."

"Oh, please mum! Please!"

Gerry got his wallet out of his trouser pocket and withdrew a fat wad of fivers. Darren's mum stared transfixed at the money and he knew he'd won.

*

Derek was having a hard time explaining to Wendy about the money – or, rather, the lack of it, what with having to put by his band earnings to pay for the EP recording, and now probably having to save for a new guitar.

"Wasn't it insured?" she asked, knowing the answer already. She jiggled the baby, Lor, on her hip. The baby kept reaching for a strand of Wendy's hair and pulling it.

"Yes, it was."

Wendy pulled a disbelieving face.

"All our gear is insured – problem is, will they pay out because we ran it over with the van? Or will they say we were negergent?"

"Negligent."

"Whatever. Anyway, it's not about the money – I loved that guitar."

"What are you going to do in the meantime?"

"Alan's lending me a spare until the insurance company coughs up."

"Alan treats you like his kid brother, if you ask me. Which is more than Chalky ever has done."

"That's not really fair, Wendy. Without Chalky, I couldn't get to the strawberry stall."

"True, but somehow there's always a price to pay for Chalky's help, isn't there? He never lets you forget it when he's done you a favour – it's like he keeps a little list."

The door to the living room opened and Sharon came in wearing her school uniform but with her skirt rolled up at the waistband so that the hem only reached halfway down her thighs. Bobby was clinging to her shin.

"Mum," she said, going over to take Lor off her. "I need one pound fifty tomorrow to pay for the school trip to Salisbury."

"Tomorrow?" said Wendy. "That's a bit sudden – why didn't you tell me before? I didn't even know you were going on any school trip."

"Forgot."

"And I hope you've not been to school with your skirt rolled up like that."

"Everyone doos it."

"'Does it'," said Wendy, automatically.

Sharon caught sight of the guitar case that her father was fiddling with and stared. It had a large tyre-mark across it and despite the fact that the Hofner was still in the case, it was crushed down to about half an inch in width. "What's that, Dad? What happened?"

"Don't change the subject," said Wendy. "We're talking about your skirt and what a sight you look."

"We only rolls 'em up on the way home," said Sharon in a plaintive tone.

"I should hope so too. You're ten years old, for heaven's sake. You can have your money for tomorrow, but make sure you give me more notice in future."

Sharon unhooked Bobby from her leg and bent over the guitar case. Derek unzipped it to show her the remains of the guitar. She leaned over and touched the jagged break in the fretboard, which was snapped almost in half. Broken strings curled out and made a discordant twanging sound as she moved her hand away.

"You see, we have other things to pay for without

forking out for you gadding about in Salisbury," said Wendy.

As Sharon was about to stand up straight again, Derek grabbed her wrist.

"Wait a minute, Sharon," he said, looking her in the face. "Have you been smoking? You have, haven't you? I can smell it on you."

"No, course not. I sat on the top deck of the bus, that's all. Loads of people were smoking. It makes your clothes smell."

"Why is it that I don't believe you?"

"Let go, Dad – you're hurting me."

Derek let go and Sharon flounced off with the baby. They heard her feet thundering up the stairs and the slam of her bedroom door.

Wendy sighed. "You need to stand up to her, Derek, or she'll walk all over you. Anyway, she's supposed to be doing her homework now, not playing with the baby."

"I'll go up and see her in a minute. Do you want a hand with the tea?"

"In a minute. Georgie's in the kitchen. He's supposed to be doing an art project for school so I said he could use the kitchen table for an hour. You back on a full day at the stall tomorrow?"

"Yep. In fact, I'll be late home. Pete is picking me up after work instead of Chalky."

Wendy raised an eyebrow.

"Just a little band discussion. Won't take long."

*

Two things were worrying Gerry. The first was the fear that Big Bertha would find out that he'd been doing a little snooping of his own. He knew Darren's mum wouldn't blab about it, but Ginny might be suspicious that she was booking taxis more frequently than she usually did. But how could they trace it back to him? No, that seemed pretty safe. The second was that handing over £50 to her all in one go now seemed like a terrible mistake. He had no idea whether she was on drugs, or just looked thin and sallow because she was depressed and run down. Perhaps she'd blow the lot on a few bags of heroin. He sighed. It was stupid worrying about it: it was done now.

He looked at his watch: 1am. Time to get back in the cab. He threw his coffee cup into the overflowing bin and got up from the table. He hated working the late-night shift. All the customers were loud, drunk and argumentative. Half of them didn't want to pay, and that included the sailors going back to their base. Last week, three of them had legged it through the gate of HMS Vernon and the stupid guard on the gate made no attempt to stop them – he'd stopped Gerry instead. As Gerry put on his car-coat, the front door of the taxi office burst open and Lenny staggered in, holding a blood-soaked handkerchief to his bald head. He lumbered over to the table and sat down.

"Bloody hell, Lenny – what's happened to you?"

"Been clobbered, ain't I?"

Gerry mentally resolved never to say yes to a late-night shift again. He persuaded Lenny to move his hand away from his head. It was a narrow but deep cut and the area around it was beginning to swell up. He grabbed a pile of clean tissues and got Lenny to press them to the cut, then went to tell Dave, the night-time dispatcher.

"I'm taking you to A&E," said Gerry.

"Nah – I'll be fine."

"Don't be daft. It's a head-wound. You might be concussed. Anyway, it's still bleeding like buggery. You sure you were clobbered, not stabbed?"

"Yeah."

"So, what happened?"

"Punter got out the cab in Eastney. I went round the back to get his bag out of the boot and when I turned around, suddenly there was this other bloke leaning in the driver's door with my cash-box in his hand. I moved towards him and he struck me over the head with it."

"And then legged it, presumably?"

"I'm a bit confused about what happened then, to be honest, Gerry. I fell to the ground by the cab. The punter was just standing there with his mouth open – couldn't believe what was happening. The other guy vanished, but I'm sure I heard a car start up, so maybe he had an accomplice. I don't know. I don't even know how I managed to drive back here, bleeding like a stuck pig."

"How much money was in the box?"

"That's the funny thing, mate. I found the box - it had just been thrown down onto the ground by the cab. So he didn't get a penny."

Gerry felt himself go cold inside. This hadn't been a robbery. This was all part of the sabotage campaign. A feeling of nausea overcame him when he thought of Darren and his mum. What had he exposed them to?

"Just gotta go for a slash, Lenny, then I'll drive you to the hospital."

In the Gents, he threw up in the wash basin.

*

Derek had packed away the stall and was waiting in the layby by the time Pete arrived. He put the unsold crate of strawberries in the boot and they drove off with a spray of gravel.

"Sorry I was a bit late," said Pete.

"That's no problem," said Derek, glancing at the unaccustomed sight of Pete in a suit and tie. Around his neck was a lanyard with a laminated badge at the end of it, bearing Pete's photo. "Where is it that you work?"

"Council," said Pete. He clearly wasn't going to add anything else, so Derek didn't ask. Pete put an eight-track cassette into the player and they drove with Pete singing along to T-Rex.

"My nipper likes this music," said Derek. "Mad about it."

In Shedfield, Pete swung the car into a drive between some imposing gateposts with stone pineapples on top of them. When they'd dropped Pete here after gigs, Derek had assumed that the drive led to flats, or a small estate of houses, and was astonished to find that it was a single house

– a vast Victorian-looking pile in red brick with lots of pointy bits and with stone steps leading up to the front door. Gables – that's what the pointy bits were, Derek recalled.

"Blimey, Pete."

Pete grinned. "I do have to share it with my parents. Not that they're here at the moment, so we've got the place to ourselves. They've taken a school class on a trip to the Lake District."

He led Derek into the hall, which had coloured quarry tiles on the floor, topped with faded and worn Persian rugs. There were gloomy old pictures on the walls and Derek thought he caught a glimpse of a stuffed and mounted stag's head, but Pete was striding out and Derek had to hurry to catch up with him. An old, scruffy-looking and rather smelly spaniel skittered across the floor towards them, whinnying with excitement. It fussed around them both.

"Don't mind Hector. He's ancient and toothless. You settle yourself in here," he said, opening a door, "and I'll be back as soon as I've fed him and let him out into the garden."

Derek entered the room. All four walls were entirely lined with books: he had never seen so many. In the window was a desk with a green banker's lamp on it. There was a sofa covered in dark velvet, and two wing chairs, both with reading lights next to them. Derek was unsure whether to sit down, or which chair to sit in, so he remained standing until Pete returned.

"Is this the library for the school?" he asked.

Pete started to laugh, but turned it into a cough instead. "No, it's just our own books."

"Have you read any of them?"

"Of course. Well, most of them, yes."

Derek shook his head in disbelief. "We never had a single book at home," he said, still gazing awestruck around the room. "Well, home was mostly a caravan when I was young, so there wasn't no room for them. We didn't get a council house until I was fifteen. But my dad didn't set great store by reading, anyway. I think he could write his name, but that was about it."

"What was it like – the travelling?" asked Pete, loosening his tie and gesturing to Derek to sit down.

"It was good, mainly. I was only a kid, so it was exciting to me, always on the move, always going to new places. A hard life for my parents, though, I think, and of course I was working from when I was about eight or nine onwards. Looking after the horse, chopping logs, doing odd jobs. You don't have many friends when you're travelling, not like my kids have now."

"When did you start singing?"

"I was always singing, but when I was ten I saved up my pocket money and bought a guitar off another travelling family." He smiled at the memory. "Battered old thing it was, with nylon strings, and too big for me to start with. One of my cousins showed me a few chords that he'd learned from some book called Play in a Day. There was a picture of this chap on the cover, with a moustache. I can't remember his name."

"Bert Weedon?"

"Yes, that's the one. I can't wait to tell Wendy about all these books. Oh …" he trailed off.

"What?"

"I've not told her about learning to read. I told her we was having a band meeting."

"I'm OK with that," said Pete. "So, let's get started, shall we?"

He picked up a book from the coffee table. Its dust jacket was black with red and green writing on it.

"The book's called 'Winners Got Scars Too – The Life and Legends of Johnny Cash'," said Pete.

He opened it to the first page.

*

"You have got to be joking!" said Pete as Alan swung the van into the drive, past the sign proclaiming this to be 'England's Premier Naturist Camp'. He gave a whoop. "Sunny Vale Camp – that's what you told us. You never told us the best bit. A naturist camp!"

"Now, behave yourself, Pete," said Alan. "And mind where you're looking! We don't want any trouble."

"What on earth's a naturist camp?" asked Derek, the words dying on his lips as the van crawled at five miles an hour past a totally naked family who were putting up a tent. "Oh – nothing to do with nature or bird-watching then."

"I'd say it's entirely to do with bird-watching," said Pete. "Did you see those two teenage girls? Talk about an all-over tan!" He peered out of the side window to catch a glimpse of them in the wing mirror. Then his face fell. "Alan – we don't have to strip off to go on stage, do we?"

"I never thought of that," said Alan, trying – but failing – to produce a worried frown. Then he burst out laughing. "No, of course not. Though if we did, we'd have our guitars to protect our modesty."

"Jessie wouldn't."

They all had a rather unwelcome mental image of a stark-naked Jessie fronting the band.

"Come on – we're here," said Alan as he pulled up the van at the rear doors of the clubhouse. Two rather elderly, scrawny men in socks and sandals walked past and cheerily wished them a good evening. Pete's eyes were running with tears of laughter and he leant against the side of the van until he had composed himself.

"I feel like I'm in a Carry On film," he said. "Any minute now, Kenneth Williams is going to appear and make some terrible *double entendre* about Barbara Windsor's tits …" He collapsed into laughter again. "I can't wait to see the look on Jessie and Chalky's faces when they arrive."

A (clothed) club steward met them in the hall as they unloaded their gear. Derek hovered nearby as Alan discussed the arrangements, finally plucking up courage to ask whether the guests would be clothed for the dance.

"Yes, of course," said the steward, smiling. "It gets chilly in the evenings."

"Thank goodness for that," said Derek as the steward walked away. "The thought of watching all those dangly bits bobbing up and down on the dance floor was too much." He gave a loud hoot of laughter and the steward glanced back at him as he went through the door to the bar. "Hey, Pete! Think you'll recognise those girls when they've got their clothes on? "

"Certainly," said Pete. "They'll probably be the only people under 60 in the whole place. Did you think naturist camps were for the young and beautiful? Forget it! They won't be able to resist me, if only because I'll out-rank the competition by about 30 years."

"Good thing they won't be seeing you naked, in that case," said Derek. "You don't want to put them off before you've even chatted them up."

*

The orange plastic chairs were bolted together in a row and Gerry shifted uncomfortably. The A&E department was packed and noisy: over by the far wall, a drunk was talking to himself while holding a blood-stained tea-towel to his nose. He still had a half-finished pint of lager in a tankard at his feet. Most people waiting looked completely stunned and it was hard to tell whether they were waiting to be seen by a doctor, or were just accompanying a patient. The lighting, which consisted of fluorescent tubes on the ceiling, was too bright, and in the background was the faint buzz of a radio tuned to a music station, a sound that could not be blotted out but whose music could not be distinguished either – a kind of ever-present white noise. Nobody seemed to be in charge. There was a metal grille over the glass front of the reception desk and a hand-written sign about staff not tolerating abuse, but any staff were markedly absent.

While Gerry waited for Lenny to be treated, he thought about the last time he had been to A&E. He'd been fourteen and playing on a building site near his home, with his mates Dave and Gordon after school. They'd found some metal scaffold poles, prised them off the scaffolding – amazing, looking back, that the whole scaffold hadn't come crashing down on their heads – and were mucking about with them. First they had tried fencing with them, but the poles were too heavy. Then they'd tried pole-vaulting over a brick wall.

A little old lady had come out of her house in her apron and curlers to shout at them, but they had just sworn at her and given her the finger, so eventually she had gone back inside. Finally, they'd had a sort of jousting contest, rushing madly with the pole from one end of the building site to the other, and this was when Gordon had struck Gerry forcibly on the arm with his pole and Gerry had dropped his pole and howled, more in outrage than pain initially. Gordon had laughed loudly and called him a 'bloody fairy' but he'd shut up when it had become obvious that Gerry's arm was broken. It hung at a funny angle and there was a white piece of bone protruding from the skin.

"You moron!" shouted Gerry, his entire, carefully accumulated vocabulary of swear-words defeating him in the panic of the moment. Gordon, a lanky boy with a shock of black hair and very pale skin, had been paralysed with fear, but thankfully Dave had a bit more presence of mind. He'd taken off his scarf and improvised a sling for Gerry's arm. The three of them had then walked him back to his parents' place. By the time his dad opened the front door, Gerry was beginning to feel sick and the arm was starting to throb. Later, his father had told him that he had passed out on the doorstep. The next thing he remembered was being at A&E, frightened at the sight of the patients there: it had been like entering a madhouse with people crying out, writhing in pain. There had been blood on the floor and Gerry had stepped in some, spending the next ten minutes wiping the sole of his shoe over and over again on a mat by the door, repulsed by the sight of it.

When the arm had been put in plaster and Gerry was beginning to feel like a battle-scarred hero rather than a victim, anxious for once to get to school the next day so that everyone in the class could sign their name on his plaster cast, his father had put him over his knee and beaten him with a slipper. He had gone back to the building site the very next day. No-one was going to tell him what he could or couldn't do.

The double doors swung over with a wooshing sound and Lenny emerged. He grinned as he saw Gerry. There was a big white bandage on his head.

Gerry willed himself back into the present and stood up.

"Lenny, mate! Can't see you pulling the birds with that nappy on your head. Unless it's to get the sympathy vote."

"Get away, Gerry," said Lenny in an amiable tone. Lenny had been married for about forty years and had never so much as looked at another woman in all that time, something that was baffling to Gerry.

"What did the doc say?"

"They took an x-ray – that's why I was so long. Nothing damaged, just a nasty bruise and a big lump. He gave me some painkillers strong enough to knock out a horse and said I should be right as rain in a week or so. I called the missus so she's not too shocked when she sees me."

"She'll probably brain you with the frying pan for waking her up at this time of night. Come on, let's get you home."

"I'll call the police first thing in the morning."

"The police?" Suddenly Gerry was nervous. "You sure you want to get them involved?"

"Yes, well – it's assault, isn't it? Attempted robbery and all that."

"Just leave all that to me, Lenny. I'll sort it. You get a few days' rest."

"Thanks, Gerry – I appreciate that. You'll let Big Bertha know, won't you?"

"Yep – she'll rearrange the shifts, don't you worry."

*

"I've already said I'll deal with it," said Big Bertha, "so don't go poking your nose in where it's not wanted." She fiddled with the gold pendant that hung around her neck, a surprisingly feminine and delicate piece of jewelry. Gerry wondered what the pendant contained – a lock of hair? A photograph of her late husband? Or of some toyboy lover? Or of her Alsatian dog? Big Bertha was a very private person and no-one knew anything about her life outside the taxi firm or was inclined to ask, for fear of incurring her wrath. "You look absolutely terrible, by the way, Gerry," she said. "Did you sleep in those clothes?"

"And you're looking lovely too, my dear. No, I wasn't sleeping in them, I was working in them. All night. Apart from two hours sitting in A&E. I'm hoping to go home now and catch up on some sleep: I'm not back on until tomorrow morning." He stood up and buttoned his coat. "So, are you telling the police about the attack on Lenny?"

"I'm not sure," she said. "I've not decided. It obviously wasn't an attempted robbery, was it? All part of the harassment campaign by some sick bastard wanting to put us out of business." She fixed Gerry with a steely gaze. He looked away and fiddled with the chair he'd been sitting in, moving it back into position opposite Bertha's desk. "But whatever I decide to do, it'll be *my* way – you OK with that, Gerry?"

"Yes, of course, boss," he said.

As soon as he left the office, feeling like he could sleep for a week, he drove to Darren's school and parked outside where he had a good view of the playground. He checked his watch. They should be out for mid-morning break in about twenty minutes. The school looked run-down and scruffy. It was a Victorian building with a new flat-roofed block that had been built in the grounds in the 60s. The façade was dingy, rain-stained concrete. The playground – though he supposed at secondary school they didn't call it the 'playground' any more – was covered in white-line markings for netball courts. There was no longer a playing field, because that's where they'd put the new block. Along the side were the bike-sheds, where a young lad was hanging about. When he saw Gerry looking, he turned away, but not before Gerry saw the cigarette in his hand. A bell sounded and the pupils poured out through the doors, the boys instantly throwing down their blazers to form improvised goalposts - someone produced a football and a game was underway within the seconds. The girls all seemed to make for the low brick wall to one side of the playground, where they sat in a row, twiddling with their hair and talking quietly. There was no sign of Darren.

Gerry was feeling twitchy by now, through stress as well as exhaustion. Unable to sit still a moment longer, he got out of the car and locked it and strode over to the school buildings. Once inside, he followed the noise to the hall, where a scrum of pupils were pushing and shoving in front of the tuck shop.

"Can I help you?" asked a female voice, in a tone that revealed what she really meant was 'who the hell are you and what are you doing here?'.

Gerry turned, giving the old bag his most charming smile. She was wearing brogues and a rather mannish skirt suit, and had a round, open face that might have been pleasant had it not been for the suspicious expression it wore. He was suddenly conscious of his appearance, his crumpled clothes and unshaved face.

"I'm looking for Darren Jackson."

"And you are?"

"Gerry Chandler from Double-A taxis." With a confidence he didn't feel, he said "Darren's mother was taken to hospital just after he left for school and I've been sent to come and collect him. She's asking for him."

Old Bag gave him a look that said she'd heard a line like that a thousand times and wasn't going to be fooled by it. Fortunately, just then, Darren appeared out of the tuck shop scrum, spotted Gerry and ran over. His tie was askew and he looked as if his trousers hadn't been washed or ironed for months. When he saw Old Bag he slowed down to a walk and ran a hand through his hair, which was sticking up in a cow-lick.

"Gerry!" he exclaimed. "What you doing here? I was coming to see you later!"

"You know this man, Darren?" said Old Bag.

"Yes, Miss."

"Well, he's got some bad news for you, I'm afraid."

Darren's face fell. "What?"

"Your mum had to go to hospital, Darren – she sent me to come and get you," said Gerry. "But don't worry. I don't think it's too serious – just a recurrence of her ... her old trouble. She's ..." he hesitated, then looking straight into

Darren's eyes, said "… being well looked after by Dr Holmes."

For a moment, Darren didn't get it, forming his lips into the word 'who?' before suddenly realising.

"Oh, Dr Holmes. Yeah, of course."

Old Bag looked from one to the other, frowning. Turning to Gerry, she asked whether he had a note from Darren's mother, or from the doctor, saying exactly why Darren should be taken out of school.

"I just rushed straight over," said Gerry, apologetically. "I didn't think I'd need a note."

"Darren is far enough behind with his work already, without him losing another day of school. And we can't just let total strangers come and take one of our pupils away. You could be anybody! We'll need to check with the office. Come with me, both of you."

She strode away, across the noisy hall and into the corridor, with Gerry and Darren in her quake.

"It's not true," whispered Gerry. "Your mum's not ill, but I needed to think of an excuse to talk to you. It's really urgent."

"I knew that. Dr Holmes – that was really clever."

Old Bag turned around to make sure they were following, and they both smiled inanely at her. They were almost outside the office door, so Gerry figured he only had a couple of seconds.

"Listen – you have to stop playing detective, Darren. It's become too dangerous. Do you understand? This is really important. You could get hurt." He gripped Darren's arm and the boy stared up at him, white-faced. Sweat poured down Gerry's face even though it was cool in the corridor.

Old Bag knocked on the office door and entered, leaving Gerry and Darren in the corridor.

"Too late," said Darren. He reached into his trouser pocket and withdrew a small piece of paper torn from a school exercise book.

"What do you mean, too late? What's that?"

At that moment, Old Bag re-emerged and Gerry palmed the piece of paper.

"I'm sorry, Mr …"

"Chandler," prompted Gerry.

"… Mr Chandler. The head will not allow Darren out of school. He can go and see his mother this afternoon as soon as school finishes. I'm sorry to have wasted your time." She turned to Darren. "Back to your class quickly now, Darren. As Mr Chandler says, your mother is in good hands so you are not to worry."

Darren managed to assume a mournful expression and shuffled away.

Back at the car, Gerry unfurled the piece of paper Darren had given him. On one side, in pencil, was a drawing of a penis. Gerry flipped the paper over – on the reverse was written 'BLU 726B' and underneath that 'black hair, mustosh, fat belly'.

There was a loud banging on the passenger window of his taxi and Gerry looked up, alarmed, his heart thumping. Three young teenage girls, all wearing an approximation of school uniform – skirts rolled up and ties at half-mast - were slapping the window with the palms of their hands and laughing. They each planted a lipsticked kiss on the window and then ran off, squealing.

Chapter Four

"OK - when you're ready, ladies and gentlemen." The engineer's voice came over the speakers and they could see him through the glass panel of the control room, smiling. He had long hair and a straggly beard and was wearing a cheesecloth shirt open to reveal a hairy chest and a medallion around his neck.

Derek and Jessie put on their headphones and the engineer gave them the thumbs-up. Derek was beginning to wish he hadn't had a can of Pepsi with his lunch as he could feel a burp forming already. He cleared his throat. The instruments had all been recorded during a lengthy morning session using just a 'guide vocal'. Problems with getting the sound right with the drums had meant they had had to do five takes of each song, Chalky getting more and more stressed with each take. They'd been lucky to recruit Richard, the steel guitarist with another local country band, to sit in for the EP recording, and his playing had lifted the whole sound. The rest of the band were in the green room now, their jobs done, apart from Alan and Pete having to patch in some harmony vocals later. It felt strange to Derek to be singing without playing the guitar: he felt naked somehow, standing at the microphone.

The duet, *Something to Brag About*, went well; the engineer congratulated them, but that didn't mean, of course, that they didn't have to go over it another three times. Derek took a break while Jessie recorded *Blanket on the Ground*, her fake Southern accent becoming more exaggerated with each take, then it was time for Derek's two solo tracks. After only half an hour, the engineer declared he was done. He swung through the doors from the control room and gave Derek a bear-hug. Derek, not being the hugging type, said rather stiffly "what was that for?"

"That, my friend," said the engineer, "was for the most beautiful voice I've had in this studio in years. I'm no fan of country-and-western, as you can probably tell – I'm more the prog rock type - but the way you sang A Good Year for the Roses brought tears to my eyes."

"I'd lay off the wacky baccy, mate, in that case."

"I'm not kidding, Derek. You've really got something special. It's a pleasure to work with you."

"A pleasure to take our money, you mean," said Derek. He laughed but there was a lump in his throat too. "It's just copying, though," he said to overcome his embarrassment.

"What do you mean?"

"I just copy George Jones."

"Who's he when he's at home?"

"He's a big Nashville star. He's the best singer there is – I try to get as close to his sound as I can."

"Maybe one day you'll find your own sound."

"Maybe. Maybe not. I'm happy with Mr Jones' sound for now."

"Let's go out for a ciggy and then we'll tackle the BVs."

"BVs?"

"Backing vocals – the harmonies." He clapped Derek on the back and led him to the fire-escape doors.

*

Derek put the book down on the table and got up, seething with frustration.

"I feel so stupid! My own children can do this – why can't I?" he said, pacing up and down the room.

"It will come, Derek, just give it time," said Pete. "You can't expect instant results. Look – let's do something different. Let's practise writing your name and address." He took an A4 pad and pen off the desk and brought it over. "Come on – another fifteen minutes and then I'll take you home."

"I'm sorry, Pete," he said, sitting back down in the wing

chair. "Actually, I can write my name, so that's one thing we can tick off the list."

He pulled the pad towards him and picked up the pen, gripping it in his fist as if he was about to stab somebody with it. He wrote his name in block capitals, a little wavery but perfectly legible.

"Relax your hand a bit," said Pete, leaning over to show him the correct grip. "There – now use your index finger on the top of the pen, and rest the pen on your other fingers. That will give you the control you need."

"Feels weird."

Just then, the spaniel - who Pete had left in the hall – started a frantic barking. Almost at once they heard the crunch of gravel as a car drew up outside. Doors slammed and there were voices.

"Must be my parents: I didn't think they were coming back until tomorrow, though. Good thing I did several days' washing up today. And replenished the Scotch." He moved towards the door of the library. "Won't be a second. Anyway, come and say hello and then I'll run you home."

Derek stood up, nervous about meeting Pete's well-educated parents and what explanation Pete would give them about why he was there. He quickly turned the A4 pad upside-down on the table and went into the hall. Pete was opening the front door with one hand and holding onto the spaniel's collar with the other.

The first words of conversation were inaudible over the frenzied barking of the dog, but the people on the doorstep were clearly not Pete's parents. The man was burly, in his early forties, and was wearing brown trousers and an open-necked white shirt with the vest showing. At his side was a very young teenage girl wearing school uniform, her long straight blonde hair obscuring much of her face. The man had his hand on the shoulder of the girl, but not in a gentle way. His fingers were white with the pressure he was exerting.

Taking his cue from Pete, Derek grabbed the spaniel's collar and took the dog out to the kitchen. He was going to stay in the kitchen with the door shut, to respect Pete's privacy, but he didn't like the look of the man or his manner, so he came back out.

"Fifteen! She's fifteen!" he heard the man say. They were still on the doorstep, with Pete using his body to block the entrance. Derek hovered behind him. The man looked contemptuously at Pete, taking in the contradiction between his neat business suit and his long hair. "And who the hell is he?" said the man, jabbing his finger in Derek's direction.

"Just a friend from the band," said Pete, licking his lips nervously.

"Well, friend-from-the-band, you should choose your mates more carefully. This is my daughter." He shook her by the shoulder, but she continued to stare down at the ground. "She's a child. You can see she's a child. HE can see she's a child. But he still thought she was fair game."

"I've never seen her before. You've got the wrong person," said Pete.

At this, the girl looked up from between her curtains of hair.

"You said you'd call me, Petey, and you didn't. I waited and waited."

There was an awkward silence. Pete didn't reply directly but addressed himself to the father. "I'm sorry," he said. "I really didn't know. She was in a nightclub – she was all dressed up, with make up and everything. She told me she was eighteen."

"Liar," said the man, shoving his face into Pete's. "She's a respectable girl. She don't go to no nightclubs. You must have been hanging around her school waiting to prey on her. I know your sort. Anyway, what you going to do about it? And how do you know she's not up the duff?"

"She's not, is she?" said Pete, blanching and unconsciously moving back a little, further into the hall.

"I am here, you know," said the girl, fruitlessly. "You don't have to pretend that I don't exist."

"Luckily for you, she's not," said the man. "But if you ever, ever, lay a finger on her again, I'll be straight down to the cop shop. On second thoughts – the cops will probably be completely useless. I'll find my own way of sorting it."

He spun the girl around, still holding onto her shoulder, and they walked off to the car. Before she got in, she turned round and gave a tiny wave to Pete while her father wasn't looking.

*

Gerry went to the school uniform shop at the end of Arundel Street. A bell over the door tinkled as he went in and a middle-aged chap wearing half-moon glasses appeared from the back of the shop. The interior was very old-fashioned, with traditional wooden draper's counters with slide-out drawers, and a glass-fronted cabinet showing the various designs of ties and prefect badges. He hadn't been in one of these shops since he was a lad: he remembered his mother complaining about the monopoly that they had and how expensive everything was, especially as Gerry outgrew his trousers and blazer so quickly. Even the Aertex shirts and plimsolls for PE had to be bought from the approved supplier. Although he'd hated the experience of going with his mother to be fitted for his uniform, and the way the assistant had talked to him in such a condescending manner, he had looked forward to taking his son there, as a kind of rite of passage, but had never been given the opportunity. Carol had moved away to Birmingham before the lad went to secondary school and Gerry had barely seen him since.

He explained what he wanted to the assistant – or more likely he was the owner - who looked slightly askance that Gerry was having to guess what size might fit Darren.

"I'm his godparent," he explained, with what he hoped was a sincere smile. "It's a little surprise for him."

"Well, in that case, the young gentleman can bring anything back that doesn't fit and we can change it for a different size."

Gerry had been asked to be a godparent once, by one of the cab-drivers he worked with. It had seemed a harmless enough request but when he had gone along to the church for the Christening rehearsal the day before, he'd found out that he was supposed to make all kinds of serious declarations about renouncing 'the devil and all his works'. "Not exactly happy-clappy, is it?" he'd said to the vicar, who gave him a quizzical look. Churches made him feel funny, anyway – he was always glad to get out of the door when he'd gone to a wedding or funeral. He couldn't remember what excuse he'd made in the end, but he had wormed out of it. Now he felt guilty. What harm would it have done to mumble a few words?

In the end, he bought two pairs of trousers, two shirts, a tie and a blazer for Darren. He paid in cash and the bloke behind the counter looked almost as if it was beneath him to touch the money – perhaps he was used to posh families writing cheques for everything with their hoity-toity fountain pens. It was rather more than he'd intended to spend, but better – surely – than just giving more money to Darren's mother, who might spend all of it on herself and none on Darren.

Next on his list was a rather less pleasant job: confronting the rogue cab driver. He'd already called in a favour with an old friend of his dad's at Fratton police station, who had agreed to give him the registered address of the car that Darren had identified, as long as he kept quiet about who he'd got it from. Gerry flipped the piece of paper with the address written on it back and forth between his fingers. He should just pass it on to Big Bertha, of course – he knew that. He'd told Big Bertha he'd stay away from it and let her handle it. But when had he ever done what he should have done? Buck the system, that was Gerry's way. Always had been. And he hadn't done so badly out of it, had he? He knew in his heart that this was complete bullshit, but he repeated it a few times and it began to have the ring of truth.

*

"You'll have to take him with you, Derek," said Wendy. "I can't have him here – I've got to take Lor into Wickham on the bus to have her vaccination, and I've already got Bobby to cope with. Georgie will be fine with you. He's over the worst of it and he'll be back at school tomorrow anyway."

Derek sighed.

"You could have mentioned this last night – I was supposed to be going to Pete's house after work to … to learn those harmonies."

"The amount of time you spend with Pete these days, you might as well get married to him instead of me. You'll just have to phone him at his work and let him know. Then Chalky can bring you home as usual."

"But what's Georgie going to do all day at the stall?"

"I don't know – you can entertain him, can't you? It's only a few hours."

"It's ten hours, Wendy. I have to endure ten hours of it every day – remember? He's going to be bored sick by mid-morning." He was conscious he was beginning to sound whiney.

"Well, make sure he takes his portable cassette player with him. That'll keep him busy. And he can help you, anyway, serving and giving people their change. I've done him a packed lunch," she said, handing Derek a Tupperware container.

Derek shouted up the stairs for Georgie, then got a bag and put the cassette player in it together with a few random tapes. As Georgie walked into the kitchen, Derek heard Chalky's car pull up outside.

"Let's go, nipper!" said Derek.

Georgie chattered all the way in the car, clearly excited to be having a change from going to school.

"Are you quite sure you're not well?" asked Chalky, after a few minutes of listening to him.

Georgie remembered that he was supposed to be ill, and drooped convincingly in the seat. He flicked his fringe out of his eyes. "Quite sure, uncle," he said. "We'll be there soon, won't we? Only I don't want to upchuck in your nice car. Perhaps I should have the window open just in case."

Chalky regarded him in the rear-view mirror and smiled to himself. "You'll be fine, Georgie. We're nearly there."

The morning passed surprisingly quickly: Georgie helped with setting out the flowers and strawberries and insisted on lugging the big A-frame board down to the end of the layby by himself. The stall was busy and the regular customers chatted to Georgie. Derek was conscious that he never did have much small-talk and that his son was rather better at this job than he himself had ever been. But by lunchtime, Georgie was wilting: it was hot and stuffy in the stall and Derek insisted that he have a lie down in the shade, under one of the trees at the back of the layby. The fact that Georgie didn't argue meant that he definitely wasn't well – it had just been the excitement of going to work with his father that had kept him going through the morning. Derek walked down to the pub at two o'clock and bought him back some orange juice.

"Aw, Dad, why didn't you get the fizzy stuff?" said Georgie as Derek handed it over.

"Because it would make you sick."

Georgie sulked a bit, then drank the whole carton.

"Can I play my tapes now?"

"Yes – just stay here in the shade and don't annoy the customers with the music. What tapes did I bring?"

"Top of the Pops from last week," said Georgie, reading the label. "And Elton John. It's an LP someone at school recorded for me. It's called Honky Chattyoo. What's 'honky' mean, Dad?"

Derek was still trying to figure out what 'chattyoo' might be. "Well, a honky tonk is an American bar," he said and was about to sing a line from a song called *I Didn't Know God Made Honky-Tonk Angels* before he decided it might not be quite suitable for a nine-year-old.

"It's got Rocket Man on it," said Georgie, waving the cassette.

"Oh yes, I like that one. No country music tapes today, though?"

"Nah," said Georgie. "If I want to hear that, I can come and hear you sing, can't I?"

By late afternoon, Derek had almost sold out and the trickle of customers had died away. Georgie, evidently feeling better, came and sat with him in the stall and they sang *Rocket Man* together, or at least the bits that Derek could remember. He liked the part about not being 'the man they think I am at home'.

"You know, you've got a nice singing voice, Georgie. Let's record a duet of this before we go home and you can play it to your mother. We can pack up half an hour early, then we'll go across into the forest where it's quieter. You can bring your machine and we'll record it over there. Then we'll come back here in time for Chalky to pick us up."

"Great, Dad!" said Georgie, immediately trotting off up the layby to retrieve the A-frame board.

Derek closed up the stall and hauled it over to the fence, fastening the padlock and chain and stacking the empty crates neatly on the grass verge. The sun was still high in the sky and he was sweating: the forest would be a welcome relief from the heat. He grabbed Georgie's hand as they prepared to cross the road, and Georgie struggled to release it. It was a ritual they often went through.

As they climbed over the ranch-style fence, they entered another world. Sunlight was filtered through a dense covering of trees; ferns covered the ground and ivy festooned every bush. The sound of traffic died away.

"If we're lucky, we might see a deer," whispered Derek.

They walked silently through the forest, towards the rutted track that the rangers used with their Land Rovers. Birdsong was a constant background, and once there was a rustle in the undergrowth as if an animal had been startled by their footsteps. Georgie was worried it might have been a snake, but Derek assured him that it was probably a rabbit. He had seen adders in the forest before, though he didn't want to alarm Georgie by telling him this.

They found a spot just below the track, where the ground sloped away, and sat down to do their recording. Georgie nobly said that they could record over part of his Top of the Pops tape. He pressed the 'record' and 'play' buttons and began to sing in a high clear voice, with Derek improvising a harmony on the chorus. Derek caught his son's eye and winked at him. He realised how little time he usually spent with Georgie, or with any of the other kids if he were honest. Out at work all day, then gigging at the weekend. This was great, he thought, just the two of them, singing their hearts out with only the birds to hear. They had just got to the second verse when there was the sound of an approaching vehicle on the track above.

"We'll have to start again when it's gone past," said Derek, breaking off. "It'll only be a minute." He turned round, still seated. "That's funny. It's a saloon car – can't be one of the rangers after all. In fact it's a taxi by the look of it. What's it doing in the middle of the forest?"

The car didn't drive by but drew to a halt above them with a crunch of gravel; they heard the sound of slamming doors and angry shouting. It sounded like two men.

Derek put his fingers to his lips. "Best keep quiet," he whispered. "Don't want to get involved if it's a bit of a barney."

*

The situation had got out of hand almost immediately. Gerry had spotted the car, a cream coloured Renault, outside the guy's home in New Road and as soon as it moved off, he blocked it in with his cab. The guy got out, swearing and gesticulating. He was shortish, about 35, with thinning dark curly hair, long sideburns and a droopy moustache. He was slightly built but with – as Darren had correctly pointed out – a big gut, probably from too many beers or too many late-night burgers. Gerry stayed in his cab, waiting, observing the guy's bell-bottomed denim jeans and tightly fitting pink shirt which appeared to have a paisley pattern on it and which was unbuttoned practically to the waist. Looks a right poofter, thought Gerry. The guy came over to the driver's door of the cab and stuck his face right up against the window, shouting and giving Gerry the finger. Gerry stared back at him, impassive. He noticed the guy even had a little gold hoop earring in his left ear. Eventually, the guy backed off a bit, then caught sight of the Double-A logo on the side of the door. 'Oh, it's a different story now, isn't it?' thought Gerry as the guy practically ran back to his Renault, got in it and tried to reverse down the road, the engine squealing in protest. 'Now you know who I am and why I'm here,' said Gerry softly. The Renault stopped reversing: a dustbin lorry had just turned into the street at the other end, so there was no way out. He laughed when he saw the guy bang his hands on the steering wheel in frustration.

It was only then that Gerry got out of his cab and strolled up the street to the Renault. He was conscious he was not walking in his usual way, perhaps because he had an image in his head of one of those men in a Wild West film who lead the posse against the outlaw from out of town. He stuck his thumb on his belt, as if he were packing a gun. He opened the driver's door.

"Park your pretend taxi over there and then come with me," he said in what he hoped was his best no-nonsense tone. He felt quite calm – the guy was a weedy poofter and wouldn't give him any trouble. All mouth and trousers.

The guy was panicking a bit and failed to start the car twice; when he did, he revved the engine too much and the car jerked away. Eventually he got it into a nearby parking space, with one wheel lodged on the pavement.

He got out.

Gerry crooked a finger and beckoned him over to the cab.

"You and me are going for a nice little ride now – and you're going to tell me all about what you've been doing and who you are working for."

"I wasn't doing anything – you've got the wrong man."

Gerry ignored this. "Daniel, isn't it? Daniel Paterson? What do your friends call you – Dan? Danny? No, wait – you don't have any friends, do you? That's because you're a little bastard who steals other people's business." He put his hand on the centre of Daniel's chest and shoved him into the passenger seat. As Gerry slid behind the wheel he pressed the lever that locked all the passenger doors. Daniel had turned pale and was biting his bottom lip.

"How do you know my name?"

"Ways and means, ways and means," said Gerry.

He started the car and drove out of Portsmouth, ramping up the speed when they got to the A27. Daniel sat silently, not responding to the barrage of questions that Gerry was firing at him. Gerry felt the rage and frustration building up inside him; a rage he'd not felt since he was a teenager. His plan was to drive to the Bere Forest and leave Daniel – minus his clothes – in the middle of the woods. That would hopefully frighten him enough to stop sabotaging the Double-A's business, but without getting Gerry into too much trouble either. But he needed to find out who else was involved and Daniel, despite the reek of fear wafting off him, was not talking.

Gerry knew that the five-bar gate which barred the entrance to the forest rangers' pathway was seldom locked during the day. He swung into the visitors' car park, which was crowded with cars. People were picnicking right next to their cars, something that always baffled Gerry. All that beautiful forest and they sat in the car park among the exhaust fumes. He wasn't bothered about anyone noticing the car – there were too many for his to stand out. He rounded the corner at the end of the car park where he was hidden from the picnickers and stopped the car in front of the gate. He took the keys out of the ignition while he went to open the gate – it would be ironic if he were the one to be left in the forest, Daniel having stolen his car. He lifted off the heavy iron chain, swung the gate open and drove through, shutting it carefully behind him. Within a few yards, the forest was deserted and the only sound was the light crunching of the tyres on the gravel path. He was sweating a bit, not so much nervous as keyed up with anticipation. He stopped the car, turned off the engine and walked around to the passenger side.

"Now get out – and don't try to run off."

He opened the door and grabbed Daniel by the front of his shirt.

"Get off me, you wanker," shouted Daniel, struggling to free himself from Gerry's grip.

"Found your voice, have you, you little poofter? You won't be so cocky by the time I've finished with you." He let go of Daniel, shoving him away from the car. "OK, now take off all your clothes."

"What? Are you mad?"

"You heard – take them off."

"Or what? You'll punch me? You wanna get done for ABH as well as kidnapping?"

"Right now, I don't care what I get done for. Anyway," he said, flipping up the lid of the boot and extracting a baseball bat, "I can see you're not going to do what you're told, so maybe this will make a difference." He smacked the bat into his own palm. It made a satisfying 'thunk'. Daniel started taking off his shirt, tearing the buttons in his haste.

"What the fuck do you keep a baseball bat in your car for?"

"For cretins like you. And in case I get an awkward customer. Now hurry up."

Daniel took off his shoes and trousers. Gerry gestured with the baseball bat.

"And your kecks as well." He was a weedy little bugger, with a concave chest and that weird wobbly belly. There was a good reason people wore clothes: they looked bloody silly without them. Gerry picked up the discarded clothes and threw them in the boot of the car.

Daniel started crying them, the snot running down his chin.

"Oh, for God's sake, shut up," said Gerry as Daniel stepped out of his underpants and took his socks off. He crossed his hands in front of his crotch.

"Now, you've got a choice. You can either tell me who you are working for, in which case I'll take you home, like the good kind person I am, or I'll leave you here in the middle of the forest and you'll have to make your own way home stark naked. I wouldn't advise hitch-hiking – one look at you and drivers would put their foot down. And if you give me any trouble, I won't hesitate to use my much-loved, genuine Babe Ruth baseball bat and break your stupid knees. It won't be the first time I've done this, I can tell you, so you needn't think I'm just bluffing." Gerry couldn't believe he was saying this and hoped that he sounded more convincing than he felt. He took a swipe with the bat at a nearby sapling.

"I'm not working for no-one! I've already told you! It was just me," sobbed Daniel. "I hate you. I hate the Double-A. I wanted to ruin you all."

"What the fuck have we ever done to you?"

"I'm not telling you. Ask Brian if you want to know."

"Brian? Brian Askew?"

"Yes, Brian bloody Askew."

" But he's dead."

"Eh?" Daniel looked completely nonplussed and forgot to hold his hands over his privates. "When?"

"Last November – heart attack. Big Bertha runs the Double-A now."

Daniel stood, his mouth hinged open.

"You complete idiot," said Gerry. "You mean to tell me this was a vendetta against Brian and you didn't even know he was dead? You tosser." His head filled with blind rage. He lifted the baseball bat up behind his shoulder as if he were about to hit a ball clean out of the forest and across the main road. As he swung it, Daniel stepped back in terror, wailing incoherently, tripped over a root and fell backwards. The wailing stopped instantly. Gerry moved forward cautiously, still clutching the bat and peered down the slight slope into the undergrowth.

*

At first, it was quite fun. Derek and Georgie lay side by side on the ferns, with Georgie giggling silently every time his father shushed him. Though they couldn't catch most of what the men were saying, Derek heard one of them starting to cry. He reached over and put his hand on the back of Georgie's head, to make sure he stayed on the ground. He distinctly heard the words 'you tosser' then, seconds later, everything went quiet.

"Stay there," he whispered in Georgie's ear. "Don't move a muscle." Georgie giggled.

Derek cautiously crawled up the slope towards the track, ducking his head down when he saw a man standing a few yards away from the saloon car. He was holding a baseball bat and tapping it against his thigh. With the other hand he was running his fingers through his hair, over and over again. "Shit, shit, shit," he was saying. He had his back to Derek. Seeing the baseball bat and the fact that there was no sign of the second man, Derek was filled with dread.

As if he'd decided something, the man turned and walked briskly to the car, threw the bat and some kind of bundle into the boot, and got into the driver's seat. Derek stayed low but got a reasonably good look at him: he was about Derek's own age, but thick-set, good-looking in a slightly-gone-to-seed way, with light brown hair and a face whose cheeks were scarred by the legacy of acne. The car's engine started almost immediately and the car roared off in a spray of gravel. The angle was such that Derek couldn't see the number plate, though there was some kind of insignia on the side of the car.

He felt a bit sick. What had the man done? He got to his feet and ran up the last couple of feet of the slope, emerging onto the gravel track. He looked up and down. Nothing. Just the retreating rear end of the saloon car.

Running back down to Georgie, he grabbed him by the arm.

"Come on – we'll be late for Chalky."

"What was it all about, dad?"

"Nothing to worry about, nipper," he said, pulling him to his feet and trotted with him back to the roadside fencing.

"Those men spoilt our recording."

"Never mind – we can do another one."

Chalky was already waiting in the layby when they got back, slightly breathless.

"About bloody time! Oh – sorry, Georgie. I've been here nearly ten minutes – thought you'd buggered off … gone off … without me."

"Sorry, Chalky. We were over in the forest doing some singing." Derek put his arm on Georgie's shoulder so that the boy would know not to say anything.

"We sang Rocket Man, Uncle Chalky."

"Did you now?" said Chalky, having not a clue what *Rocket Man* was. "You're feeling better, then?"

"Yes thank you."

"School tomorrow then, in that case."

Georgie pulled a face and they drove off. Derek sat in the back with Georgie, pale and silent. Chalky didn't seem to notice.

*

As he approached the five-bar gate, Gerry glanced in the mirror. To his horror, a man was silhouetted on the track behind him. He was very slim, with a thin face and dark hair; he had his hands on his hips and was wearing a white shirt and dark jeans with some kind of big buckle on the belt. He was staring down the track at Gerry, who took his eyes off the rear-view mirror for a split second while he negotiated a turn in the track. When he looked back the man was gone.

"Damn, damn," said Gerry, banging on the brakes in front of the gate and hurrying out of the car to unhook the padlock chain. His heart was beating loud in his chest and his hands shook so that he fumbled the chain twice before lifting it over the vertical bar of the gate. He drove through and out of the forest, without stopping to shut the gate behind him, but remembering to drive slowly through the car-park in case he drew attention to himself. His hands were sweating on the steering wheel.

What had the man seen? Calm down, he told himself. He might not have seen anything. And anyway, what had Gerry actually done? Nothing. Daniel had fallen backwards – that was all. If he had hurt himself, that wasn't Gerry's fault, was it? In his mind, he heard his father's voice: "You think you're so clever, don't you, lad? Well, don't forget, there's clever and there's bloody clever. When you start doing bloody clever things, you're getting above yourself and that's when you'll be found out."

Think, man, think, he said to himself. He had a raging thirst and as he passed a pub, he desperately wanted to stop off for a pint of lager, but was rational enough to realise that the fewer people who saw him, the better. Best to get straight back to Portsmouth as quickly as possible.

Going through Portchester, near the Smiths Crisps factory opposite the harbour, he was still going over and over what the man on the track might have seen, and almost didn't notice when a police car loomed up in his mirror, overtook and then flashed the 'stop' sign in the rear window. Gerry licked his lips, which felt dry and cracked. He pulled over behind the police car and sat waiting, both hands still on the wheel. The beat from his heart was in his ears now, pounding and pounding. How could they have found out so quickly? Had the man read the car's number plate and phoned it in? He wound the driver's window down as the copper approached but didn't manage to raise one of his winning smiles.

"Is this your taxi, sir?"

Gerry said nothing for a moment, his mind a complete blank.

"Yes, officer," he said eventually, rooting around in the glove box for his licence.

The policeman examined the licence for what seemed like hours.

"Anything the matter, officer?"

The copper now peered into the back seat. Gerry was terrified that he'd ask to see in the boot where the baseball bat and Daniel's clothes were.

"Are you on your way to pick up a passenger?"

"No ... I ... I'm off duty."

"Were you aware of what speed you were doing?"

Gerry felt a surge of relief. So this was about speeding. He almost laughed. "Forty, I think."

"This is a 30 limit. And you were doing well over 40."

"I'm very sorry, officer."

The copper handed the licence back to Gerry and looked him in the eye.

"You cabbies are all the same. Always in a hurry. I won't do anything this time – just consider this a friendly warning."

"Yes, officer. Thank you, officer."

Gerry had used the word 'officer' so many times now

that he began to worry that the copper would think he was taking the mickey.

The policeman tapped twice on the roof of Gerry's car in a gesture of dismissal and then walked back to the patrol car. Gerry waited until the police car was a speck in the distance, then rested his forehead on the steering wheel for a few minutes before starting the engine again. Four hundred yards down the road was a big litter bin. He pulled into the layby, took Daniel's clothes out of the boot and stuffed them into the bin, burying them under some drinks cans. Then he headed for Tipner, where he drove down the road towards the greyhound stadium. He looked around carefully: there was no-one about. He took the baseball bat out of the boot and flung it as hard as he could into the harbour mud where it sank with a small 'glooping' noise. He laughed as he got back into the car.

Chapter Five

The following night, at a scruffy working-men's club in Portsmouth where the band were announced as the 'bingo interval' – at which Alan just rolled his eyes - the incident in the forest was still preying on Derek's mind. That morning, after waving Chalky off, he had not set up the stall immediately, but had crossed the road and climbed over the fence into the forest. As he walked up the slope towards the track, he'd seen two police cars up on the ridge, one with its lights flashing. He had retreated hastily and gone back to set up the stall. An ambulance had gone streaking by moments later, but it hadn't been until lunchtime that a police car had cruised slowly into the layby, two uniformed cops inside. It had seemed to take an age for them to get out of the car, during which time Derek had been telling himself over and over again that he hadn't seen anything – which was true, surely? He had no reason to think anyone had got hurt: it had just been an argument. The other bloke must have run off. But that couldn't be right – why would the police be there at all? Why had an ambulance turned up? He'd then remembered the baseball bat the man had been tapping against his leg. By the time the two cops reached him, Derek had been trembling, almost as if he had something to feel guilty about. He'd debated whether to tell them what he had heard, but decided he couldn't put Georgie through that – it wouldn't be fair on the little lad – so he'd said none of it. He'd told the police he'd seen nothing and heard nothing: he'd been alone at his stall all day. They had gone away happily enough, especially after he'd given them a punnet of strawberries each. They never revealed why they were asking, and Derek hadn't asked, for fear of looking too curious.

While the bingo-caller was doing his clichéd best to rouse some enthusiasm into the crowd, Derek made his way to the bar to top up his pint. On the way, he passed a table where the local evening newspaper was spread open to the first double-spread, next to a packet of crisps and an overflowing ashtray. There was a big picture in the middle of a scene in the forest, and a great big screaming headline with an exclamation mark after it. In the second set, Derek muffed the words to *Livin' on Easy Street*, causing Jessie to miss her cue for the second verse. Her look could have turned strong men to stone but she covered it with a big insincere smile, only cursing Derek after they got off stage. The applause at the end of the evening had been muted and Derek knew his mind had not been on the performance at all.

"Everything all right, mate?" asked Pete, as they packed up. He was trying to look casual about it, but Derek could tell he really was concerned.

"Yeah – sorry about that. I messed up Folsom Prison Blues as well, didn't I?"

"Happens to us all. Even George Jones probably has an off-night now and again."

"I couldn't squeeze in another lesson this week, could I, Pete? Say – Tuesday night? There's something in particular that I want to read."

Pete hesitated.

"Oh sorry," said Derek, seeing his face. "I expect you've got other plans."

"No, that's fine. Let's make it early evening though, then I can still go out on the pull afterwards."

Derek laughed, though Pete hadn't probably meant it as a joke.

When Derek got home, he still felt wired, so went and made a cup of tea and sat in the kitchen drinking it. The house was silent. He crept up the stairs and checked on Wendy and the kids. When he looked into Georgie's room, he saw the cassette player lying on the floor, picked it up and took it back downstairs with him. He closed the kitchen door so they wouldn't hear. A bit of Georgie's sweet singing voice would be just the thing to settle him down before he went to bed.

He rewound the tape and clicked 'play'.

*

Gerry put his beer can down on the coffee table, on top of the *Portsmouth News*, where it made a wet ring over the rather blurry picture of someone being loaded onto an ambulance on a stretcher. He looked again at the headline 'BODY FOUND IN FOREST' and shook his head in disbelief. Police were, apparently, 'treating the death as suspicious'. As the victim was naked, he had not yet been identified and one line of enquiry was apparently that it might have been a homosexual encounter that went wrong. Gerry made a snorting sound through his nose. He tried to picture Daniel Paterson in a 'gay tryst': he had looked a bit of a poofter, after all. He didn't object to poofters, but one dirty old pervert had come on to Gerry when he was about 16. Gerry had gone into the public toilets near the market when he was working on his dad's stall and there'd been a hole in the wall of the cubicle. While sitting there, Gerry had idly stuck his fingers into the hole and been horrified to have them grabbed by the bloke in the next cubicle, who'd immediately invited him to insert something else into the hole if he wanted to. Gerry had kicked out hard at the floor-level gap between the cubicles and the guy had let go of his fingers. He had stormed out of the toilets, heart beating hard, banging his fist on the door of the guy's cubicle before he left. Afterwards, he felt a bit of a fool. It had just been a sad old bloke, after all.

He read again the bit in the paper about police appealing for witnesses. They wouldn't get far with that – there'd been none. Except for that skinny geezer on the track afterwards, but there was no way he could have identified Gerry because he was already driving away when the man appeared. And the cab was surely too far away by that time for him to have been able to read the numberplate.

And at the end of the day, he'd not done anything. Daniel had fallen – that's all. But who'd have believed that he would actually die from falling back like that?

Gerry drank the rest of the beer and crumpled up the can, drop-kicking it in the general direction of the waste-paper basket, but missing it entirely.

He supposed the police would put out a picture and someone would come forward and identify Daniel. Had he been married? A father? A brother? Gerry realised he knew nothing about him – not even the reason he had been waging such a vendetta against Brian Askew, a man who Daniel hadn't even known had died months before. Askew had always been such a mouse: Gerry couldn't believe he'd be the cause of any ill-feeling, let alone a plan to sabotage the Double-A.

'No way can they trace it to me,' he said confidently to his reflection in the mirror over the gas fire. But that was the beer talking. He sat down again and got out a stubby red biro – one of the many he had nicked from Ladbroke's over the years – and on the back of a taxi receipt pad, began to list anything that could link him to what had happened. For a long time, the pad was absolutely blank. Then he began to think properly. He wrote a figure '1' and drew a circle around it, adding the name of his dad's old mate at Fratton police station – the one who had given him Daniel's address, though he was intensely loyal to Gerry's dad and would surely never say anything because he'd be putting his own job in jeopardy if he did. Also, he was getting on in years and most probably was up for retirement this year. Number two was Darren, though he wouldn't say anything either, especially when Gerry gave him the new school uniform tomorrow – likewise his mother. Number three was when he confronted Daniel in New Road. He paused for a while after he wrote this one down: a densely packed street of terraced houses, it must surely have been witnessed by several people, twitching their front-room curtains. He remembered how he had walked cockily down the middle of the road, something he now felt embarrassed about. By the time he'd got to number seven on the list, Gerry was beginning to feel a whole lot less confident. He could tackle the list one by one: make sure he was covered. Or perhaps he should just cut out the waiting and go round to the cop shop now – tell them exactly what happened. He sighed and turned on the TV to watch the last few minutes of *Columbo*. The detective, played by Peter Falk, was wearing that grubby beige mac again and looking like he'd spent the night in a skip. He went out of the door of a posh-looking house and just when the murderer had a look of relief on his face, he popped back in again. 'Just one more thing…' he said, and you knew he'd cracked the case.

*

The singing on the tape suddenly stopped and there was a loud rustling noise and some muffled conversation, followed by the sound of Georgie's giggle. Then, faint but clear, came the words 'get off me, you wanker!'. Derek turned up the sound. It was all there on tape, right through to Chalky saying that it was "about bloody time" when they got back to the stall – Georgie must have forgotten to press the 'stop' button and the recording had continued through to the end of the tape. Derek carefully ejected the cassette and sat holding it, wondering what to do. In the end he climbed onto one of the kitchen stools and reached up to the top of the cupboard, placing the cassette into a storage jar for coffee that they never used.

*

When Pete came to collect Derek, Sharon answered the door.

"Dad!" she shouted, over her shoulder, without saying a word of greeting to Pete.

"Just coming!" Derek picked up the rolled-up newspaper and hid it inside his zip-up jacket. Sharon left Pete at the door and drifted into the kitchen, pulling a face.

"What's that in aid of?" said Derek.

"Weird!" she whispered.

He grinned. "See you later, love. Tell your mum I won't be long."

When he got to the door, he saw the reason for Sharon's reaction. Pete was wearing close-fitting, purple flared trousers that had crushed-velvet patch pockets on the front, teamed with a purple-and-pink striped shirt with an oversized collar. Derek – clad in his usual straight denims and white shirt - had a job not to laugh.

At Pete's house, he lost his nerve about the newspaper and asked instead if they could read some more of the Johnny Cash book. Pete looked puzzled but didn't say anything, so they ploughed on with chapter two. Pete was his usual patient self as Derek struggled through sentence after sentence. When Derek got up to leave, Pete reached over and picked up Derek's jacket. The newspaper fell out.

"You've been reading the newspaper? That's great," he said.

"It's Saturday's," said Derek. "I like to look at the car advertisements. In case I ever have enough money to buy a car."

"Right," said Pete, his eyes fixed on Derek's face. Neither man moved. "That's why you brought it with you tonight then? Tuesday night?"

"Yes," said Derek. "Well, no - not really." He fiddled with the zip on the jacket.

Pete said nothing.

"There was something I wanted to know about. You see – it happened opposite where I works on the strawberry stall." He spread the paper out at the double-page story, the one with the big photograph of the ambulance and the police cars at the scene. "Does this mean the bloke is dead?" He pointed at the opening paragraph.

Pete swiveled the paper around and read the story out loud, including the part where police were assuming the death was suspicious. Derek slumped back in the chair.

"Did you see anything, Derek? They're asking witnesses to come forward."

"No, I seen nothing," said Derek, rather too quickly.

"The police was round at the stall asking afterwards. I told them I seen nothing."

"The victim was found naked, apparently, with the back of his head smashed in. They don't even know who he is yet. Nasty business."

"Yes."

"Better take you back now, Derek – I've got a date and she's a hot one."

"Oh, I'm sorry," he said, getting up out of the chair.

"Only kidding. I'm just going to have a drink with a couple of mates at a wine bar in Southampton and see if I can find any nice young lady who might be looking for company."

"Stay away from Derby Road then, Pete – they're all looking for company there."

*

At the other end of the line, the phone was picked up quickly.

"Hello, Carol."

Carol was silent fractionally too long and his heart sank. "Oh, Gerry … it's you. What do you want?"

"Were you expecting someone else?"

"No, no – that's fine."

"Is Joe there? I was hoping for a quick word."

"No, he's gone to watch Aston Villa."

"That's nice. With his mates?"

"No, just with John. He's got a season ticket."

Gerry remembered that John was Carol's latest boyfriend, the latest in a long line. Carol had high standards and usually booted them out after a few months, just as she'd booted out Gerry. Or maybe it was just that she was a bad judge of character, so hooked up with anyone who took even a mild interest in her, only to find out later about their multitude of faults and inadequacies. John obviously had a bit of cash, though, if he'd forked out for a season ticket for himself and the boy. Carol had been a really good-looking bird when she was in her teens – Gerry had first met her at a coffee bar near the Guildhall when he was 17. She liked the Beatnik style and had affected black polo-neck jumpers, slim jeans, and long straight hair. She had smoked Gauloises, which Gerry thought was very sophisticated, and spent a lot of time listening to records by artists he'd never heard of and drinking coffee that had a lot of foam on the top of it. These days, she was a brassy blonde with a permanent tan, a gin habit, and too much time on her hands, though Gerry still fancied her something rotten.

"I was wondering if I could come up one day next week – take Joe out somewhere. You too, if you wanted." As soon as the last sentence was out of his mouth, he realised that it had been the wrong thing to say.

"No, I don't think so, Gerry. We've got a lot on next week."

"Only, I've not seen Joe for quite a while now. And he's on school holidays now, isn't he?"

"It's not my fault you've not seen him– it's because you're always working shifts."

"I know. I'm sorry."

"Maybe the week after? I've got a golf tournament, but you could take Joe out."

"Golf? You've taken up golf?" He laughed. "Bit middle-class, isn't it?"

"Well, I am middle-class these days, Gerry. Gone up in the world. Unlike you."

"Does this 'John' play golf?"

"Don't say it like that. And no – he doesn't."

"You'll tell Joe that I called, though, won't you?"

When he put the phone down, he felt restless. He looked again at the newspaper, at the photofit of the 'victim' in the forest – he supposed they had to use an illustration: they couldn't really take a photograph of a dead man's face. Imagine seeing that if you were the mother or the wife. The police were appealing for anyone who recognised him to get in touch. He put down the paper, grabbed the big carrier bag containing Darren's new uniform and headed out of the door.

*

The gig at the Irish Club was going well. Alan had picked up the first pressing of their EP earlier that day and had brought a stack of them to display at the front of the stage. At the interval, Derek and Jessie were kept busy signing copies and the money was rolling in. Alan had been visibly jittery about the prospect of Derek signing but Derek had assured him he could manage.

"At this rate, we'll get our costs back in no time at all," said Alan with a grin as he went to the bar to get another pint.

They were a friendly crowd at the club – or at least, until they'd got a few drinks inside them. There were always requests for the band to play *The Forty Shades of Green* and other sentimental Irish country songs and they always had a meat raffle halfway through the evening. The last time they played there, Derek had struck lucky and won a leg of lamb, which had delighted Wendy a lot more than the £4 he usually came home with.

As Derek went out to the Gents just before the band were due back on stage, he was aware of an altercation at the back of the hall. Someone had got their hands round the neck of some other bloke and was banging his head against the wall and shouting something. Derek moved nearer – though not too near in case the fight spread – and realised with horror that it was Alan who was being assaulted. A small dark-haired, wiry man, who might have resembled a leprechaun had it not been for the venomous expression on his face, finally removed his scrawny hands from Alan's neck as a steward pulled him away.

"Juss don't ever shing it again, y'hear?" he said to Alan over his shoulder as the steward marched him towards the door. "It was rubbish, so it was. Ye can't shing it, so juss don't try."

Alan dusted himself down and adjusted his collar.

"You OK?" asked Derek.

"I'm … I'm fine. Just a bit shaken."

"What was that all about?" He moved aside to allow the barman through, who was bearing a large glass of Jameson's for Alan.

"Thanks, mate," said Alan to the barman, taking a large swig. "He didn't like the way I sang Little Old Wine Drinker Me."

Derek laughed. "You're kidding me?"

"No, that was his only grievance, apparently."

"Well, he's gone now – shall we have it again, by popular request?"

"Good idea."

The second set got underway and the crowd all stamped their feet on the floor while Alan sang a reprise.

*

Darren's mum opened the door just a crack. Gerry could only see one of her eyes through the gap. It looked tired and her skin looked whiter than ever. He had hidden the bag of clothes behind his back, so it would be a surprise, but she didn't look in the mood for surprises.

"I thought we was done," she said. "He got you the reg number, didn't he?"

"Yes, he did a brilliant job. I wasn't going to ask him to do anything else. I just wanted to say thank you."

"OK." She inched the door open a little more and gestured for Gerry to go in.

It was hard to negotiate the narrow hall because there was a mattress, old and stained, propped up against the wall. He edged past and into the kitchen. On the formica table was a half-drunk pint of cider and an ashtray with several butts in it.

"I was just ..." she began, waving her hand in the direction of the glass. "Do you want one?"

"That would be grand. Thank you." He tried once more to think what on earth her name was. While she was getting the cider bottle out of the fridge – still empty of food, he noted – he saw a letter on the worktop from the council addressed to Miss Tina Jackson. She never was married to Darren's dad, then.

He drank the cider she poured and they struggled to make conversation. As he finished the glass, he got up from the table and reached down for the large paper carrier bag at his feet. He'd seen Tina glancing at it, curious as to what it was and whether it was some kind of present. He handed it over rather clumsily with an awkward little speech about wanting to help Darren. Tina clutched the bag without looking inside.

"It's a few bits of school uniform for the autumn term, that's all."

She looked down at the kitchen table, sticky with glass-rings and scattered with crumbs.

"Come through – there's nowhere to put it down here." She led the way out of the kitchen and into Darren's bedroom.

It was a typical boy's room. The bed was unmade, there was a row of scuffed shoes and plimsolls in front of the wardrobe, and the walls were covered in posters of footballers and pop stars. A large handwritten 'KEEP OUT' sign was taped to the door of the room. The room was poky and smelt unaired; a box room rather than a bedroom.

Tina put the bag down on the bed and took out the contents one at a time, holding each item up. By the time she got to the blazer with its school badge she was crying.

"These are wonderful. You're so kind, Gerry," she said, letting the tears course down her cheeks and making no move to wipe them away, as if they were nothing to do with her.

"Don't look so bloody miserable about it, then," said Gerry, taking the blazer and trousers and hanging them neatly over the back of a chair. He patted her rather awkwardly on her bony shoulder. "It's nothing really – but I'm sure he needs this stuff, doesn't he?"

"He does. It's just … " She went quiet.

"What?"

"We're not used to people being kind."

His heart lurched. It was true what his mum always said: you never know what cross other people are bearing. It seemed to have taken him until now to realise the truth of it.

Tina turned towards him and let out a sob. He put his arms around her, gingerly at first, then suddenly they were kissing and he was pawing at her breasts, lifting her T-shirt, and she was clawing at the belt on his jeans, undoing the buckle and grabbing for the zip. He noticed her fingernails were dirty, then reprimanded himself for noticing. He tipped her back onto Darren's bed, landing on top of her, but keeping his weight off her with his elbows. He laughed, trying to catch her eye – he was used to a bit of light banter when he bedded a girl – but she didn't smile: she looked desperate, like she was starving, like she'd been in some concentration camp for months and was seeing her first glimpse of daylight. He kissed her deeply; her mouth tasted slightly bitter, but not unpleasant. She'd taken his shirt off by then, so he thought he'd better reciprocate and pulled her T-shirt over her head. She wasn't wearing a bra: her body was emaciated, with her ribs showing, and there were a couple of strange marks on her torso, like burn-marks. Gerry registered this without even stopping his frantic kissing. When he entered her, she cried out as if in relief.

He was tender with her afterwards, lying with his arm around her until Tina asked him to get her fags from the kitchen. He found a packet of ten Player's Number Six on the kitchen worktop together with an old dented Zippo lighter. He also grabbed a tin ash-tray from the kitchen, conscious all the while of his nakedness in the harsh daylight; conscious too of his slight paunch. As he lay back on the narrow bed, his feet sticking out over the end, he wanted to tell her about the mess he was in; about the confrontation with Daniel and the police, but of course she was the last person he could tell. She'd go mad if she thought he'd put Darren in any danger. Anyway, there'd be no reason for him to see her again after this. He'd paid his dues.

He looked again at the marks on her body and put his finger gently on one that was just under her ribs, on the right hand side. He turned his head sideways and caught her eye.

"It's nothing," she said straight away. "Just caught myself with a hot pan."

He smiled, both of them acknowledging the lie without saying anything.

When he left, he had to wait on the external staircase while a fat woman laboured up the steps, a clipboard tucked under her arm. Her dark hair was tightly permed and she was wearing the kind of clothes that nobody in this maisonette block wore – a smart black suit with a light blue silky blouse, and court shoes.

Gerry stepped aside and made an overlarge courtly gesture, sweeping his arm as if he were Sir Walter Raleigh laying down his cloak for the queen. The woman laughed as she went past. He turned to see her stop outside Tina's front door and was caught between relief that he'd only just got out in time and curiosity as to what she was doing there. Tina clearly hadn't been expecting anyone. He realised he was starting to feel protective not just of Darren, but of Tina too. Big mistake, he admonished himself: what's done is done. Time to move on now. He ran down the stairs, juggling the bunch of car keys in his hand and whistling the chorus from *I'd Like to Teach the World to Sing*.

Chapter Six

The children clustered round the radio in the kitchen, as Wendy fiddled ineffectually with the dial, trying to get Radio Solent.

"Give it to me," said Georgie, snatching it impatiently. Wendy sighed. "Got it first time!" he crowed as the sound of a country song filled the air. When it finished, the announcer then droned on interminably, listing various C&W events in the area that coming weekend.

"Come on!" said Sharon. As if she'd made it happen, the sound of their father's voice rang out, pure and true, with the opening line of *A Good Year For the Roses*.

"He sounds even better on the radio," said Wendy. "You wouldn't know he wasn't American, would you?"

"Just wait until the interview," said Sharon. "I bet he sounds right Meon Valley then."

"Nipperrr!" shouted Georgie.

They all laughed, but were each overawed that Derek was on the BBC, just like he was someone famous.

*

Canute House, where Radio Solent was based was a right rabbit warren, thought Derek, as he and Jessie followed their guide up and down corridors and staircases, all painted cream and green. Derek wondered why Jessie had worn her fringed jacket and boots: didn't she realise it was radio? It reminded him of pictures he had seen of old-time presenters in the studio, all done up in bow ties and dinner jackets, even though the listeners couldn't see them.

"This used to be the old Cunard offices," said the slim young man in the purple shirt as he sidestepped a pile of old tape-recorders and reel-to-reel tapes stacked outside a doorway before leading them into the waiting room. They could see the presenter through an internal window. He gave them a cheery wave as he introduced the next record.

"While this record is on, I'll take you through to the studio," said the guide. "You'll sit opposite and I'll give you some headphones to wear. Once the record finishes, he'll do a trailer and then play your track. So, he can have a few words with you while it's playing – then when it finishes you'll be live on air. Best of luck."

Derek and Jessie exchanged apprehensive looks.

"Don't worry – he'll put you at your ease," said the young man. "We had Pat Campbell in here last week. You know – 'stay right on the dial with Country Style'."

"We've met Pat Campbell," said Jessie, pulling a comic face for Derek's benefit. "He judged a talent show at The Ponderosa a few months ago."

She was just about to tell him how Campbell had disapproved of Jessie singing *These Boots Are Made For Walking,* and suggested she sing some 'proper country', when they were called into the studio. There was no more time to be nervous.

*

"Why's Jessie going on and on about being auditioned for the band?" wailed Sharon. "That were ages ago. She's supposed to be talking about the EP."

"Shush," said Wendy.

"She's jealous," said Georgie.

"Shush."

"But she is," he said, reducing his voice to a whisper. "Cos they played Dad's track and she's not on it. They weren't supposed to play that one – they were supposed to play the duet."

The interviewer smoothly brought Jessie to a halt by asking Derek a question about his admiration for George

Jones. Now it was Georgie's turn to say 'shush'. They all stared hard at the radio, willing Derek to say the right things.

*

"It's no good yelling at me," said Derek as he and Jessie rejoined her husband in the reception area. "It wasn't my fault." He looked across to where Jessie's little shadow, her self-effacing husband, was waiting glumly in an orange imitation-leather chair, clutching a cup of coffee. "The chap who showed us into the studio - he's in charge of production. He should have told them which track to play."

"What – that young lad, barely out of short trousers?" Jessie snatched the cup from her husband's hand, swigged down the rest of his coffee and banged the cup down on the table. "What did he think I was doing there? Just coming along for the ride?"

Derek sighed.

"Anyway, the main thing is that he gave us a good plug – and it should sell a few copies," he said. "And when people buy the EP, they'll hear you, won't they?"

"I suppose so," said Jessie, grudgingly.

"You were great, darling," said her husband.

"Hmm," she said. She ran her fingers through her blonde hair to fluff it up, then looked sideways at Derek. "What was all that about a record competition? I didn't really take it in – I was trying to think up what I could say next."

"I don't really know. Something about putting the EP in for a country music prize. I'll have to ask Alan what it's all about. So long as we don't have to pay to enter."

"And as long as the prize isn't a night out with Pat Campbell," said Jessie, finally cracking a smile. As they crossed the street to where the car was parked, she said: "Oh, we were going to do some shopping while we're in Southampton. Are you OK to get the bus?"

Jessie always did like to win. He was sure she must keep count of grudges and tick them off every time she managed to land a tit-for-tat. He pretended not to mind and headed off towards the bus station.

*

Gerry, idly browsing in Weston Hart's on an afternoon off, picked up the EP of the Smith & Wesson Band and flipped it over to look at the track listing. It caught his eye because it was displayed on the counter next to the till, with a sign saying 'local band'. He was queuing up to buy the *Machine Head* album by Deep Purple. As soon as he realised that Smith & Wesson was a country band, he put the EP back onto the stand. His tastes ran more to rock these days.

The girl behind the till stuck out a languid hand to take the album from him, but Gerry wasn't looking. Something struck him about the picture on the front of the EP.

"Are you buying this or what?" she said.

"What? Oh, sorry," said Gerry, handing over the album. "I'll take this as well." Impulsively he picked the EP up again and passed it over the counter to her.

"Don't see you as the boots and Stetson type," she said, forgetting for a moment to maintain her bored and uninterested persona.

He laughed, wondering whether she was flirting with him and whether it was worthwhile summoning the energy to flirt back. He decided not.

"Nah – it's for my mum," he said.

Outside in the cab, he took the EP out of the bag and looked intensely at the band's picture. In the centre was a girl with a lot of blonde hair and big teeth. She was done up like Dolly Parton on a bad night, but wasn't as pretty. The guys flanking her were holding guitars, and crouching down in front of them on one knee was an old-fashioned looking bloke with slicked-back hair and a bootlace tie, who was holding drumsticks. One of the guitarists had a great frizzy halo of hair like an Afro and another was a tall, relaxed-looking geezer who would look right at home in Nashville. It was the man standing next to the blonde that caught Gerry's eye. He was slightly built with dark hair and a thin face. He was holding his guitar upright in front of him, resting his hand on the top of its neck and looking at the camera with only a slight smile. With his Western-style shirt and black jeans he wore a belt with a large and distinctive buckle. Gerry flipped over the EP sleeve to look for the names of the band members on the back. 'Hank Wesson' – that was the man. That was surely the man he had seen on the track as he drove out of the wood.

"You're going mad, Gerry Chandler," he told himself, flinging the EP down onto the passenger seat. "Seeing things. Paranoid, that's what you are."

*

Gerry sat in the Double-A offices, drinking a cup of tea and turning the pages of *The Sun*. It was a quiet time and he had another fifteen minutes of his break left. He could hear Ginny, the despatcher, sending Lenny and a few of the others out on jobs but things wouldn't really liven up until later in the afternoon. Reluctantly turning the page after having spent some considerable time admiring the assets of the 'Stunna' of the day, and comparing them rather unfavourably with Tina, a small news item caught his eye. It was well down the page and it didn't have a photograph with it. 'Mystery body identified' was the headline. It only took him a second to read the two-paragraph piece, another couple of seconds to throw on his coat and run out of the door.

"Where you going Gerry?" shouted Ginny to his retreating back.

"Be right back!" he said, waving an arm. He ran down the street to the nearest newsagents, arriving breathless and cursing his lack of fitness, picked up the *Portsmouth News* but couldn't find the *Southern Evening Echo* on the rack.

"Not come in yet, mate," said the shop-keeper.

"Holy shit."

"No need for swearing."

"Sorry," said Gerry.

As he went to leave the shop, the *Echo* delivery van

pulled up outside and the driver unloaded a bundle of papers tied up with string. The shop-keeper seemed to deliberately take an age to find some scissors and snip the string, then he insisted on putting some papers in the rack and onto the display shelves before he would let Gerry buy a copy.

"Keep the change," said Gerry, handing over a pound note and running out of the door, leaving the shop-keeper open-mouthed with amazement.

As he reached the offices, he had second thoughts about reading the papers in there, so headed for his car instead. He propped the papers up against the steering wheel. The story was on the front page of both papers, and identified the body found in the Bere Forest as being Daniel Paterson, aged 32. There was a rather smudgy photograph of Paterson which looked as if it had been taken at a wedding a few years previously. He was wearing a suit with a flower in the buttonhole: his hair was shorter and he didn't have a moustache but it was recognisably the same man. Neither of the papers seemed to have much more information and the stories just repeated what had already been published about the discovery of the body. What was new was that it was Paterson's neighbour who had reported him missing, having found the Renault 4 parked with one wheel on the pavement and the keys still in the ignition. The article said that police had now seized the car for examination. Well, they wouldn't get much from that, thought Gerry, biting at his thumbnail. The skin was all red where he'd bitten it down to the quick. He wiped it on his trousers and stuck his hand into his coat pocket.

Daniel Paterson had apparently been unemployed and the full-time carer for his 85-year-old grandmother, Gwen Hayward, with whom he lived in New Road. The grandmother had been found by the neighbour, dehydrated and without any food in the house, who had heard her banging with a stick on the wall. She had apparently been on her own in the house for three days: after an overnight hospital stay, she had now been moved to a Council nursing home. Gerry felt a bit sick when he read this. He wound down the car window to let in some air.

The *Portsmouth News*, unlike the *Echo*, which just had the standard police statement, focused more on the Bere Forest angle, as that was on the paper's 'patch' and had managed to get a quote from the brother, who lived in Scotland. He described Daniel as a quiet man who had been through some tough times in recent years but had recently been beginning to get his life back together. He didn't think Daniel had ever been to the Bere Forest, nor could he think of any reason for him to go there with someone. The police were apparently working on the theory that Daniel had been kidnapped for purposes unknown. They were not revealing the cause of death, but were appealing for witnesses.

Well, Gerry knew of one witness – but what had the bloke actually seen? Gerry swinging the baseball bat? And what did that prove, exactly? It's not as if the bat had made contact with anything other than air. Surely, if the bloke had intended to go to the police he would have done so straight away? Perhaps he was worrying unnecessarily. Then something else struck him: something that made him throw the papers down onto the passenger seat and grip the steering wheel so hard that his hands hurt. He stared out of the windscreen. New Road – how could he have been so stupid? There must have been a dozen witnesses in those houses when Daniel was screaming at him in the street. He rested his forehead on the steering wheel. Suddenly, the driver's door was flung open and Gerry sat up straight, his heart pounding.

"Mr Chandler, my dear, are you having a nap or are you ready to start your next shift?" Ginny said teasingly, leaning into the car. "I've been calling you – did you not have your radio switched on? Only you've got a pick-up at Hilsea to do."

"Sorry, Ginny," he said.

She laughed, chucked him under the chin, closed the door and went back up the stairs to the office.

Gerry started the engine.

*

"Delivery for Miss Tina and Master Darren!" Gerry called out chirpily as he rapped twice with his knuckles on the front door.

The door opened to reveal Darren. Gerry put a finger to his lips and winked. Darren, as quick to catch on as ever, made not a sound but stood aside to let Gerry in.

"Thlee chicken chow mein, two flied lice, thlee spling lolls," said Gerry in his best comic-book Chinese accent, moving past Darren and heading for the kitchen. The mattress was still there, blocking half the hallway. He swung the carrier bags past it and put them on the table. Darren peered into each bag excitedly.

"Please to find plates," said Gerry.

Darren picked three unmatching plates off the draining board; one still had a smear of baked beans on its edge. When he turned back, Gerry was holding up chopsticks, juggling with them and then using them to beat out a rhythm on the edge of the table.

"What on earth's going on?" said Tina as she came into the kitchen, looking like she had just woken up.

"Chinese banquet for pletty lady," said Gerry, laughing.

"Come on, mum – before it gets cold."

Tina smiled and ran her fingers through her hair.

"This looks great, Gerry – what a nice surprise. Darren – go and wash your hands before you sit down."

Darren gave his hands a perfunctory dunk under the cold tap of the kitchen sink while Gerry and Tina opened up the steaming foil containers.

"I've got some beer, if you'd like one, Gerry."

"No thanks – I'm on shift later."

As he reached for the rice, she caught hold of his shirt sleeve, moving the cuff back above his wrist.

"What's this then?" she said, revealing a heavy gold identity bracelet and weighing it in her hand as if to assess its value.

"Just a little something I treated myself to," said Gerry. "You're not the only ones to get little treats, you know."

"Very nice," said Tina. "There's nothing engraved on it yet, then?"

"I've not decided what to put."

"What about 'Gerry'?" said Darren.

"I'd never have thought of that," he said, cuffing Darren playfully around the head. "What a genius this boy is!"

They all laughed.

"This is like being a family, isn't it, Gerry?" said Darren merrily, chopsticks poised in midair.

There was a moment of silence before Gerry said: "It is, Darren." He moved his feet further under the table so that they gripped one of Tina's ankles. "It is."

Chapter Seven

The Rosemore Nursing Home was on a quiet wide street, set back from the road, though what might have once been a front garden had been tarmacked and turned into a car park. It was a big Edwardian double-fronted house with huge bay windows. There was no sign of any roses or any other vegetation. Its status as a Council nursing home was immediately apparently from the cheap sign on the front to the plethora of typed and handwritten notices sellotaped to the walls of the reception area. Not a home for 'distressed gentlefolk', that was for sure.

Gerry breezed into Reception with his best winning smile ready. He'd parked the taxi two streets away and congratulated himself on his clear thinking.

"I've come to visit Gwen Hayward," he said to the sourfaced old dragon behind the desk. She did not seem to find his smile remotely winning: maybe she was related to that old cow he'd met at Darren's school, he thought.

"And you are?"

"Roy Jones – I telephoned earlier."

"Ah yes. Mr Jones," she said as if she immediately knew it was a made-up name.

Gerry fiddled with his tie while the old dragon bit her cheek and tried to think up reasons not to let him in. Eventually she sighed as said: "Gwen is in the conservatory at the moment. Straight through those double doors and turn left."

"Thank you." He adjusted the wrapped bunch of carnations in his hand, gave the old dragon a nod and walked purposefully off. Once he was out of her sight he flagged down a young woman wearing a nurse's uniform.

"I wonder if you can help me, love," he said. She paused – an attractive dark-haired girl of about twenty-five. "I'm visiting Gwen Hayward but the thing is – I don't know what she looks like."

The nurse frowned. "You're not press, are you?"

"Goodness, no – I'm a friend … was a friend … of her grandson, but I've never met her."

"That's OK then – it's just that we've had some press snooping around. Terrible thing, about her grandson. Who would want to do a thing like that, eh?"

"Terrible," agreed Gerry.

"Come on – I'll show you where Gwen is," she said, walking off briskly and leaving him to follow. Her uniform made an attractive rustling sound as she walked.

"Thank you. No need to mention this to the old drag ... the lady in Reception, is there?"

The nurse laughed.

"Gwen's settling now well now, but obviously she was fairly distressed when she was first admitted. You'll find her quite shy and reserved. She's not got over the shock of Daniel's death yet."

The conservatory was a large light-filled room overlooking a scrubby patch of lawn and the backs of the houses in the neighbouring street. The smell of overboiled cabbage was less noticeable out here than in the corridor. Almost every seat was occupied, but no-one was talking to anyone else: the residents were all slumped in their chairs staring vacantly into space, apart from one who was doing a crossword. Gerry was grateful for the young nurse's help, particularly as all the old ladies looked identical to him.

"Visitor for you, Mrs Hayward," she said, walking up to a diminutive white-haired lady seated in a wheelchair. On the table attached to the front of the wheelchair was a packet of birdseed that the lady was trying to pour into a bird-feeder. She looked up as the nurse approached and Gerry hoped this meant that she wasn't deaf and he wouldn't have to shout his entire conversation for everyone in the conservatory to hear.

"He's bought you some lovely flowers, too. I'll go and

find a vase for them, shall I? Perhaps he'll wheel you out into the garden in a minute and you can set up the birdfeeder on the stand." With that, the nurse scooped up the bouquet of carnations and swished off.

"Hello, Mrs Hayward," said Gerry. "I know we've not met before, but my name's Roy." He felt awkward bending over her chair. "I was a friend of your grandson's."

Tears immediately sprang into her eyes and she reached out a scrawny hand and gripped Gerry's arm with surprising strength.

"I'm so glad you've come. Pull up that chair – you're the first of Daniel's friends to visit me. In fact you'll probably be the only one." He eyes were blue and very clear. As Gerry looked into her face, he could see the resemblance to Daniel.

"Well, as it's a nice day, why don't we go into the garden and have our chat there?" he said, anxious to be out of the hearing of the others, all of whom had inclined their heads greedily towards Gwen, not having visitors of their own. He grasped the handles of the wheelchair firmly and pushed it towards the French doors. A sprightly old boy with a stick walked over and opened the doors for them. Gerry feared he might follow them out, but he sank back into the nearest armchair again.

Gerry pushed Gwen into a patch of sunlight next to a bench, and followed her instructions on how she wanted the blanket arranged over her knees. He hung the birdfeeder on the stand and they sat back waiting for the birds to detect its presence. He was unsure what to say next but, remembering that the nurse had told him that Gwen was quite shy, he thought he ought to lead off.

"I don't want to upset you by talking about Daniel if you'd prefer not to."

"That's alright, dear. Perhaps in a minute."

He tried again: "I was sorry to hear you were in the house for so long on your own. It must have been frightening."

"Yes, you see Daniel was my full-time carer and he was always so careful to tell me where he was going and when he would be back. He said he would only be an hour."

I bet he did, thought Gerry – each little outing just long enough to nick another booking from the Double-A.

"Then it got dark and I couldn't reach the light switch and I was frightened. I didn't mind not eating, but as the hours went by I finished all my water and I was so thirsty. I couldn't understand where he'd got to."

She was twisting a corner of the blanket in her hands now, clearly distressed. Gerry felt worse about what she'd gone through than what he'd done to Daniel, the bumped-up little poofter. She seemed a good sort.

"Remind me – how long had Daniel been looking after you?"

"Since he lost his house. Three years ago now, it must have been." Gerry smiled encouragingly. "What with my daughter and son-in-law in Australia, and Malcolm in Edinburgh, there was no-one else. And it came after all that – you know, all that trouble that Daniel was having, so it worked out well for us both. He had somewhere to live and I had someone to look after me."

A blackbird alighted on the bird-table and started cautiously to peck at the seed-holder, looking around after each peck to see whether it was in danger. Its eyes were bright and hard. They both watched it for a while. Then came the question that Gerry had dreaded.

"Were you and Daniel friends for a long time, Roy? Only, I don't think he had many friends and he never seemed to want me to meet them."

He'd prepared for this, but still felt like an obvious fraud.

"Well, I hadn't seen so much of him recently, to be honest." He didn't meet her eye.

"He was very upset when he was thrown out of his home. So unfair, I thought."

"Yes, indeed," said Gerry.

"I mean – it's not as if it was illegal any more. Mr Askew was just being vindictive."

Gerry tensed. Brian Askew?

"Do you think," she continued, before Gerry had had

time to formulate a response, "that he went with a man to the forest for .... well, you know what?"

"It's possible, I suppose," said Gerry. "Do the police have any theories?"

"I don't think they know what to think, to be honest." She stared at the bird table as if it might provide an answer. "I'm glad to have met you, Roy. You seem nicer than the few friends of Daniel's who I did get to meet."

He licked his lips. "Thank you."

Through the window, they watched the young nurse arrive in the conservatory accompanied by a uniformed policeman and a man in a suit. They had an agitated air.

"Oh dear," said Gwen. "Here they are again." She turned to Gerry. "Do you think you would mind visiting me again next week? I've enjoyed your company."

"It would be my pleasure," said Gerry, not insincerely. "I'd best slip out through the garden, if you don't mind."

He got up, pecked Gwen on the cheek, and headed around the side of the house towards the street, his heart beating hard in his chest.

*

Gerry put the EP on the turntable. Seemed a shame not to play it now he'd bought it. He grabbed a bottle of beer from the fridge and sat down to listen, holding the record sleeve in one hand. The first track was one of those typical up-beat rather corny country duets: he didn't particularly like the song but had to admit that the woman had a good voice and the lead guitar had a nice crisp sound. He looked again at the woman's photograph. She was a bit overblown for his taste. He had a swig of his beer. When the second track started, he was astonished to find tears springing into his eyes. He put the beer down on the table. It wasn't just the words, though the line about the lip-print on a half-filled cup of coffee made him think of Carol straight away. It was something about the voice, the way the singer bent the notes, the break in his voice as he went into the chorus. It seemed to be speaking some essential truth; communicating some unbearable sense of loss; and cutting through what might otherwise have just been a sentimental song. When the record finished, Gerry just sat there, ignoring the click of the stylus arm as it returned to the resting position. After a few moments he wiped his eyes. 'For God's sake!' he reprimanded himself. 'You sentimental idiot.'

Then he remembered why he'd bought the record in the first place. He looked again at the picture of Hank Wesson – surely not his real name as the band were British – and at the thin face, the slicked-back hair and the distinctive belt buckle on his jeans. The more he looked, the more he couldn't decide whether he was going mad or not. He decided to find out where the band was playing next: he was sure that if he saw the bloke face-to-face, he'd know. He'd also know whether the bloke recognised him too. Quite what he'd do if this turned out to be the case was not something he even wanted to consider yet.

*

"So it's all just stopped? Just like that?" said Gerry. He leaned forward, putting his hands on the edge of the desk and drawing close to Bertha's face. In the interests of sincerity, he looked her straight in the eye.

"It has," she said, clearly weighing up what he might be getting at.

"Nah," said Gerry. "You did something, didn't you, Bertha? Little genius, aren't you? I bet you found out who was doing it and threatened to set your dog on them." He picked up the pen from her desk and spun it round in his fingers.

She smiled. "No, I didn't have to do a thing. Presumably they just got bored with messing us about."

He put the pen down and rocked back onto his heels.

"Unless you stuck your nose in, of course, Gerry?"

"Course not. You told me to stay away from it and I did."

She didn't respond but let the silence draw out – a silence that he had to force himself not to fill by adding to what he'd already said.

"Talking of dogs – I've got a joke for you," he said eventually.

"I hope it's a filthy one."

"Yeah, well, it's about this bloke I met in the pub last night. I ask him what he does for a living and he says he has a stage act. Him, the wife and the Alsatian. They go on stage, and he has it off with the wife while the dog watches, then the dog and the wife have it off, then all three of them do it. I said "that sounds an interesting act - what do you call yourselves". 'The Debonaires', he says."

Bertha allowed herself a brief snort of laughter.

"Incidentally," she said, "that young boy that keeps hanging around outside the office – you know the one I mean? The thin lad with bad teeth?"

"That'll be Darren."

"Is he hanging around waiting for you?"

"Yes, he … well, me and his mum we're …" He looked down at the desk.

"I see," said Bertha. "Bit of a looker is she? You always did have an eye for the ladies."

"She couldn't hold a candle to you, Bertha," he said, grinning, relieved that the tension had passed but feeling guilty that he hadn't immediately said what a looker Tina was. Which she wasn't, of course.

"Get away with you, Gerry."

Gerry left the office, passing the framed picture of Brian Askew that sat on the top of the metal filing cabinet. Brian was a square-faced bloke with eyebrows that always gave him a surprised expression. He had a fleshy mouth and a dimple in his chin. His hair was dark brown with a very precise parting: he must have been the last bloke in the country to still be using Brylcreme. In the framed photograph, he was wearing a Pompey team shirt and was looking a bit miserable, probably because his team had just lost. A funny picture to want to use to preserve his memory. Gerry wondered again what connection there could have been between Daniel Paterson and Askew. Maybe he'd make that his next task.

The gig at Eastney Working Men's Club was going well and by the second set Derek even felt that there was a slight flicker of chemistry between him and Jessie, which was a rare enough occurrence. During *Something to Brag About* he moved over to Jessie's microphone to sing the chorus with her, their heads close together, their mouths barely two inches apart. The crowd loved it; Jessie's husband shifted uncomfortably in his seat.

Dancers packed the floor and people were standing three deep at the bar. As Derek sang 'let's get married in the not too distant future' and Jessie gave the answer-back 'we'll rent a little flat on 29th street', he smiled across at the crowd. A man standing near the doorway caught his eye. He was looking straight at Derek – nothing unusual about that, when Derek was centre-stage. But it was something about the way he was standing that nagged at Derek's memory. It was a solid stance, with the weight evenly balanced between his two feet. He looked to be in his thirties, with light brown hair. As he turned to put down his empty pint glass on a nearby table, the lights picked out the acne scars on his cheeks. Derek almost missed his cue for the final chorus trying to remember where he'd seen the man before – he was useless at remembering people's names but faces weren't usually a problem. Not one of their regular followers. Maybe one of his strawberry stall customers. Then suddenly he knew with chilling certainty who it was.

At the end of the gig, Derek saw the man head for the Gents, so he quickly put down his guitar, muttered something to Alan about nipping outside for a moment, and hurried out through the fire doors to the car-park at the back of the club.

He stayed close to the wall of the club, not wanting to be spotted should the man suddenly appear. It was dark and the car park was still fairly full: all the cars looked the same, their hunched shapes indistinguishable from each other and Derek, thinking it was pointless, turned to go back inside. Just then, a couple walked up to a yellow Ford Capri and got in. As the driver put the headlights on, ready to drive away, the light shone on a car in the next row. An insignia on the door was visible: two interlinked 'A's. Derek was sure that was the symbol he'd seen on the car in the forest. As the Capri pulled away, he stepped forward to peer at the insignia more closely and as he did so, there was a crunch on the gravel immediately behind him. He turned.

"Need a taxi, mate? Only I'm not on duty tonight."

"No, that's fine," said Derek, feeling stupid at being caught so easily and trying to keep his face turned away from the light. He moved away from the man and the car, towards the club's firedoors, but he could feel the man staring after him.

"Goodnight, Hank!" shouted a woman from across the other side of the car park.

Great, thought Derek. So much for creeping away without him seeing my face.

"Yes, goodnight, Hank," said the man dryly as he unlocked the driver's door of the taxi and got inside.

*

Gerry was sweating as he turned the car onto Eastney seafront. He told himself to calm down and think it through. Obviously this Hank character had recognised him from the forest, otherwise why would he have been peering at the taxi-cab in the dark? Why hadn't he stayed with the rest of the band to pack up the equipment? He'd also looked a bit flustered when he'd spotted Gerry in the club earlier and their eyes had met. Or was that just Gerry's imagination? Maybe the bloke had just gone outside for a fag after the gig? On reflection, it had been reckless of Gerry to go to the club in the first place, but he'd needed to know whether 'Hank' was the man he'd seen on the path: now he was convinced that was the case. The question was how much had Hank seen that day and could he identify Gerry? However often Gerry told himself there were other explanations, he knew in his gut that Hank had seen it all. He was probably calling the police right now. Gerry's head started to hurt. He leaned it back on the headrest.

When he got close to home, he changed his mind, turned the car around and headed for Tina's place instead. She'd still be up, surely? A bit of mindless sex was just the thing to empty his head of all this.

*

Libraries were not exactly Gerry's natural territory. In fact the last time he had been in one was when he had signed his boy up for a library card when he was about seven. Joe couldn't believe that he could exchange four little bits of cardboard for four books and had watched in delight as the books were stamped. The librarian – younger than most and a bit more unbending – had even allowed him to play with the date-stamp, until her sour-faced colleague had returned to the desk. He wondered if the boy still read books. The fact that he didn't know started to make him feel depressed, so he deliberately cast off the impending bad mood by bouncing up to the counter with one of his winning smiles.

If this wasn't the same sour-faced librarian as it had been six years ago, then it was her identical twin. Gerry explained what he wanted and she reluctantly led him over to a large table, sighing audibly. She pointed at the huge bound volumes on the shelves.

"They are all here. Make sure you put them back in the right order."

"I will."

"And please don't use a biro to take any notes, in case you accidentally mark the pages."

"There's no index, then? I just have to go through every page?"

"We have card indexes for Hampshire Magazine, but not for the daily paper."

Now it was his turn to sigh. He didn't know exactly what date he was looking for: Daniel's nan had said it was about three years ago that he'd lost his home, but who was to say that it was anything that might have made the papers? And what exactly was Brian Askew's connection to that?

"Thank you," he said, smiling ingratiatingly at Sour Face.

Impervious to his charm, she pursed her lips and stalked off. Gerry settled down with the first volume. The library was silent and at first Gerry itched to have a bit of background music to help him concentrate. He looked around for distraction, but the only person visible was an old bearded guy sitting in the reference section and he seemed to be asleep. Gerry returned to the huge volume, scanning headlines about weddings, council meetings, mayoral ceremonies, shipping movements, city planning, altercations outside pubs and arson attacks. After an hour, he craved a coffee; after two hours and three volumes of papers, his stomach started to rumble. Eventually he went over to the desk and told Sour Face that he'd be back in a while. She nodded, like a jailor reluctantly giving permission for a prisoner to go out into the exercise yard.

After a hot sausage roll and a mug of coffee at a caff on the corner, he was back at the reading table. The sun was streaming through the window and the newspaper pages were tinged with green and red from the stained-glass. It was a bit like a church, thought Gerry – a church where people worshipped books.

It was after three o'clock when he found it, and he had to suppress a whoop of delight. It was a tiny news item, down in the bottom corner of the page and he might have missed it entirely except that his eye had been drawn to a photograph of the Miss Hayling Island beauty-queen winner that accompanied a story in the next column.

LANDLORD CAUTIONED FOR ASSAULT

A Portsmouth landlord who owns three houses that have been converted into flats has been cautioned by police for assaulting one of his tenants. The complaint had been brought by Daniel Paterson (29) against landlord Brian

Askew of Southsea. Mr Paterson, who rented a flat in a property in Albert Road, alleged that in evicting him and another unnamed tenant, Mr Askew had used unnecessary force and he had sustained an injury to his shoulder, which meant that he would have to take long-term sick-leave from his job as a precision tool-maker. Speaking to the *Evening News*, Mr Askew defended his actions and said he had every right to "evict tenants who were bringing his property into disrepute." Asked whether he meant that he did not accept that homosexuality was now legal, Mr Askew said that they were "his houses and therefore his rules". Mr Paterson declined to comment when contacted by our reporter.

*

Derek sat at the kitchen table while Wendy went through all the figures again. Across the table were spread unpaid bills from the electricity, gas and water boards. She had a lined notebook open in front of her, and was writing columns of figures. She'd always been good at maths; he guessed it came from those Saturday jobs she'd had as a teenager working at the grocer's in Wickham.

"We owe Chalky, too," she said, bouncing Lor on her knee when the baby started to grizzle. "Ten pounds, isn't it?"

"Yes, but Chalky don't mind waiting a bit longer."

"It's no good, Derek. Whichever way I add it up, you're just not earning enough for us to make ends meet. The kids are starting to get picked on at school."

"What do you mean?"

"Well, sometimes it's about their clothes and sometimes it's that they don't go on trips like the other kids do." She tapped the end of the pencil up and down on the table.

"Sharon went on that Salisbury trip," he pointed out.

"One girl, one trip – it's not enough. What if I was to get a part-time job?"

"Are you mad? How could you possibly manage that, what with Lor and Bobby to look after?"

"Well, the others are practically grown up now – they could do some more minding for me, after school. They're looking for workers over at Hill Pound Farm. I could get there on the bus."

"No, it's out of the question."

"Why? Your male pride would be offended, would it?"

Derek was about to deny it, but then laughed.

"You're right, Wendy. My male pride. We'll just have to hope that the band's EP is a hit and then we'll be rolling in it." He grinned.

"Huh," she said doubtfully.

"I'll think of something, love. Don't you worry."

That night, he lay awake, thinking about the man at the club and fretting about money. He hadn't even told Wendy yet that the insurance company had refused to pay out for his ruined guitar. Then there was Pete: he owed Pete £20 too. Wendy snored lightly. He got out of bed and went over to the window. There was a high wind and the clouds were scudding across the face of the moon. Suddenly, he knew how he could solve his money worries. And the answer didn't lie in becoming an overnight chart success either. It lay much closer to home: in a coffee tin, in fact.

Chapter Eight

"Is that Burntwood Records?"

"That's us, man," said a man, sounding friendly. "Can I help?"

"Well my name is Dave Townsend. I'm a promoter and I'm looking to get in touch with someone who's recorded for you - but all I've got is his stage name: Hank Wesson."

"Oh yeah. From Smith & Wesson – they did an EP with us a few weeks ago. What a voice that guy has got! Sent shivers up my spine, I can tell you. You looking to book them?"

"I am, but it was Hank in particular who I wanted to talk to, so I wanted an address for him, rather than the band's agent or anything."

"I get your meaning. Striking a deal direct is always the best option. Hold on a sec." There was a thud as the handset was put down and Gerry heard the man walking away. The metallic sound of a filing cabinet drawer opening and shutting was followed by the footsteps coming back to the phone.

"I don't know what his real name is, I'm afraid, and I don't have an address for him. That's because the lead guitarist, Alan King, signed the contract on behalf of the band – I can give you his address and phone number if you want."

"No, that's OK. I'm sure I can find him," said Gerry, cursing silently.

"I think he did say that he lived out Wickham way, if that helps. Runs a strawberry stall or flower stall or something."

"It does help. Many thanks."

"Make 'im famous, Mr Townsend!"

Gerry laughed. "I'll do my best."

*

Derek went down to the phone box and lifted up the directory onto the little shelf alongside the phone. He knew the taxi company had two interlinked 'A's on the door, but did that mean it was called the 'AA' or maybe 'Two As'? He looked at both, his reading skills confident enough now for him to run his finger down the page and try to spot the name. There was an 'AAA Taxis' but that didn't look like it was the right company. He also looked under 'T' in case it was 'Two As' but there was nothing. Frustrated, he put the directory back in its slot and tried to think. If it was a taxi firm, it would be in the phone book, surely? He looked again at the front of the directory and the map that showed the area it covered: Southampton and its surrounding towns and villages. Maybe the Double-A was from another area? Winchester, maybe, or Portsmouth?

There was a tap on the glass door of the phone box and Derek turned to see a young, gum-chewing girl standing outside. She was wearing a very short skirt and shoes whose heels were worn down and scuffed. He vaguely recognised her: one of the Harvey daughters from the farm up the road who was at the same school as Sharon but a year above. He opened the door slightly.

"Yes?"

"You gonna be long, Mr Fry? Only my boyfriend's phoning this box at six."

"OK," said Derek, sliding through the gap in the door and holding it open for her. "Hang on a minute."

"What?"

"Where do you find phone numbers for firms if they're not in this book? Like, if they're in a different book?"

"Dunno." She blew a bubble of gum.

"Never mind," he said.

*

The story was in the *Evening News* on page seven. 'Do you recognise these clothes?' was the headline over a picture of a pair of flared jeans, a pink paisley shirt, a pair of briefs and socks, and some dark lace-up shoes. Gerry gripped the newspaper more tightly in an effort to stop his hands shaking. The article said that police had reason to treat the items as suspicious and possibly to have been involved in a crime. They were keeping tight-lipped about any other details and were not revealing how these items had come into their possession.

The bin where Gerry had dumped the clothes was miles from where Daniel had died – surely they wouldn't connect the two? Except, the paisley shirt was quite distinctive. What if they showed the picture to Daniel's nan? Would she recognise the clothes?

He ran his fingers through his hair, massaging his head with his fingertips. Turning it over and over in his mind was no help: he needed to get out there and do something. Maybe he should see Daniel's nan again – see what she knew? Should he risk it? Anything was better than sitting around worrying about it. He grabbed his car-keys off the table and headed out of the flat.

*

"Sorry," said Gerry, rolling off Tina and reaching over to the bedside table to reach for the cigarettes. He lit two of them and passed one to her.

"It's alright. It happens," said Tina. "You worried about something?"

"No, everything's fine, love. Just a bit tired, that's all." He sat on the edge of the bed to pull on his T-shirt then found to his surprise that he was crying. He rubbed his eyes with his knuckles, the way a small child would do.

"You're obviously not fine. What is it?"

"It's just that someone I knew has died." He still had his back to her. "Someone I'd only just met, really. I don't know why it's upset me so much."

"A customer?"

"No, an old lady who was a friend of a friend of a friend, if you know what I mean." He turned to look at her. "She was in an old folks' home. I went to take her some flowers today, and she was gone, just like that. She passed away in the night, they said."

Tina put her arms round his waist and rested her head on his back.

"Why don't you go out somewhere tomorrow with Darren – you're not working Saturday, are you? Cheer yourself up a bit."

"Yeah, you're right. Give Darren an outing. Want to come?"

"No, I got … stuff to do here."

"What kind of stuff?" She was always vague about what she did when he wasn't there: he imagined it was all about queuing for her Giro, or fending off the social workers. Or worse: he tried not to think about worse.

"Just stuff, you know."

"Hey – I could take Darren to Brighton. Would he like that?"

"Like it? You're kidding – he'll be over the moon."

Once Gerry was back in the car, he took the envelope out of the glovebox. 'Roy Jones Esq' it said on the front in neat handwriting with a little flourish on the tail of the 'y'. The envelope was blue – Basildon Bond, which reminded Gerry of that awful 007 joke about 'the name's Bond: Basildon Bond'. He hadn't opened it at the home when the nurse handed it over, partly because he was stunned to hear that Gwen had died and partly because he wanted to get out of there as quickly as possible before they asked him too many questions.

He opened it carefully and extracted the single sheet of paper that was inside.

'Dear Roy,' it read, 'I was so pleased to meet you last week and I wanted to write and thank you for the flowers, but I did not have your address, so I hope you will forgive me if I hand you this thank-you in person next time you visit. You were a good friend to Daniel, I think, and I hope you find out what really happened to him, because my heart is breaking at the loss of my grandson. Yours sincerely, Gwen Hayward (Mrs).'

Once more the tears started to course down Gerry's cheeks and he couldn't work out whether it was genuine sorrow at her death, or just self-pity: his emotions seemed to be all mixed up these days.

*

"I'll draw it," said Derek. He pulled the pad towards him and carefully drew two interlinked 'A's before turning the pad around and pushing it across the table to Pete. "Does that mean the firm is called 'AA'?"

"Maybe. Have you tried the phone book?"

"Yes, but I needs a Portsmouth one. Or maybe a Winchester one."

"Yellow Pages is what we want. Come on – grab your coat."

Derek followed Pete out to the car and they drove into Fareham and parked outside the Post Office. Inside, along one wall, was a row of telephone kiosks and a whole bank of phone directories suspended from a metal rack.

Pete picked out the one for Portsmouth first.

"See – it's organised alphabetically by the type of business. You look under 'taxi firms' and all the Portsmouth ones will be listed." He thumbed through the directory.

"There it is!" said Derek, recognising the logo with the interlinked letters on the large display advertisement.

"Double-A", said Pete, "That's what they are called. Shall I write down the phone number for you?"

"Just the address, please."

Pete wrote the address clearly on a piece of paper and handed it to Derek.

"Now we're going to drive back home and you're going to tell me what's going on."

"It's nothing. I just need to go and see them, that's all."

"Looking for a job?" asked Pete. "Because it's a bit far away, isn't it?"

Derek shook his head but didn't reply.

"Is it connected to what you showed me in the newspaper? That body they discovered in the forest?"

"No, of course not," said Derek. "Why would you think that?" The car swung in through the gates of Pete's parents' house and Pete said no more about it.

*

"Whoo-hooh!" shouted Darren as Brighton seafront loomed into view. He had the window fully down and his hair was streaming in the breeze. His feet, in scruffy plimsolls, were up on the dashboard despite Gerry having told him twice not to do it.

"Where to first, then?" asked Gerry as they parked the car. "The beach or the pier, or an ice-cream. Or the amusement arcade?"

Bemused by all these enticements, Darren couldn't get his words out.

"Don't worry – we can do all of it," said Gerry, laughing. "We've got the whole day to enjoy ourselves."

By the time they were on the beach – Darren with his trousers rolled up and carrying the most enormous ice-cream cornet with a Flake stuck in the top of it – the tight knot of pain in Gerry's chest was starting to ease. He sat down on the slightly damp sand and licked at his ice-cream while Darren paddled. Despite the fact that Southsea beach was only a couple of miles from Tina's flat, Gerry got the impression that Darren never went there. His life seemed to be circumscribed between school, flat, the shopping parade, and of course hanging out outside the Double-A.

The sun had come out and he felt its healing warmth on his face. He looked around at other families setting out their beach-towels and blowing up rubber rings for the kids. He wondered if he should have brought some swimming trunks and a towel for Darren.

"Oi!' he called.

"What?"

"Can you swim?"

"Nah – never learnt how," shouted Darren.

Gerry kicked off his shoes and ran down the beach towards Darren, roaring like a bear. Once there, he picked up Darren, flung him over one shoulder in a 'fireman's lift' and then ran straight out into the waves. The water was much colder than he'd anticipated. Darren was screaming, either from fear or exhilaration. Once the water had reached thigh-height, Gerry put Darren down and they splashed each other with water, laughing like idiots. Somewhere along the way, Darren had dropped the remains of his ice-cream cone.

They walked back out of the water, hand in hand, both soaked through from the waist down, and flung themselves onto the sand. With his hair all wet, Darren looked thinner than ever.

Once they'd dried off a bit, they went onto the pier where there was an amusement arcade, full of flashing lights – just the sort of place to issue a siren call to any young lad. Gerry changed a pound note into coins and they fed a couple into the table football machine. He'd spent much of his early teens playing table football at the youth club in Somerstown and although he hadn't played for years, the technique quickly came back to him. It was a good five minutes before he remembered that he needed to let Darren win, without making it too obvious. Darren fired a shot into goal as Gerry futilely spun the handle, his back line in the wrong place and upside down when the ball went through. He gave a quiet grin when he saw Darren's victorious face.

Afterwards, they sat on the pier and ate fish and chips straight from the newspaper.

"I wish you was my dad, Gerry," said Darren, stealing a handful of Gerry's chips and cramming them into his mouth.

"Oi! You little blighter! If I was your dad I'd have to give you a good hiding for that." Darren looked crestfallen and Gerry was horrified to see tears in his eyes. "Only kidding," said Gerry, ruffling Darren's hair.

After a couple of minutes, during which a dozen seagulls had clustered around their feet, hoping for a fallen titbit, and

Gerry had shooed them off, he said: "What was your dad like, Darren?"

"Can't remember him. He left when I was three or something."

"He's not kept in touch, then?"

"Nah. He don't want to know about us." He screwed up his empty newspaper wrapper and stuck it in the bin, wiping his greasy hands on his jeans as he walked back. "Mum's had lots of boyfriends since, but I hated all of them. They're not nice like you." He sat back down on the bench. "They do bad things to mum."

Gerry's throat felt constricted. He looked out at the sea for a moment; a light breeze had sprung up and the waves had small white crests on them. Someone was on a lilo that had a dragon's head and they were paddling it out determinedly, as if they were aiming for the French coast.

"I can't be a dad to you, Darren. I'm not good enough, and that's the truth. You deserve someone better. Anyway, I've already got a son."

"What? You never said nothing about no son!"

"I don't see him very often, to be honest, Darren. I split up with his mother years ago. She lives in Birmingham now with a new bloke."

"What's his name?"

"The new bloke?"

"No, stupid – your son."

"It's Joe. And don't call me stupid – it's rude."

"How old is he?"

"Same age as you - thirteen."

"So, if you stay with my mum, he could be ... like ... a brother for me. A long-distance brother."

Gerry pictured taking scruffy, skinny, tooth-missing Darren round to Carol and John's doubtless-perfect little house to stay for the summer holidays. He gave a bark of laughter.

"What's so funny?"

"Sorry, Darren. " He wanted to ask him what the bad things were that these men did to Tina, but perhaps it was best not to know. And best for Darren not to dwell on them, either.

By the time they got back to the car, Darren was exhausted and before they'd got as far as Lancing, he was fast asleep, his head resting on Gerry's shoulder.

*

"So, where the hell were you? And why did you have your radio switched off?" Big Bertha paced up and down the tiny office, while Gerry stood by the door.

"It was my day off – I booked it ages ago."

"No, you didn't." She stabbed a stubby finger at an entry in the desk diary. "I told you – Lenny was going to his nephew's wedding in Maidstone and you couldn't both be off at the same time, especially with two navy ships in. It was *next* Saturday you booked, you complete dolt."

"I'm really sorry, Bertha. I must have got muddled up."

"I even got one of the lads to go round to your flat to see if you weren't well. No answer, which I couldn't quite believe – I mean, it's not as if you've got any friends to go out with, is it, you poor saddo?"

"Oh, thanks a lot!" Gerry was ceasing to feel guilty now and beginning to get annoyed. The Alsatian, lying under the desk, sensed the change in mood and got to its feet.

"As a matter of fact, I did got out with a friend and we had a very good day." He realised how pathetic this sounded and shut up. He reached behind for the door knob.

"There's something else, Gerry," said Bertha, sitting down and crossing her legs. He ankle chain chinked softly. Gerry thought about her and Brian, the sort of landlord who turned queers out of his properties and didn't care who knew it. Probably did the same to Jews and blacks too. "Are you listening?"

"Sorry," he said again, snapping out of his reverie. "You were saying?"

"When you handed your cashbox over on Friday, it was £15 light."

He suddenly remembered borrowing the fifteen quid in

order to go to Brighton, intending to put it back before Ginny did the week's accounts on Monday morning. He reached for his wallet, but there were only three pound-notes in it. He checked his watch.

"I'll nip round to the bank now – back in two ticks."

"Gerry, you're a good driver and we don't want to lose you, but you need to get your head out of your arse and concentrate on the job."

"Yes, Bertha. I know. And I will."

"By the way, the police want to interview all the drivers tomorrow. I'm calling everyone back in at noon. They'll call you in one at a time and take your statements in the office."

Gerry felt the colour drain from his face.

"What's this all about?"

"I told you on Friday, but you were counting clouds or something." She sighed. "They're investigating a suspicious death and a Double-A cab was seen stopped in the street the day the bloke died. They're just going to ask where you were and if you saw anything that could help them."

"Where was this?"

"New Road. Three weeks ago."

Gerry shook his head and kept his expression blank.

"No, doesn't ring any bells. Why don't you just look at the bookings log and see who picked up a call for New Road?" He began to feel more confident: there'd be no record of him going there. "Who was the victim? Not one of our regulars, I hope?"

Bertha looked down at her notepad.

"Someone called Daniel Paterson."

"Never heard of him."

"Me neither," said Bertha.

Gerry was good at reading upside-down. The only thing written on Bertha's notepad was 'toilet roll' and 'Winalot'. Lying cow, he thought as he left the office to go on shift. He chucked Ginny under the chin as he went past, blowing her a kiss. If the police were getting statements from all the drivers, that meant the witness didn't get a registration number. So Gerry was home free.

Chapter Nine

Derek was nervous as he waited at Fareham railway station for the train to Fratton. He was sure that Wendy had seen straight through his story about having to go and meet the owner of the Queen's Hotel in Southsea, about a possible series of bookings. Alan always did the bookings for the band, but Derek told Wendy that Mr Shufflebottom had asked for him especially, because he had heard the EP. She didn't question him further, mainly because Georgie had gone into hysterical laughter at the thought of anyone being called 'Shufflebottom' and that had set them all off. He'd caught the 69A bus to Fareham, then walked the length of West Street to the station. It was hot but a stiff breeze was blowing. The railway platform was empty. Derek brushed the dust off his jeans and adjusted his belt buckle. Wendy had insisted he wore his best white shirt, since he was allegedly seeing this important man. They'd had to tell Chalky too, so that he could arrange for someone to cover at the stall.

Derek looked at his watch again. About three minutes before the train was due. He wandered over to the other edge of the platform and looked across at the trees on the other side. As he turned back, he caught sight of Roy and Anne sitting on a bench, presumably waiting for the Southampton train. They were both wearing jeans and checked shirts and were holding hands and talking quietly. He moved quickly to retreat to the Portsmouth-bound platform, but they had noticed him.

"Hank!" called out Roy, getting up from the bench. Derek sighed, hoping that they didn't ask him what he was doing there. At that very moment, the Southampton train pulled noisily into the platform so he was spared a lengthy conversation. Roy and Anne shook his hand quickly then got onto the train, pulling down the window straight away so they could lean out and talk.

"Your record – absolutely fantastic," said Roy.

"Thanks, mate."

"Will you sign my copy for me, next time you're at the Ponderosa?"

"Yeah – be happy to."

The train started up, but Roy was still talking. Derek couldn't hear what he was saying – something about a competition – but he smiled and waved anyway.

*

Lenny came out of the office whistling *Long Haired Lover from Liverpool* and doing a little soft shoe shuffle.

Gerry got up from his chair. "So?"

"They were fine, Gerry. I'd never heard of this bloke Paterson other than what was in the paper and I didn't have a pick-up on New Road that day. So, nothing more for them to ask. You're next, by the way. In you go!"

Gerry took a couple of deep breaths and opened the door. Two coppers sat behind Bertha's desk, one of them a young woman. Quite a dishy bird too, thought Gerry, with blonde hair in a neat bun and with a smile on her oval face. Lovely teeth, too. He couldn't resist glancing down but her legs were hidden by the well-named 'modesty panel' on the front of the desk.

"Mr Gerald Chandler?" said the bloke, looking down at his notebook. He had great big hands with hair on the back of them and when he looked up, he had a five o'clock shadow even though it was only lunchtime. He wasn't smiling and he didn't introduce himself, neither did he invite Gerry to sit down. Instead he pushed a photograph across the desk.

Gerry knew very well it was a picture of Daniel Paterson, but he made a show of studying it carefully.

"No, I don't recognise him. I mean – I did see the

picture in the paper when his body was found, but he wasn't one of my customers."

"Where were you at 3pm on Wednesday 10th July?"

"I've absolutely no idea, I'm afraid. We just go where Ginny – she's the despatcher – sends us. One day merges into another, really, unless we get a long run, to the airport or something. She keeps a weekly sheet, but nothing further back than that as far as I know."

"To make sure you're not pocketing the fares?"

Gerry didn't know what to say.

"I'm not accusing you, Mr Chandler. I meant the purpose of the sheet is to prevent any driver from pocketing the fares."

"Yes."

"You don't keep your own records?"

"Nah – no point." He thought about Lenny. "Some drivers do, though."

The copper said nothing but didn't take his eyes off Gerry's face. The blonde smiled encouragingly.

"Oh, wait a minute," said Gerry. "I'm sure I was off that day. The rotas'll be in the office diary."

The bloke jerked his head at the blonde and she got up and went out of the room, returning a minute later with a large hardback ledger. She handed it to the bloke who licked his finger before turning the pages to 10th July.

He shut the book and gave it back to the blonde.

"Do you use your taxi on your days off?"

"Well yes – it's the only car I've got. I always take the taxi sign off the roof, of course, when I'm not working." He tried to keep looking at the bloke so that it would seem he was telling the truth, though of course he vividly remembered deliberately leaving the sign on that day.

"But the car still has its insignia on the doors?"

"Yes. They're a transfer - you can't remove them."

The bloke wrote something else in his notebook.

"And do you have any occasion, on your days off, to travel along New Road?"

Gerry pretended to be thinking. "No … I don't. In fact, definitely not."

"Very well. That'll be all for now. WPC Slade will prepare a statement for you to sign. Can you call at the station later this afternoon?"

Gerry nodded, inwardly cursing that this would be Fratton police station, where his dad's mate worked – the very man who had looked up Daniel's address for Gerry.

"Could you send the next driver in, please?"

"Will do." He paused with one hand on the doorknob. "Do you think one of our drivers was involved in Daniel Paterson's death?"

"We're following a number of lines of enquiry at this stage," the bloke said crisply. "Kidnap and manslaughter are the charges we are looking at."

Gerry nodded dumbly and fumbled with the doorknob, unable even to switch on his usual smile and aim it at the blonde, who he now knew to be WPC Slade. He finally made it out of the room and nodded to Young Dave, who was smoking a fag.

"Better stub that out, mate – you're next in."

*

Derek got off the train at Fratton and started walking. He wasn't fond of Portsmouth: too many terraced houses crammed into too many back streets, all looking identical with their rows of bay windows and little weed-strewn forecourts. He looked down at the address Pete had written on a piece of paper and felt a huge sense of achievement in being able to read it – and it was all down to Pete's time and patience with him. Soon, he'd tell Wendy what he'd been doing, but he needed to get this little matter out of the way first.

He spotted the Double-A offices from a hundred yards away, thanks to the line of silver-grey cabs outside. They all looked identical, and Derek realised he had been stupid not to have taken the registration number when he saw the taxi at the club. And what if he couldn't actually identify the driver once he'd seen him? They obviously had lots of drivers: maybe they didn't always drive the same cab, either. Maybe it was a pool of taxis.

The frontage of the office was scruffy; blobs of chewing gum littered the pavement outside and the sign over the door was faded and spattered with pigeon droppings. A pigeon perched on the ledge above the sign gazed down at Derek with what he thought looked like defiance. He hadn't really thought about what to do when he got here – he knew exactly what he wanted to say, but that relied on seeing the man in the first place. Without knowing the man's name, Derek could hardly go in and ask for him: all he could do was wait and hope to see him.

He checked the line of cabs – all empty – then retreated across the road to watch the entrance.

An oldish bloke emerged from the offices, dressed in one of those fake suede car coats with the fluffy lining. He had thick grey hair, with a curious square bald patch on the side of his head. The man got into a cab parked in the centre of the row and drove off. Litter blew past the doorway in which Derek was standing. He polished the top of his shoes by rubbing them one at a time on the back on his trouser leg. When he was a kid, his dad had always insisted he had well-polished shoes and it was always Derek's task before he went to bed to polish the shoes of his younger brothers and sisters, lining them up in the caravan by the door. He wasn't sure why it was so important: after all, none of them went to school much and they weren't the kind of family for formal outings. It was about self-discipline, his father had said: people judged you by your shoes. Derek clearly remembered the time he found a dead frog and put it into his sister's shoe after he'd cleaned it. He'd had a good strapping from his dad the next day, though he'd resolutely continued to deny his guilt and the strapping had been worth it just to see his sister's face when she'd put her foot unsuspectingly into the shoe. He smiled at the fact that it had taken him ten years before he finally admitted to her that it had been him, long enough for her to be able to laugh it off. Chalky had never let him forget it, though. Chalky was still working on his grudge list from 1959.

He looked at his watch, wondering how much longer he

could stand there. Maybe the guy wouldn't show up at all. He hummed a little of *Right Won't Touch a Hand That's Filled With Wrong*, one of the most melancholy George Jones' songs in the band's repertoire, about 'the road I'm on don't lead me back to home'. It suited his mood just now.

A cab drew up and Derek held his breath, but the driver who got out was nothing like the man in the forest – this one was over six feet tall and rail-thin, with long brown hair down to his shoulders. Derek sighed. He was hot, thirsty and bored. This was ridiculous: he should just go into the office and describe the man and ask for his name. They'd ask why he wanted to know – maybe he could make up some story about having left a bag in the taxi. No, that was no good. Oh, sod it, thought Derek and strode across the road. As he did so, the door to the taxi office swung open and two coppers emerged. One was a big bugger with buzz-cut hair; he looked even bigger once he'd put his helmet on. Alongside him was a WPC, petite and blonde. She looked like she belonged to totally different species. Derek immediately changed direction and veered off along the pavement towards the shop at the end of the street, his heart beating wildly. Maybe the police already knew about the driver? When he felt a safe distance away, he turned around – the coppers were walking side by side, chatting. As he watched, the WPC tugged at her skirt to pull it down at the back. They stood aside to allow a gaggle of young boys to walk past: the boys were shouting out cheerily at the big policeman, who clearly knew them. As they parted to let the boys through, Derek caught sight of the police car – a blue-and-white Marina - parked on the corner. He stood still, unsure of whether to go back or to call it a day when a familiar figure bounded down the steps of the taxi office, holding a polystyrene cup of coffee. The figure waved to the boys and one of them called out: "Aw right, Gerry?"

Derek broke into a run, reaching the cab just as it was about to pull out. He held onto the handle of the driver's door and banged on the window. Gerry's face turned in alarm. For a couple of seconds neither man moved, their eyes locked on each other's. Then Gerry opened the door fast and forcibly, taking Derek by surprise and causing him to fall backwards onto the pavement. Gerry leant over him, his face angry and set. He grabbed Derek by the front of his shirt and hauled him up.

"You! What exactly do you want, Mr Country Singer? Not a taxi, though, is it?"

Derek found that he couldn't speak. Gerry let go of the shirt and made a mocking feature of brushing the dust off Derek's jacket.

"Come on, then – speak!"

Still Derek couldn't say anything. He felt sick with fear.

"What's your real name, anyway? And don't tell me it's Hank because you've got a Meon Valley accent I could cut with a knife."

"Derek. It's Derek."

"Well, Derek-alias-Hank, I have to admit you've got a beautiful singing voice. I bought your EP, in fact."

"You did?" Derek was completely wrong-footed by this.

"But you didn't come here so I could compliment you on how you sing A Good Day for the Roses, did you?"

"A Good Year – it's A Good Year for the Roses."

"Whichever. Reminded me of my ex-wife, anyway. And not in a good way."

They stood in silence, Gerry leaning back against the door of the cab.

"I seen you," said Derek eventually. "That day in the forest – I seen you."

Gerry looked entirely indifferent at this news, glancing down the street as a young woman walked past.

"And what ya gonna do about it?" he said. "Not told the filth, have you? No, because you didn't see anything. Because nothing happened for you to see."

"I seen you with the baseball bat. And I heard you."

"What were you doing lurking about in the forest anyway? Shagging your girlfriend under the trees? A bit of al fresco, eh?" Gerry made a lewd gesture with his fist.

Derek couldn't understand why Gerry seemed to be treating this all as a joke. He just didn't seem to care.

"You killed him," said Derek, cursing inwardly at the

way his voice cracked.

"Don't be ridiculous," said Gerry, laughing. "You're just wasting my time now – I'm supposed to be on duty. Get back to playing cowboys and leave me alone." He made a move to push Derek away.

"I got it on tape."

Gerry's hand paused in mid-push.

"You what?"

"On tape – it's all recorded. What you said to that man you killed. Everything."

"In the car!" said Gerry. "Now!"

Derek opened the back door and got in. Gerry sat in the driver's seat and eyed him through the rear-view mirror.

"You're bluffing."

"No, I swear. My son had his cassette recorder on – he taped it by accident. I've not played it to no-one. I've kept it safe."

Gerry sighed. "What do you want?"

Derek began to feel more in control of the conversation.

"Money," he said to the eyes in the rear-view mirror. "I wants money."

*

Derek watched Wendy giving Lor a bath in the little plastic tub, which she'd put on top of the kitchen table. Lor was giggling but started to cry and arch her back when Wendy tried to wash her head. Derek softly sang a few bars of *Sweet Dream Baby*, leaning over the bath with his mouth close to Lor's ear. He looked up at Wendy as he did so.

He thought about the first day he had set eyes on Wendy. They had both been fifteen years old. He'd gone into the newsagents with his younger brother Henry, to buy some sweets – and, if he was being honest, to see if he could nick a few while he was at it. There was a skinny girl of about the same height as him, with long straight brown hair. She was staring at the pick-and-mix display. She'd glanced shyly up at him and Henry as they approached and watched as they chose some sherbet dips. She didn't seem to have a purse or bag with her and after a while she'd wandered away towards the door. While Henry paid for their sweets and asked for – and been refused – a packet of ten Players - on impulse, Derek had palmed another sherbet dip. He moved towards the door and slipped the sherbet into the pocket of the girl's shirtwaister dress while she was fiddling with the door handle.

Outside the shop, she'd loitered on the pavement for a minute. Derek thought she was bound to have her eye on Henry, always the better-looking one. At fourteen, his shoulders were beginning to fill out and he made the most of it with his tight white T-shirt, the short sleeves rolled up to reveal his growing biceps. His hair was cut in what they called a 'duck's arse' style, and he affected sunglasses even when there was no sign of any sun. But it had been Derek that the girl wanted to talk to. She had a thin face with dark brown eyes and she lisped a little when she talked. Her manner was quite serious, quite intense. He was smitten straight away. When Henry walked off in a huff, unused to not being the centre of attention, Derek asked her out. They'd been together ever since. Her family were working-class and lived in a rented house in Bishops Waltham, but had been a bit sniffy about Derek because he was from a travelling family, even though by then they had settled into a council house and had the market garden to run. Derek didn't know what class came underneath the working class, but he knew they regarded him as part of it.

Lor was still grizzling.

"I don't know what's wrong with her today," said Wendy, taking her out of the bath and drying her gently. "I'll try and get her settled down now. What time are you off to the gig?"

Derek glanced at his watch.

"About half an hour," he said. "Better get changed."

"Is it the Acorn Club at Fair Oak again? Wasn't great last time, was it?"

"No. We went off like a damp squid."

Wendy laughed. "Damp *squib*, you mean."

Derek looked puzzled.

"No I don't - that doesn't make no sense. It's 'squid'. They live in the sea, they get damp, it's obvious. What's a 'squib' when it's at home, anyways?"

Wendy shook her head and carried Lor upstairs.

Lor had been named for Loretta Lynn, who in Derek's view was one of the best female country singers in the world, though he still carried a bit of a torch for Patsy Cline. Loretta Lynn had done a song about her poor beginnings in Kentucky – *Coal Miner's Daughter* it was called – and look at her now! Top billing at the Grand Ole Opry, a string of hits and gold records. Derek looked around the kitchen, with its old scratched formica units and the lino curled up in one corner where it had come unstuck and knew that no-one was ever going to tell the story of his life: his rags-to-riches tale was just a dream. Of course, Loretta Lynn wrote all her own material. Derek thought for a moment then went upstairs to put on his fringed shirt and to brush his Stetson.

*

Gerry turned off his headlights and his engine as he approached the layby and coasted to a stop under the trees. He looked back at the pub but it was in complete darkness. He pulled on his black knitted hat, grabbed the torch out of the glove-compartment and put his hand on the door handle ready to open it. Was he ready for this, he asked himself? The truth was, he didn't really know, but he needed to do something or he'd go mad. Something decisive, something that would fix the problem. Or one of the problems, anyways. He glanced at himself in the rear-view mirror: his face looked paler than usual in the dim overhead light.

He stepped out of the car, zipped up his dark anorak, put on his black leather gloves and walked round to the boot, opening it with the key and taking out the metal can of petrol. Car headlights appeared in the distance so Gerry quickly shut the boot and moved into the shadow of the trees until it had gone by.

The white-painted wooden strawberry stall was pushed back against the forest fence, its shutters clipped down and two big wooden chocks holding the wheels in place. Gerry realised that unless he moved the stall further out into the layby he risked setting fire to the trees as well. He put down the can, removed the chocks and got his weight behind the corner of the stall.

"Bugger, it's heavy," he said. How that scrawny Derek bloke managed to move it on his own, God only knows, he thought. Then he noticed the chain and padlock. He was about to give it up as a bad job when he realised the chain had only been looped over the fence and could quite easily be lifted off. After another full minute of pushing with his hands and then with his back, the stall finally shot out of the mud and he had to grab at it to stop it rolling into the road. He steadied it and then walked back into the shadows to catch his breath. The road was empty and the pub still in darkness. Now was the time, he thought. He twisted the cap of the petrol can but it wouldn't budge. Rust flaked off as he tried to turn it. He took off his gloves to get a better grip, but it just left the indent of the serrations around the cap on his fingers and hurt like hell. After swearing at it a few times, he began to laugh at the absurdity of the whole situation. The can had been in the boot of the car for about a year: he'd shaken it that afternoon to make sure there was plenty of petrol in it, but it had never occurred to him to try and open it. He went over to the car and rummaged in the boot for a pair of pliers, then remembered he had some WD-40. That did the trick and within a minute or two the can opened easily. He instantly felt calmer.

There was a scampering noise in the trees behind the fence and Gerry froze, can in hand. His heart was thumping and his mind raced through the possible excuses he could make for being there at the dead of night holding a petrol can and with a box of matches in his pocket. In the darkness he saw a fox break cover from the fence and dart across the road into the forest, its tail spread out behind it like a pennant. He wiped his mouth with the back of his hand, then started to circle around the strawberry stall, dribbling the petrol as he went. When he had completed a circuit, he sloshed the remaining petrol up the sides of the stall.

He put the can back into the boot and, almost as an afterthought, opened the driver's door of his car and pushed the vehicle twenty yards down the road. He might be an idiot, he thought, but setting fire to his car as well as to the stall would have been a bit too much, even for him. Another set of headlights approached, this time belonging to a big truck, which seemed to slow down as it passed him. Gerry ducked down but could see the driver turning to look at the stall and the car.

Quick – he had to be quick. He ran back to the stall and struck a match. His hands were shaking so much that the first two matches he threw went well clear of the poured petrol, but the third struck home and with a whumping noise, the fuel caught alight. Gerry ran back to the car, got in and watched through the rear-view mirror for a moment or two to make sure the fire would not peter out. But the wood was old, dry and ready to burn. When the flames curled up onto the sign at the top of the stall that read Locally Grown Strawberry's, he knew the job was done. He started the engine, turned the car around and drove away. As he did so, a light came on in an upstairs window of the pub.

Chapter Ten

When post came through the door, it was usually a bill. Derek scooped the letters off the mat and put them on the hall table for Wendy to deal with. British Telecom, the Gas Board – it was the usual stuff, except for the envelope on the top, which had a little symbol in the top left hand corner, showing the head of a guitar with the letters 'BCMA' underneath it. It was addressed to 'Hank Wesson' and it had a London postmark. Derek tore it open and unfolded the single sheet that was inside. As he read the first two lines, he felt proud that he could decipher most it for himself without having to ask Wendy to do it for him, even though it was slow-going. What it said, however, was something he just could not take in. He went through the first sentence again:

Dear Mr Wesson
We are writing to congratulate you on winning our Country Music Vocal Track of the Year award, the prize for which is an all-expenses paid trip to Nashville.

It was some kind of hoax, thought Derek. He hadn't even entered a competition so how could he have won? Maybe it was a practical joke that someone was playing on him? The letter went on for a full page, but Derek couldn't make out a single word after this first sentence, which kept reverberating around his head. If it was a joke, then it was a cruel one, he thought. Angrily, he flipped up the lid of the kitchen bin to throw it in, but then something made him stop and put it into his pocket instead. He went to the phonebox and called Pete.

*

It was 8am and Gerry was having a lie-in; he wasn't due to be on shift until 11am. He'd had a restless night, kicking off the bedclothes because he was too hot, then pulling them on again because he was too cold. His mind was too active, that was the problem. He remembered someone telling him that worrying was like being in a rocking chair – you went backwards and forwards but never got anywhere. Very true, but at 3am you always convinced yourself you could think through whatever it was that was worrying you and come up with a solution.

Gerry was pretty sure that no-body had seen him by the strawberry stall and even passing traffic would not have got a really good look at him, so he had no real fear of being arrested for it. But had he done enough to make Hank back off about the money and the tape? Maybe he should have called his bluff – asked him to bring the cassette tape and he'd swap it for the money … then destroyed the tape right there and then. But Hank might have copied the tape. No, this had been the best way: just to send a clear message about who he was dealing with. A frightener: and Gerry knew how to frighten. He'd had plenty of practice.

A banging at the door brought these complacent thoughts to an instant halt. There was no door knocker and the bell had stopped working ages ago, but this wasn't a polite tap on the door – it was a hammering with both fists. Police: it had to be.

Gerry's first thought was to ignore it. Then he remembered those scenes on TV programmes where police broke down the door of a suspect to get in. Best to let them in. He rolled out of bed and grabbed his jeans off the floor.

"Just coming!" he shouted, tugging them on and searching for a T-shirt.

He took a deep breath and opened the door, barefoot, unshaven, and with his hair all stuck up from where he had been lying awkwardly. The sight that greeted him was not the one he had expected. On the doorstep was Darren, in his school uniform. As soon as he saw Gerry, Darren began sobbing and trying to talk at the same time.

"I can't understand a bloody word you're saying,

Darren. Here …" he reached for a handkerchief in his jeans pocket. "Take this and blow your nose and then try telling me what's wrong." He stood aside from the door and pulled Darren inside by his shoulder.

The boy's face looked all contorted and he was even paler than usual.

"It's mum," he finally said. "She won't wake up. I'm frightened, Gerry." He burst into tears again.

"Did you run all the way here?"

Darren nodded.

"Good lad – that was the right thing to do. Let me get my shoes and coat and we'll go and see what's the matter. She's probably taken a sleeping pill or something, that's all. Nothing to worry about, I'm sure. Now while I get dressed, you go into the kitchen and have a glass of water."

*

Chalky was in a cheerful mood for once, as he drove Derek over to the stall for what would be one of the last days of the season. The sky was clear and there was a pleasant autumnal bite to the early morning air.

"Looks like I've got that promotion at the Mill, nipper," he said, drumming with his fingers on the steering wheel as he drove.

"That's great news," said Derek. "So … you'll be what, now?"

"Foreman."

"Foreman! They won't be able to call you 'Chalky' now."

"It'll be 'Mr Fry' from now on – no, not really. I expect I'll still be 'Chalky' to the lads."

"Do you get a pay rise too?"

"I certainly do. Thought they're switching to paying me monthly instead of weekly, so it'll take a bit of getting used to."

Derek felt a pang of jealousy: there was Chalky, with no wife or kids to worry about, getting a pay rise, and here he was, trying to do the impossible by scraping by on what

Chalky paid him and his earnings from the band. Still, all that would change once that taxi-driver paid him what was only his by right. The pang passed and he was able to feel genuinely happy for his brother.

"So don't worry about that money I lent you, nipper. I don't need it back," said Chalky, glancing over at Derek and grinning.

Derek now felt guilty at even slightly resenting Chalky's good fortune.

"That's very big of you, Chalky. I really appreciate it but I'll still pay you back one day."

They rounded the bend in the road and the pub came into view. Chalky put the indicator on to pull into the layby.

"What the hell's happened here?"

He pulled up sharply and the two men looked through the windscreen at the blackened shell of what was barely recognisable as the strawberry stall.

*

Gerry pounded up the stairs to Tina's flat, with Darren following on his heels. When they got to the front door, he had to take the key off Darren, whose hand was shaking so much that he couldn't put the key in the lock properly. He patted the boy's head.

"Calm down, now Darren – I'm here and I'll make sure everything's all right," he said with a confidence he didn't really feel. His mind was still on the burning of the stall and he wouldn't allow himself to think that anything really was wrong with Tina. Probably just hung over or something.

Darren's breakfast bowl was on the kitchen table, his Frosties half-eaten. Gerry made Darren sit down while he went into the bedroom. Tina was lying on her back in bed, her mouth slightly open.

"Tina, love – it's Gerry. Time to wake up now," he said, shaking her by the shoulder, at first very gently and then with more vigour. There was no response. Her face was pale, but then she was always pale. He tapped her cheek with the palm of his hand. Nothing. He bent down, so that his head was very close to her mouth and was relieved to find that she was breathing, though it seemed slow and shallow. As he looked up, he noticed two bottles of pills on the bedside table, both nearly empty. He read the labels.

"Shit!" he said. "Darren? Run down to the phone box and dial 999 and say you want an ambulance. Can you do that? You don't need any money: it's free to dial 999. Just give them your address. I'll stay here with your mum."

Darren's frightened face appeared in the doorway.

"OK, Gerry. Mum's going to be all right, isn't she?"

"Of course she is. Does she always take these pills?" he said, holding up the two bottles.

"If the man brings them round, yes," said Darren. "He doesn't always turn up. She says he's unreliable."

"What man?" asked Gerry. "No, forget it - I'll ask you about that later. Just run as fast as you can now."

Darren vanished and Gerry heard the front door slam behind him. He began to feel sick, a combination of the sleepless night and the shock of finding Tina like this. He sniffed his hands and thought he could still detect a whiff of petrol on them. He turned Tina onto her side and drew her hair gently back from her face. He found he was crying.

"Please God," he said – he who was an ardent atheist – "please let her be alright." He remembered with a stab of guilt the lie he told about Tina being ill when he went to the school and collected Darren. He also remembered the way that lately he'd only gone to see Tina when he was in need of sex; how he'd never even taken her out anywhere, as if he were ashamed of her. He had been ashamed of her, that was the truth, but he vowed all that would change if only God would let her pull through.

Darren seemed to be taking forever, which gave him an unwanted time to think about the pills 'the man' regularly brought her and to finally acknowledge what he'd really known all along: that Tina was a drug addict. That it seemed to be prescription drugs didn't make it feel any better. It explained her constant lack of money. It also probably explained the visit of that woman he'd seen on the stairs – clearly a social worker – and he then began to feel frightened for Darren. Would Darren be put into care if they knew what Tina was taking? What if Tina died? What would happen to him then?

Darren burst through the door at that moment shouting "they're coming!" then fell quiet when he saw his mother. Gerry put his arm around him and held him close him until they heard the ambulance's siren.

*

Derek pulled the cream enamel coffee tin off the shelf, wrenched off the lid and thrust his hand inside. It was empty. He peered into the tin as if there was somewhere the tape could be hiding but there was nothing.

"Georgie!" he shouted.

"Out on his bike," said Wendy from the next room.

Derek went into Georgie's room and rifled through a stack of music cassettes that were strewn haphazardly across the table where he was supposed to do his homework, but never did: he preferred the kitchen, where he could sit with Sharon instead and mess about, putting her off her work. Derek tried to read the labels, but he could only make out the words on a few of them and Georgie's looping handwriting didn't help.

"What you trying to find?" asked Wendy, leaning against the door opening and holding a big pile of ironing.

"A cassette tape of Georgie's. It had me and him singing Rocket Man on it."

Wendy put down the ironing on the bed and had a desultory look through.

"They all look the same – same cases, same scribbled titles. How did you think you were going to recognise that one?"

Derek longed to tell Wendy that he was learning to read, but the time wasn't right.

"I think it had a blue sticker on it," he said, trying to sound vague.

"You'll have to ask Georgie when he gets back. A duet, was it? I'd like to hear that – he's got a sweet voice."

That was one recording, thought Derek, that she could never listen to. Bobby started up with a loud wail from the living room and Wendy went to see what the problem was.

Derek was panicking now. He had to find that tape. He thought back: he definitely remembered putting it into the coffee tin. Why on earth would anyone look in there? The jar hadn't been used for years. And if someone had found it, why hadn't they said anything? Surely Georgie would have asked him what it was doing in there?

The back door banged and Sharon came into the kitchen, carrying a bag of shopping, which she dumped onto the table. She shrugged off her coat and draped it over the chair.

"Got everything on the list?"

"Yeah."

"Well done, girl," said Derek. "That's a great help to your mum, what with Lor being a bit poorly, she's got her hands full."

"What's this doing here?" said Sharon, picking up the coffee tin and the lid that lay alongside it.

Derek didn't know what to say, but took the tin from her, replaced the lid and put it all back on the shelf.

"Just looking for something, that's all."

"Hoping there might be a few pound notes in it, Dad?"

"Well, yes, I was actually," said Derek.

"You'd be lucky – Georgie's always looking in those empty tins to see if there's any biscuits. He'd have found your stash ages ago if you'd put it in there."

Derek forced himself to smile. He ruffled Sharon's hair. It was dead straight, just like Wendy's, but she'd had it done in a feather-cut by a friend's mum last month. It was short on top with longer sides and showed up her fine features and dark eyes. Wendy had thought the school might object to the haircut, because it was a bit like a skinhead style, but they hadn't said anything.

"Don't, Dad!" said Sharon. "You'll mess it up!"

Bobby waddled into the kitchen, cooing with delight at seeing his big sister. She scooped him up and carried him off into the living room.

Derek tapped with his fingers on the kitchen table. He

supposed he'd just have to wait until Georgie got home. Then he had a thought, rushed into Georgie's bedroom and searched for the cassette player. He found it under the bed; there was a tape in the machine and he pressed 'rewind' and then 'play'. The batteries were nearly flat, but the clear tones of Georgie's voice could still be heard, singing 'She packed my bags last night pre-flight'. Bingo! He ejected the tape, put the player back under the bed and then tugged at the exposed bit of dark brown magnetic tape that showed through the plastic casing between the two spools, pulling it all out until it formed a long tangle. For good measure, he then put the cassette on the floor and trod on it hard with the heel of his boot, cracking the casing. He put the whole lot in the metal dustbin outside, hiding it under some kitchen waste.

He thought Georgie was unlikely to ask where the tape had gone, since he must have known he shouldn't have been looking in the coffee tin in the first place. He began to feel better. From now on, he'd forget all about the man in the forest and just get on with his life. They were square now, surely? The man had given his warning and Derek had heeded it. That left the painful question of his lack of money, of course, but he figured he'd just have to find an answer to that on his own. Maybe Chalky could get him a full-time job over the winter at the Mill, now he was a foreman? Or maybe money was part of this award that he'd apparently won, if indeed it was true.

He grabbed his coat off the hook in the hall and shouted through to the living room: "Just going down to the phone box – won't be long!" He could at least put in a call to a few friends to see if they had any wood going spare and make a start on rebuilding the stall.

*

The ambulance men looked at Gerry as if he were scum. They shoved him quite rudely into the kitchen and told him to stay there while they worked on Tina. He showed them the pill bottles and it was obvious they thought Gerry was her dealer or at the very least was complicit in her taking the drugs. He and Darren sat in the kitchen, not talking, listening to every sound from the bedroom, hoping to hear Tina's voice. After about a minute, one of the ambulance men pounded down the stairs and returned with a stretcher.

He popped his head round the kitchen door.

"We're taking her in now. You can follow if you want. Is the boy yours?" he said, jerking his head at Darren.

"'The boy, as you put it, is Tina's son. I'm just a friend of the family." He felt like St Peter must have felt, denying Christ: that was the one Sunday School story that had stuck with him all his life, especially the bit about the cock crowing.

"The police will be in touch – and social services too I expect. What she was doing with this quantity of pills, Gawd only knows," said Mr Sensitive. "Full name?"

"What, mine?" asked Gerry.

"No." Mr Sensitive sighed theatrically. "The name of the patient."

"Tina Jackson. Christina."

"Date of birth?"

"I don't actually know. Look, shouldn't you be getting her to hospital? We can sort out all this later."

"OK. Don't think time will make too much difference, to be honest."

Gerry felt chilled when he heard these words. Darren started whimpering.

As the men went out the door with Tina strapped to the stretcher, an oxygen mask over her face, Darren ran out onto the landing.

"Mummy! Mummy!" he cried and Gerry felt choked up to hear him.

*

"This is amazing," said Pete, holding the letter, perched on the arm of one of the leather-upholstered wing chairs in the library of his house.

"But is it real?" asked Derek, "or is somebody playing a joke on me?"

"Looks real to me. It's for A Good Year for the Roses and says you were nominated for the award by BCMA members across the country. You know what this means, don't you? Think of the publicity, Derek," he said, getting up from the chair and pacing up and down the room. "You'll be in all the country magazines, on the radio and goodness knows what else. The EP is going to get a boost – the whole band will benefit. And you get to go to Nashville." He waved the letter in the air.

"I can't, though."

"Why ever not?"

"I don't even have a passport. I've never even been on a plane. I wouldn't know what to do, or where to go. I've never really been away from Wendy for more than a day or two."

"Have you told her yet?"

"No, I wanted to see you first – see if it was genuine, like."

"It'll be fine. I'll help you all the way. A week, expenses paid - how can you turn that down? It says here that you will get a guest spot on the Grand Ole Opry. This could be your big breakthrough."

"Why isn't the award for the band, instead of just me?"

"Because the award is for the vocals."

"I can't leave the stall for a week, anyhow. Oh …"

"What?"

"Well, the stall's not there any more."

"What do you mean?"

"I'll tell you. But I think I need a cigarette first, to clear my head."

They went through to the cavernous kitchen and opened the back door. The spaniel lurched out into the garden, whinnying with pleasure. Derek lit up and took a deep drag on the cigarette before telling Pete about finding the burnt-out shell of the stall.

"Just kids? Or has someone got it in for you?"

"No, it ain't nothing like that."

"Landlord? You're not behind on the rent, are you?"

"No, it's not that."

They stood in silence for a moment.

"So," said Pete tentatively, "you know who did it, don't you?"

Derek sighed. "Yes, I think I do."

"Have you called the police?"

"I persuaded Chalky not to call them."

Pete looked out into the garden, to where the spaniel was enthusiastically digging at the base of one of the apple trees, earth flying up from between his paws.

"You're not thinking of taking this into your own hands, are you?"

"No," said Derek, carefully stubbing out his cigarette on the brick wall and then holding the butt until he could dispose of it properly. "It was a warning and I'm taking the hint. I'm walking away from … well, from the situation that caused it."

Pete closed his hand around Derek's arm, near the elbow and gave it a quick squeeze.

"Well, if I can help, you know you've only got to ask." Derek didn't reply, so Pete tried again: "Maybe this prize if just what you need to give you a fresh start – something to look forward to."

"Shame it's not cash instead of a trip. And of course when Jessie finds out I've won, there'll be hell to pay. I can just imagine her face!" Derek managed a brief laugh.

"Come on – let's go inside and go through the letter again and see what you've got to do. The first thing is for you to accept the award – you need to write them a letter. I'll write it and you can sign it. We'd better get a form from the Post Office, too, for you to apply for a passport. And you'll need a visa."

He left the back door open and they went back into the library, where Pete took the cover off a portable typewriter, rummaged in the desk drawer for a sheet of paper and rolled it into the machine.

"The arson attack – it's nothing to do with that article in the paper about the body in the forest, is it?" said Pete, turning round to face Derek.

"No, of course not," said Derek, feeling his face flush.

Chapter Eleven

As they got out of the lift, Gerry felt Darren's hand slip into his. Surprised, he looked down but could only see the top of the boy's head. He squeezed the hand, but Darren withdrew it as they approached the ward. Gerry checked his watch to cover any embarrassment Darren might feel. Two minutes to go until visiting time. He adjusted the bouquet of flowers he was carrying and pushed open the grey swing doors. Immediately, his path was blocked by what Gerry could instantly see was a bossy cow in matron's uniform. He knew the type.

"You're too early, I'm afraid," she said with what looked suspiciously like pleasure. "You'll have to wait in the corridor."

"It's two minutes, for Christ's sake," said Gerry and was about to argue further when Darren spotted his mother in a bed halfway along the main ward and burst out crying.

The matron gave a theatrical sigh.

"Go on, then. And stop crying, young man, or you'll upset the patient. Are you family?"

"Yes," said Gerry firmly. Darren had broken away and was already by Tina's bedside. Gerry walked past the rows of beds, appalled that men and women had to share the same ward. Tina was sitting up in bed and looked pale and wan. Her hair could have done with a brush and there was a half-eaten bowl of mush on a tray next to the bed. Her water jug was empty. Gerry put down the flowers, turned to look at her and suddenly felt choked with tears.

Darren had draped himself across the bed, his face buried in his mother's lap. Gerry looked into Tina's eyes, which had dark circles underneath them.

"Tina, love," he said. "I thought …" His voice cracked and he cleared his throat to disguise it.

"I'm sorry," she said, her voice raw and raspy.

"Don't apologise." He stood for a moment in silence. "Did you … did you mean to do it?"

She looked away.

"There's so many things I don't know about you, Tina."

"Yeah, well when you find them out, I won't see you for dust." She fussed with the edge of the blanket.

"That's not true. I just want to be here for you, to help you." He sat down in the visitor's chair and watched her absently stroking the top of Darren's head. "What can I do?"

She didn't say anything.

"Is there anything you need from the flat?"

"No. The doctor said I can probably go home on Monday."

"What about the police?"

She gave him a sharp look. "Darren," she said, untangling him from the blankets. "Go and get yourself a Coke from the machine." Gerry fished out some coins and Darren scampered off.

"Won't there be an investigation?" said Gerry. "About where you got the pills?"

"They're prescription."

"Yeah, but they're not your prescription, are they?"

"Course they are."

"Tina – I know they're not."

She looked annoyed, picked up a plastic cup to drink from, but it was empty. Gerry grabbed the water jug and went over to the sister's desk in the corner of the ward.

"Could you give me some water, please? Miss Jackson's jug's empty."

The sister pulled a face.

"I'll do it when I've got time. Just leave it here."

"She's dehydrated – she needs it now."

"I can't be at everyone's beck and call at every minute of the day."

Gerry felt the old anger well up in him.

"Look, you may think you can boss your patients around because, God knows, they're ill and they're just going to have to take it. But don't try that on me. Just get me the water."

The sister grabbed the jug from Gerry's hands and turned away, muttering under her breath.

"What did you say?" said Gerry, grabbing her arm.

She looked down at his hand until he removed it.

"I said we would do without overdosers like her, wasting our time." Gerry was dumbstruck. "Who are you, anyway?" she said. "The husband?" She was openly sneering now.

"No," said Gerry quietly, "not yet, but I'm going to be."

"Well good luck with that!" she retorted, walking off towards the nurses' station.

Gerry stood for a minute, watching her go, and then went back to Tina's bedside.

As he got alongside the bed, Gerry dropped onto one knee.

"Tina," he said. "I love you. Will you marry me?"

Behind him the entire ward burst into applause.

*

Derek was lurking by the dressing-room door, but overheard the confrontation between Jessie and Alan.

"You have got to be joking!" said Jessie, her face blank with disbelief.

"It's true," said Alan. "But remember it's an accolade for the whole band, not just for Hank. We're all delighted about it."

"But it's Hank who gets to go to Nashville," said Jessie, putting her face close to Alan's. "I'm sorry but that's just not on. It was the band's record, not Hank's, and it's the band who should win the award."

Alan laughed, which made Jessie more furious and drew her husband nearer the stage. He was looking anxious.

"I'm sorry, Jessie, but the award is for best vocal, not for best track. There's nothing we can do about it – Hank gets the prize but we all benefit."

"Bullshit," said Jessie, succinctly. "Perhaps you'd like to rename the band, too? 'The Hank Wesson Band' maybe? In which case you can manage without me." She turned on her heel and walked away.

"Good grief," said Pete. "What a drama queen! Never mind – she'll come round." He clapped Alan on the shoulder.

"Not until she's extracted the maximum amount of fuss from it, she won't." Alan sighed.

"Maybe telling her just before a gig wasn't exactly the best tactic?" said Pete, lightly. "Well, what's done is done – I'm off to get changed now."

He put his bass back on the stand and crossed the hall to the dressing rooms, otherwise known as the store cupboard. The small room was crammed with spare chairs, a bingo machine, a tombola drum, some crates of beer glasses, and a life-sized cardboard cut-out of Liberace. Derek was adjusting his bootlace tie in a small mirror, one foot up on the seat of a wooden chair.

"What on earth is that doing here?" said Pete, pointing to Liberace in this sequined costume. "Surely he hasn't played this dump, has he? On the other hand, maybe I should have my hair done like that? A nice bouffant."

"Thought you already had!" said Derek.

There was hardly room for the band to hang up their stage clothes, never mind change into them. They had to shuffle round as Chalky came in with his clothes on a hanger.

Pete looked at Derek's reflection in the mirror.

"Looking good, Hank."

"How did Jessie take it?" asked Derek, smiling.

"It could have gone better." He fiddled with the pearl buttons on his stage shirt. "Put it this way, I don't think she will be pursuing a career in the diplomatic service anytime soon."

"Is it safe to go out there?"

"Well, she's stormed off, trampling that meek husband of hers underfoot as she did so, but I dare say she'll be back in time for the first set. I'm getting used to her little winning ways."

"Don't mention winning!"

Pete laughed. "Good point. Right, that's me ready."

"New shirt? Very nice."

"I've got a young lady coming along tonight to see the band. In fact I must have a quick word with the man on the door, to make sure she gets in OK."

Derek looked quizzical.

"How young, exactly, is this 'young lady'?"

"Don't worry: she's definitely over the age of consent. Or that's what she told me last night, anyway."

*

"Where the hell have you been? And God, you look awful."

"Nice to see you too, Bertha." Gerry made his usual jokey response, but his heart wasn't in it and the smile faded quickly from his face. At first he was reluctant to say that he'd been at the hospital but then he remembered the shame he had felt about his attitude to Tina and the promise he'd made.

"My girlfriend – my fiancée - was rushed to hospital yesterday. I had to take her boy home with me, then I had to take him to school and see the headmaster about it, then I had to take him to visit her."

"I'm sorry to hear that," said Bertha, not looking in the least bit sorry. That's the feral-looking boy who's always hanging about outside, right?"

"Yes, that's Darren."

"Looks like he could do with a good meal inside him. And a visit to the dentist."

Gerry waited for Big Bertha to ask how Tina was or to express any sympathy, but she said nothing.

"I may need to take more time off," he said. "I've got to go back to the hospital later to see if she's allowed visitors yet. And I need to make sure Darren gets home from school OK."

"Well this time, just phone in and let us know. I can't have you just swanning off whenever you feel like it. You've made mistake after mistake recently – and this isn't the first time you've gone missing."

Gerry tamped down the surge of rage that welled up within him and forced himself to speak calmly and to adopt a reasonable tone.

"I am sorry about the previous times, but when it's life or death," he said quietly, looking down at the desk, "I'd hope that you would show some compassion and some understanding. Tina is out of danger now, but she might not have survived. Or are you just as unfeeling as your husband was?"

"What did you say?" Bertha rose from her chair – in her boots with the platform soles she was still shorter than Gerry but considerably more sturdily built. The dog staggered to its feet as well, sensing a confrontation.

"You heard me. Brian was an intolerant bigoted bastard and he made a lot of enemies because of it."

"That's it!" shouted Bertha. "Stop right there! You've gone too far this time, Gerry. You never even knew the man."

"No," said Gerry, "but I've recently found out things about him that tell me everything I need to know about what kind of bloke he was."

"You're fired! Get out of here! I never want to see your stupid face in here again."

"Fine by me. I've had enough of driving scuddy cabs anyway. Going to get me a proper job."

"A proper job? Don't make me laugh!"

The dog was growling now and emerged from under the desk, looking up at Gerry, its ears cocked. He went out of the door and closed it firmly behind him.

As he walked briskly out through the front office, Ginny glanced up from the bookings sheet, a smile on her face.

"Not blowing a kiss to me today then, gorgeous?" she called, ready for a bit of banter.

Gerry walked over to the hatch behind which Ginny was sitting, bent through the opening, grabbed her head with both hands and gave her a lengthy and expert French kiss.

"You're wasted here, Ginny," he said when he finally stood up again. "Goodbye, darling. You've brightened many of my days and I'll miss you."

As he went out into the street he was aware of her staring after him, a bemused look on her face.

Chapter Twelve

"That's it, Mr Wesson. Just move slightly to your right – and angle the EP cover so that it's facing me." The black-clad photographer looked through the lens again, then went over to Derek and reached out to adjust his jacket slightly. "Perhaps you could tilt your hat back just a tad? It's causing a shadow on your eyes at the moment."

Derek moved it by the smallest possible amount: there was a very precise way in which a Stetson should be worn, and he wasn't going to change that for this snapper, even if the snapper did work for *Country Music World* magazine.

Finally, the photographer seemed satisfied and banged off a whole series of pictures.

"Right you are, then," he said, calling over to the reporter, who was having a cigarette and a coffee at a table in the far corner of the room. "I'm done!"

The reporter got up, stubbed out the cigarette and walked over to Derek, who was still standing in front of the giant mural that depicted the front of the Ryman Auditorium, home of the Grand Ole Opry. She had short curly blonde hair and was wearing flared denim jeans and a cheesecloth top. She was younger than Derek had expected – probably only in her late twenties.

"Madeleine Ferre," she said, sticking her hand out for Derek to shake. "But call me Maddie. Is it OK to call you 'Hank'?"

He smiled.

"You know that's my stage name, not my real name."

"Stage name is fine with me," she said, opening her notebook and gesturing to two nearby chairs. They both sat down.

Derek tried to remember what Wendy had told him about the interview: what he should say and not say, but it was already getting muddled in his mind. He was conscious that he needed to give the band a good plug, so they wouldn't feel left out, though nothing was going to appease Jessie.

"So, how do you feel about winning this award, Hank?"

"It was a total surprise. I never knew I'd been entered for it until I got the letter telling me that I'd won best vocal."

Maddie took notes as he talked; the interview progressed in a predictable fashion for the next ten minutes or so and Derek began to relax a little.

"You clearly like traditional Country music and traditional vocal styles, Hank," she said suddenly. "What about the New Country that's emerging in Nashville – the so-called 'Outlaws'?"

"You mean people like Kris Kristofferson and Waylon Jennings?"

"Yes, and Tompall Glaser too, maybe. And wild cards like Kinky Friedman."

"I haven't heard of Kinky Friedman, but I don't think any of those others have a place in true Country music. Real Country is Hank Williams and Slim Whitman and George Jones and those kind of singers, and it always will be. These 'outlaws' are hippies, in my opinion, and they belong in pop or rock, not country."

"Well, you may encounter one or two of them on your trip to Nashville. And I hear you're going to get a guest spot on the Grand Ole Opry, so you may be sharing the stage with some of your heroes." She smiled, put away her notebook and stood up, indicating the interview was at an end. "I take it you've not been to Nashville before?"

"I've not been out of the country before. Oh – I probably shouldn't have said that."

"It's fine – I'm not going to put that in the article."

Derek took off his Stetson and held it in both hands in front of him, turning it around the brim.

"You like this Outlaw sound yourself, I reckons," he

said. "You being young and that."

"I do. I think it's the future."

"Do you play or sing at all?"

"Yes, I play fiddle in a Western swing band. We're called Aces High."

"Fiddle is traditional," he pointed out, putting his hat back onto his head.

"Not the way I play it, Hank." She smiled, shook his hand again, called the photographer over and they both left.

*

"Hello, Dad."

Alf, who was bending over getting a crate of oranges from the floor at the rear of the stall, wheeled round, an astonished look on his face.

"Gerry," he said. He put the crate onto the stall display, angling it so that the customers could get a good view of all the fruit. "What brings you here?"

His dad, as usual, was wearing a neatly pressed brown overall over his clothes: he'd always been a stickler for a smart appearance. Gerry became conscious of his own scruffy jeans and noticed the rime of dirt on the sleeve of the coat that he should have taken to the dry cleaners weeks ago.

"I'm allowed to come and see you, aren't I?"

"Of course, son. I'm just surprised, that's all. It's been a while since we've seen you." Although his tone was neutral, it made Gerry instantly feel guilty.

"I know. I'm sorry about that. Things keep getting in the way. Is Mum around?"

"Gone to the hairdresser's."

"She still go to that Raymonde bloke in Southsea with the phony French accent?"

"Yes." His dad laughed. "What a ponce! She likes the way he does her hair, though." He broke off to serve a customer, deftly putting fruit and veg into a series of brown bags and twisting the tops to keep the bag secure, chatting and joking all the while. He'd always had a good line in banter with the punters: it came with the trade.

"So," he said, turning back to Gerry. "Not working today?"

"Truth is, I've been fired, Dad." Gerry was irritated to feel his face flush: this was like being a little boy again and owning up to something he'd done wrong. He'd done plenty wrong in his time and his father had been handy with the belt and the slipper. He was hoping his father wouldn't ask why he'd been fired.

"I imagine you've come to borrow some money, then?"

"No – no, not at all. I've got savings that'll tide me over till I get something else."

The noises of the market swelled around them, the meat man shouting about best pork chops, the man on the sweet stall next to Alf's rattling sweets into the metal scales, and a chap with a microphone on the household goods stall conducting a Dutch auction for what looked like perfume rip-offs.

"You're applying to another taxi firm then?"

"I'd like a change, really," said Gerry, contemplating how Big Bertha would spread the word about him vindictively around all the other firms in the city. "I was wondering whether you might need a hand with the stall?"

Alf laughed. "I thought you hated the stall?"

"Yeah, well I've done some growing up since then."

Alf carried on re-arranging the cabbages, which looked to be already perfectly arranged.

"We couldn't really afford to pay you a proper wage."

"No, I realise that," said Gerry. He looked at his watch, wondering if it would soon be time to pick up Darren and go to the hospital. "Sorry to have asked."

"I tell you what we do need, though …"

"Yes?"

"We're paying too much for our stock. If we had someone to go up to Covent Garden a few mornings each week, and buy direct from there, it would work much better for us."

"Really?"

"Would you be up for that? You'd have to be reliable,

though. And it's a middle-of-the-night job, you know. And you'd need to do some tough bartering."

"I'm not sixteen any more, Dad."

Alf nodded. "Let's discuss it with your mother."

"OK. I need to shoot off now – I need to visit my … visit a friend in hospital."

"How's Joe, by the way? Your mother is really put out that she never gets to see her grandson. Doesn't seem fair to her."

"I know, Dad. I don't see him either, really. Two or three times a year – that's all Carol will allow. Got a photo the other day, though." He pulled out his wallet and withdrew the school photograph, showing Joe in blazer and neatly knotted striped tie, with his well-cut blond hair slicked back, giving a big smile for the camera. He had braces on his teeth and looked squeaky-clean: just the kind of lad you'd want to boast was your son. He was nothing like Darren: Gerry quickly pushed away that thought because it felt disloyal.

"Always was a nice-looking boy," said Alf. "Private school still, eh?"

"Yeah."

"Carol still with that geezer who flogs posh people's houses?"

"Yeah. She's even taken up golf now."

Alf rolled his eyes.

*

Lor lay in her cot on her back, her face flushed, her mouth open slightly. She had stopped thrashing around and now lay still as a doll. Derek looked down at her. Her eyes seemed huge.

"If you can just leave me with her for a few minutes …" said Dr Taylor, opening his medical bag and withdrawing a stethoscope.

"Yes of course," said Derek, ushering Wendy out of the door and down the stairs.

"Oh Derek, what's wrong with her?"

"Don't fret, love. Probably just a bit of fever. Let the doctor sort it out."

They'd known and trusted Dr Taylor for many years – since Sharon was born, in fact. He was an 'old school' doctor who never minded making home visits and who still wore a three-piece suit with a fob watch on the waistcoat. Derek never liked going to the doctor, though – when he was young the family never really had access to a GP, though his brothers had shown up at A&E a few times with broken wrists or broken legs. One time, Chalky had gashed his leg on a barbed wire fence trying to take a short-cut across a field and Derek, being only five at the time, had fainted clean away when he saw the cut. Chalky had put on a brave face suitable to his 'older brother' status and never even cried when the nurse put iodine on the cut.

"Let's put the kettle on," said Wendy. "Dr Taylor would probably like a cup."

They went into the kitchen but hadn't even filled the kettle when they heard the doctor thundering down the stairs. He came into the kitchen, unsmiling.

"Do you have a phone?"

"No, sorry," said Derek. "Nearest one is down the road."

"Run down there, Mr Fry, and dial 999. Tell them we need an ambulance and we need it now. Tell them I said so."

Wendy made a whimpering noise and clutched the tea towel to her mouth.

"Is it …?"

"I'll talk to you about it in a minute. Just get that ambulance on its way." He pounded back up the stairs.

Derek, his heart thumping, ran all the way down the road. The phone box, as usual, was occupied by a teenage girl, this time with one of her friends crammed into the box with her. Derek opened the door, seized them both by the collar and pulled them out.

"Oi! What do you think you're doing?"

He grabbed the handset, rattled the metal rest and dialed 999, keeping the door shut with his free hand. The girls banged on the panes, indignant faces pushed up against the glass.

*

Gerry looked through the money in his wallet. Not enough. He shoved it back into his pocket and got out his chequebook instead.

The ring wasn't the one he'd really like to have bought Tina, but it was pretty nevertheless, with a solitaire diamond in a white gold setting. Of course, he didn't know her finger size, but the jeweler said he'd be able to alter it if it was too big. Gerry thought of Tina's scrawny little hand and skinny fingers, like those of a child. She didn't wear jewelry of any kind and he hoped she'd feel able to wear this. One day, he swore, he'd buy her a whole set of jewelry. New clothes too. If he could make it work with the Covent Garden runs, they might even be able to open up a second stall somewhere else, so Gerry could build his own business.

As he wrote out the cheque and the jeweler put the ring into a box, Gerry could see Darren pacing up and down outside. He'd pulled his school tie down from the collar and untucked his shirt and Gerry smiled at the contrast between Darren and that photo of Joe. He'd made Darren wait outside: he didn't want him to know what he was doing just yet.

On the way to the hospital, Darren was chatty and bright, talking about a girl at school who he thought might fancy him. He obviously had as much interest in his lessons as Gerry had had at his age.

"Oh, by the way," said Gerry. "Don't come round the taxi place any more – I'm not working there now."

"I seen the taxi-meter was gone from the dashboard," said Darren, fiddling with the mounting that had held it. "What about the Double-A sticker?" he asked, winding down the window and leaning out to look at the side of the door as they went round the Rudmore roundabout.

"For goodness sake, get your head back into the car!"

"Sorry."

"I'm taking the stickers off tomorrow."

"Are you still going to be a driver?"

"Yes, in a way. I'm going to be driving up and down to

London a lot."

"London?" said Darren excitedly. "Can I come? I've never been."

"We'll see." He realised he sounded just like his dad. "We'll have to ask your mum. It would have to be in school holidays, but you might be able to give me a hand with my work. For pocket money, like."

Darren grinned, put his feet up on the dash and hummed to himself.

At the hospital, Tina was looking much better. Her face had some colour and the drip had been removed from her wrist. The nurse with the chip on her shoulder had evidently taken it somewhere else, and her desk was occupied by a young blonde with a curvaceous figure and a big smile. She was happy to tell Gerry that Tina would be discharged in two days' time. Gerry slipped into the flirting mood that attractive young women automatically released in him, then remembered that he was now engaged and struggled to adopt a more formal tone. He put his fingers to his lips to indicate the nurse should not say anything, then took the ring-box from his pocket.

"Oooh! Someone's a lucky girl!" she said. "Unless you're proposing to me, of course."

Over at Tina's bed, Darren was telling a complicated story about the gears on his bicycle.

"Never mind that," said Gerry, "We've got something important to tell you, me and your mum."

His face fell. "What?" he said warily.

"Me and your mum are going to get married."

The next couple of minutes were complete bedlam: Darren was beside himself with joy and excitement, hugging Tina, then hugging Gerry, and dancing a little jig on the spot.

After the boy had calmed down a little, Gerry took the ring-box from his pocket and gave it to Tina. When he slipped the ring onto her finger – not too big after all – her eyes filled with tears.

"It's beautiful, Gerry. Thank you."

"Just get well, love, then we'll set a date for the

wedding. Come on, Darren, let's go down to the machines and get us all some drinks to celebrate. Back in a minute," he said to Tina over his shoulder. She was still gazing at the ring.

They walked down the long green corridor to the lift lobby, where there were drinks machines. Darren immediately went over to gaze longingly into the display in the chocolate machine. There was another young lad there, meticulously counting out his money into the palm of his hand. His dark fringe kept falling over his eyes and he kept flicking it back. Gerry got three bottles of Coke and tossed one over to Darren who caught it one handedly.

"You should play cricket, son," said Gerry. He saw the expression on Darren's face. "What?"

"You called me 'son'."

"So I did," said Gerry, embarrassed. "So I did."

Darren grinned and flipped the bottle up in the air, making it somersault.

The other young lad had put his money back in his pocket and was starting to shuffle away from the machines.

"Hey!" called Gerry. "What's up? Haven't you got the right money?"

"No. I'm 5p short, " said the lad. "Don't matter." He had a strong Meon Valley accent. There was something familiar about him, his sharp features and the way he stood, but Gerry couldn't pin it down.

"Here – take 5p from me," said Gerry, holding it out.

The lad looked cautious.

"Mum always says I'm not to take nothing from a stranger."

"Your mum's right. I'll introduce myself, then I won't be a stranger. My name is Gerry and this is Darren. We're here visiting my fiancée, Darren's mum, just down the corridor there."

"I'm Georgie," he said, reaching out for the five pence piece. "My baby sister is ill. We're all here, all the family."

He went over to the machine, put in the money and selected a Kit-Kat. When it didn't drop down into the tray, he gave the machine a practised thump and the chocolate appeared.

"Thanks, Mister Gerry." He ripped the wrapper off the Kit-Kat and offered Darren a piece. Darren obviously wanted to take it, but looked up at Gerry first for permission. Gerry nodded.

"I hope your baby sister gets well soon," said Gerry. "Come on, Darren – let's get back."

Georgie walked away and as he turned the corner of the corridor Gerry heard him singing a snatch of the Elton John song, *Rocket Man*.

"Well, we certainly cheered him up, didn't we?"

*

The arrival of Derek's passport, the package dropping through the letterbox with a pleasurable 'thump', was a major event in the house and a welcome relief from the hours of worrying about Lor. Sharon was first to the door and ran excitedly into the kitchen, waving the envelope. Derek put down his mug of tea.

"Open it, Dad!"

"No, you open it for me, love."

Sharon carefully unsealed the package and drew out the dark-blue, stiff-backed passport with the royal crest on its cover. She turned to the first page and hooted with laughter at the sight of Derek's photograph. Georgie and Bobby came in, Bobby reaching up with sticky fingers for this alluring prize, but Sharon held it up high.

"You look like a criminal, Dad," said Georgie, leaning over to see the picture. In the image Derek was stern-faced, having been cautioned by the photographer not to smile, and a bit of hair over his right ear was sticking out at the wrong angle.

On the opposite page was his name, his date of birth, his height, and his occupation, which read 'market garden trader'. Against the line that read 'distinguishing marks' had been written 'none'.

"They should have put 'singer' as your occupation," said Georgie. "Then everyone would know."

"Don't think I'd have been allowed to wear my Stetson for the photograph, though!" said Derek, laughing. "Or to call myself 'Hank'."

"You're all set to go to Nashville then?" asked Sharon.

"Not quite. I've got to go to the American Embassy to get a visa, and to the BCMA to pick up the tickets. Pete is coming with me to London to lend a hand – he knows his way around all this form-filling. I haven't a clue. And then there's Lor ... I can't go at all unless Lor gets better."

Sharon put the passport back into the envelope. Both children were silent: only Bobby continued to burble to himself.

"She will get better, won't she, Dad?" asked Georgie eventually, drawing rings with his finger in the puddle of tea that had spilt on the kitchen table.

"I hope so, son. I really hope so. We can visit again this afternoon, after school. Chalky said he'd take us over there." He felt his voice shaking and coughed to disguise it.

"Is mum going to stay there all the time?"

"Yes. You'll have to put up with me being your dad and your mum for a while longer. And that means not playing me up. So grab your school things – the bus will be here in five minutes. I'm going to drop Bobby off next door." He picked up Bobby in one arm and a large bag of toys and nappies in the other and headed out across their scrubby front patch of lawn to the next house, where Dawn – who had a baby and a toddler of her own – was going to look after Bobby for the day.

*

Gerry and Darren arrived at 'A Lick of Paint' in Fratton Road as soon as it opened on Saturday morning. Inside, it was a bewildering array of brushes, rollers, scrapers, paint, wallpaper, paste, scissors, buckets and quite a few things that Gerry couldn't identify. They worked their way around the shop, picking out things and piling them onto the counter. The assistant, a man in his twenties with hair down to his shoulders, stayed behind the counter, yawning into his hand and making no effort to help them.

"We'll use rollers – it'll be quicker," said Gerry, picking up a gallon tin of magnolia emulsion. "Now, what about your bedroom?"

"What about it?" said Darren.

"Go over there and choose some wallpaper you like. I expect they've got stuff for boys."

The assistant raised a languid hand and pointed to the end of the display.

"And get two rolls because we'll only have time to paper one wall – we can paint the rest," said Gerry.

Darren came over to the counter with two rolls of paper that had designs of sports cars all over it.

"Good choice."

Darren grinned.

"Did you check the batch numbers?"

"What?"

Gerry explained and showed Darren how to check that the batch number was the same on each roll.

"Now," said Gerry, turning to Mr Languid. "What discount can you give me for this little lot?"

Mr Languid made a noise that could have been a scoff but hastily turned it into a cough when he saw Gerry's expression.

"Are you 'trade'?"

Gerry just stared.

"Well, shall we say ten percent for cash?"

"It's a deal," said Gerry, getting his wallet out.

Back at the maisonette, they set to work, piling what little furniture Tina owned into the middle of the lounge. Gerry showed Darren how to wash down the walls with sugar soap, which Darren declared was 'boring'.

"Don't worry – I'll show you how to use the paint roller in a minute. You can do the main part of the walls and I'll do the edging." He remembered helping his dad, whose decorating was always very organised and precise, just like the way he ran the stall. He'd taught Gerry the importance of good preparation – like Darren, he'd declared it at the time to be boring, but he now appreciated his father's good teaching, though that hadn't stopped him delegating the drudgery to Darren, he acknowledged.

By lunchtime the lounge was done and Gerry had even glossed the skirting boards.

"Shouldn't the council do all this stuff?" Darren asked, whilst painting 'MUM' in big letters on the wall of the hall that he was about to emulsion.

"Yeah, but it's no good waiting for them – you've gotta just get on with it. Take responsibility yourself." He thought of the state of his own place, unpainted and largely untended for some years, and then for the first time realised that he'd be moving into Tina's place and giving up his own flat. What would it be like? He'd not lived with anyone since Carol, and that had been like walking on eggshells all the time. How well did he know Tina, anyway? Hardly at all, he realised.

"Right – time for burger and chips!" he said. "You stay here and finish that wall – I'll nip down to the Wimpy. Do you want a Coke too?"

"Yes please," said Darren.

When Gerry got back with the food, they sat on the floor to eat it. Gerry dipped his finger into the paint and put a blob on Darren's nose. Darren was offended to begin with, then realised it was a game and put a blob on Gerry's nose. They were still laughing when the doorbell rang.

"I'll go," said Darren.

"No, I'll go. But leave it a minute. Might be a bill-collector."

The bell rang again. After the second time, the letterbox flipped open and a voice called: "Tina? I've got some sweeties for you."

Gerry looked at Darren, who looked away.

"Just the man what brings the stuff for Mum," he muttered, staring down at the floor.

Gerry got up, went into the hall and flung the door open. The bloke on the other side practically fell into the hall, he'd been leaning so close. Gerry grabbed his collar and hauled him up. The bloke was small and scrawny, with a ginger goatie beard and funny unfocused eyes. He reminded Gerry of that lead singer from Jethro Tull, the one that played the flute. Ian somebody.

"Tina's not here," he said, with his face a couple of inches from the bloke's. "What do you want with her?"

"Nothing, nothing – I'm just a friend, you know, looking after anything she needs. You working for the council?"

Gerry picked up the bloke by the collar and hung him by his jacket on the coat-rack in the hall. He went through his pockets as he was dangling there. The bloke kicked out a few times, but fairly feebly. Even his swearing was a bit mundane.

"Shut up," said Gerry reasonably. "I've heard it all before. "

Gerry extracted half a dozen bottles of pills, unscrewed the lids and threw them contents over the maisonette's balcony to the ground below.

"It was you brought her the last lot of 'sweeties' was it? The lot that has put her in hospital?"

"Me? No, that would be someone else," said the bloke. His voice was rising in pitch: he'd be pissing himself in a minute, thought Gerry. Obviously this was just the delivery boy, not the main man, who doubtless would be packing a bit more muscle.

"So who do you work for?"

"No-one."

Gerry turned to Darren, who had retreated to the lounge.

"Darren? Come here and bring the paint roller with you."

He took the paint-laden roller off Darren and rolled it up and down the bloke's clothing, from head to foot.

"That's my best leather jacket," said the bloke, helplessly.

"Not now, it isn't. And tell your boss if I ever find one of his men coming here trying to sell stuff like this to Tina, I will kill him." He unhooked the bloke from the coat-rack and shoved him out of the front door, rollering the back of his clothes and kicking him in the arse for good measure.

The bloke ran off down the stairwell.

"Jonno," said Darren as they went back into the lounge. "I've remembered now. That's his name – Little Jonno."

They looked at each other and both burst out laughing at the same time. They were both splattered with paint, with identical paint blobs on their noses, like a couple of circus clowns.

Darren had paint in his hair and was still holding his half-eaten burger with one hand.

"What must we have looked like!" said Gerry. "The decorators from hell!"

"Would you really kill him?"

"I didn't know you'd heard that. No, 'course not. Just trying to frighten him off, that's all. Your mum doesn't need those pills any more, not now she's got me. Come on – we've got a lot more to do this afternoon before we go to the hospital. And remember: not a word to your mum about what we're doing. It's got to be a surprise for her when she comes home."

"We could get some flowers too," said Darren.

"Good idea. See if you can find any jam jars or anything to put them in. Tomorrow we'll do your room and put the wallpaper up."

"I love you, Gerry," said Darren.

"Get away with you, you soppy git."

Chapter Thirteen

Getting the visa to visit America turned out to be an exhausting business and Derek was glad that Pete had come with him. It had been bad enough arriving at Waterloo station and trying to work out which tube train to catch and where they needed to change. Derek's reading was progressing well, so he could read the station names, but that didn't help with working out the route. London was so crowded and everyone seemed to know exactly where they were going.

"Have you really never been to London before?" asked Pete, incredulously.

"I've not been anywhere, really."

"Right – well, when we've got the visa and the tickets, let's take in a couple of the sights."

The intentions were good, but the queue for visas snaked out of the building and halfway down the street and by the time they reached the desk they both felt ready to pass out with boredom and hunger. The officials were brusque and unsmiling and made Derek feel guilty for applying, even though he had no reason to. Eventually, his passport was endorsed with the right stamp and Pete advised him to zip the passport into the inner pocket of his jacket.

"The last thing we want now is for you to have it stolen," he said cheerily. "Let's grab a bite to eat – we've got plenty of time before we need to be at the BCMA." He headed for the nearest pub, a crowded Victorian place called The Audley with huge ornate mirrors behind the bar. Pete ordered a large whisky but Derek shook his head at the idea of alcohol.

"Just a lemonade for me, please."

He sat at a table watching Pete chat up the barmaid – a girl with a skinhead haircut and wearing a lot of mascara - then walk over with the drinks.

"Two steak-and-kidney pies are on their way. Now, let's talk about what happens with the band while you're in Nashville. We've got two gigs – the Woolston Social Club on the Friday and a wedding on the Saturday – and Alan has told them both that you won't be fronting the band. They were a bit miffed to start with and we offered to cancel so they could find another band, but when they heard you would be on the stage of the Grand Ole Opry at the time, they were fine about it."

"I won't exactly be on the stage," said Derek. "Just visiting, I think."

"Don't be too sure."

Their pies had arrived and Pete gave the barmaid a wink as she set down the plates. She smiled at him.

"Jessie's getting agitated about covering the whole set …" he began, but Derek interrupted him.

"Sorry – but one thing I have to ask. How do you do that?"

"Do what?"

"Win over all these girls?"

Pete laughed.

"Must be my good looks." Derek tried not to smile then realised Pete was winding him up. "No, seriously – you just ask them about themselves and look like you're listening to the answers. That's the secret. Come on, Derek – you must have had loads of girls waiting for you by the stage door."

"I've never known what to say to them. Anyway, I was married to Wendy by the time I started with the band, so I wasn't really interested." He forked down the last of the steak-and-kidney pie. "Have you not met no-one you wanted to settle down with, Pete?"

"No. I'm happy just playing the field. Come on – let's go get those tickets."

At the BCMA, a small office suite amid a warren of similar offices, Derek was greeted warmly and given the air tickets and an itinerary for his week in Nashville. There would even be a car to meet him at the airport and a driver would be at his disposal for the entire time he was in the country.

"This is some prize," said Pete as they emerged onto the street.

Derek fingered the envelope containing all the paperwork.

"It all depends on Lor getting better. If she doesn't, I won't be able to go and that's that."

"They understood that. All we can all do now is pray."

Derek looked up, surprised. He hadn't figured Pete for a religious man.

*

It had been a good homecoming. Tina had cried when she saw all the things that Gerry and Darren had done at the flat. Darren made sure she noticed the bunch of carnations he'd put in the kitchen and then dragged her into his bedroom to show her his new wallpaper and bed cover. Gerry had stocked the fridge with food and bottles of beer and they celebrated with a curry that night. Tina seemed happy but ate little, just moving the food around her plate with her fork, but Gerry put that down to her still feeling weak and not fully recovered.

He stayed over that night but woke up when he heard a slight noise. It was pitch dark. He looked at the illuminated face of the alarm clock: 3am. When he turned over, he realised Tina was not in the bed. After a while, he got up and padded into the kitchen. Tina was standing barefoot on a stool rummaging in some boxes that were stored on top of the wall units.

"What're you doing?"

Tina turned around, one hand still in an open box.

"I was hungry. I thought we still had some biscuits in one of these tins."

Gerry just looked at her.

"I put them up here so that Darren can't reach them," she said.

He felt sick to his stomach.

"I can get them for you," he said. "Don't want you balancing on a stool in the middle of the night, do we?" He tried to sound light and jokey.

"No," she said, too quickly. "I can do it. Anyway, there's none here. I've already looked." She jumped down from the stool, holding onto the kitchen worktop.

"I can make you a sandwich if you want. You didn't have much dinner, did you?"

"No, that's fine. I'll come back to bed in a minute, Gerry. Just need to go to the loo first."

There was something in the pocket of her dressing-gown. Gerry told himself to forget about it. When she eventually came out of the bathroom, she got into bed and seemed to fall asleep almost immediately. Gerry lay, wide awake, for the rest of the night, finally dropping off a few minutes before the 7am alarm.

The man would come back, he knew that. Not Little Jonno, but one of the others. It was only a matter of time. And Gerry would be ready for them. In the meantime, he needed to do a thorough search of the flat.

Next morning, after Darren had gone to school, he removed the Double-A stickers from the car – they left behind a filmy residue, so that the outline of the logo was still visible – and threw the rooftop 'taxi' sign into the dustbin. As he did so, he felt a sense of relief and knew that this was not just because he was leaving the taxi business but because the police were still investigating Daniel's death and not being part of the Double-A any longer might lead the police to overlook him.

Tina still hadn't woken up, so he made himself a coffee and took it out to the car, where he made a list of all the things he needed to do, including giving notice on his own flat and seeing his dad to finalise all the details of his new job. He also needed to agree with Tina what date they would get married: he wrote it down then almost crossed it out again. He took a deep breath. This was all going so quickly: one minute she was just a casual girlfriend, the next he was marrying her. Gerry was not a man given to much introspection, but he realised that it was all wrapped up with his guilt about Daniel's death, about feeling sorry for Tina and wanting to do something for Darren, his irrational sorrow at the death of Daniel's grandmother, and his abiding hatred of a man he'd never even met: Brian Askew. What had tipped it over was that stupid cow in the hospital.

"Christ, I'm mixed up," he said out loud.

He realised that he also needed to call Carol and tell her he was getting married again – maybe arrange to see Joe so he could explain it to him face-to-face. But could he explain it to himself, even?

He looked up to find Tina tapping on the window. He rolled it down and gave her a kiss.

"You're looking better, love," he said, not meaning it.

"Yes, I feel OK today. I'm going over to pick up my Giro. Then I thought I might buy some material to make some curtains for Darren's room. Will you still be here?"

"I've gotta go and see my dad about the arrangements for the new job. Then I need to start sorting things back at my flat. "

She dangled the spare key in front of him.

"You might be needing this, then."

"Thanks," he said, grabbing the key. "You fancy fish and chips tonight?"

"That'd be great. Hey, when you move in …"

"Yes?"

"Well I'll have to tell the Social, won't I? Because of my benefits."

"True. No need to bother them just yet, though, eh?"

As soon as she'd turned the corner, Gerry sprinted back to the flat. He reasoned she wouldn't keep the pills anywhere that Darren might find them, so he started with her wardrobe.

*

"Carol? It's Gerry." He heard the clink of a glass on the other end of the line. He looked at his watch: 10.30am. Surely she hadn't started on the G&Ts this early?

"What do you want, Gerry?"

"I'd like to arrange to take Joe out for the day. Have you got your diary handy?"

Carol sighed and there was a thump as she put the phone down on the telephone table, followed by the sound of her heels clicking on the hall floor.

"I'll have to ask him if he wants to see you," she said, as if already convinced that Joe would say no.

"OK. There's something I want to tell him."

"Oh? What kind of something?"

"I'll tell you too when I come to pick him up."

Carol didn't press him any further, presumably not sufficiently interested in finding out. They agreed a date.

"What would he like to do for the day, do you think?"

"Something that costs a lot of money, I expect," said Carol. "So be prepared."

Gerry was annoyed when he hung up the phone: after all, Joe was unlikely to care whether his dad remarried or not, and Carol certainly didn't give a monkey's, as long as the alimony payments kept coming every month. Which reminded Gerry: he needed to go and see his own father, to get started on his new job.

He was just grabbing his keys when there was a knock at the front door. The bell had long since stopped working, and visitors had to rap on the glass panel of Tina's door. The letterbox flap was hanging off, too, and Gerry mentally added it to the list of things he needed to fix around the flat. Through the obscure glass, he could see the outline of a figure – female for sure, so not Little Jonno or one of his cronies. He moved towards the front door, then quickly stepped back to scoop the bag of empty pill bottles off the kitchen table and thrust them into a cupboard. On the doorstep was the plump middle-aged woman he had seen a few weeks earlier on the stairs: smartly dressed in a rather fussy fashion, she had the whiff of the Council about her. Gerry turned on his winning smile.

"Good morning. I've come to see Miss Christina Jackson," she said, not returning the smile.

For a split second, Gerry couldn't think who Miss

Christina Jackson was.

"She's just stepped out, I'm afraid. I'm only visiting, doing a few little jobs around the place."

"I'm Mrs Grimble from Social Services. I have an appointment to see Miss Jackson this morning." She put her foot over the threshold but Gerry did not stand aside to let her pass. She peered around him. "It certainly looks in a rather better state than when I last visited. She's even got a phone now, I see. May I have the number?"

"I don't actually know the number, I'm afraid," said Gerry, putting on a sincere expression, and hoping the number wasn't printed on the dial.

"And Darren Jackson – is he at school today?"

"Yes – I drove him there myself this morning."

She gave him a speculative look and Gerry realised that it had made him sound rather more than an odd-job man.

"Miss Jackson has been in hospital, I understand," she said, consulting a paper on her clipboard. Gerry tried to read it upside-down, but she hugged it to her chest.

"I don't know. Perhaps it would be better if you came back when she was here? I can't really answer any questions on her behalf and I do have some decorating work to get on with."

"I could wait," said Mrs Grimble with a tight smile.

"I don't think so," said Gerry, closing the door gently but firmly in her face. From the sitting-room window he watched her emerge from the building and get into her car, a maroon Austin 1100. Stupid cow.

After she'd driven away, he left the flat to go to Charlotte Street to see his dad. The bag of empty pill bottles lay forgotten in the kitchen cupboard.

*

The big blow-up came when the band played the Ponderosa, the South's top country-and-western venue. They'd been boosted up to the headline act instead of the support and Jessie had been pleased with that – right up to the moment that the compere, Tom Butler, said: 'Ladies and gentlemen, please welcome onto the Ponderosa stage the award-winning Hank Wesson and his fabulous band'. Jessie's toothy smile froze in a ghastly grimace and all through their set, Derek could feel her radiating hatred and bitterness. When they sang *He Don't Deserve You Any More* she seemed to spit out the words. Derek didn't know what to do – it was hardly his fault that Tom Butler got it wrong and, as for winning the competition, it was bringing the bookings rolling in.

He sang *A Good Year for the Roses* as their final number and the whistling, stamping and applause continued until they were off the stage and in their dressing room.

"That's it!" shouted Jessie. "That's the last straw!" She tried to undo the clasp of her suede waistcoat but in the end tore it off and flung the waistcoat onto the floor.

Pete opened his mouth to say something but caught Derek's eye and shut it again.

"I quit!" she yelled, sticking her face right up close to Alan's. "You hear me? I quit!"

"Don't be hasty, Jessie," said Alan, sounding calm and soothing but retreating slightly.

"Hasty, my arse! I've watched him …" She pointed her finger at Derek, who noticed that her red nail-varnish was peeling slightly. "… I've watched him suck up all the glory. He's been loving it. And now he gets to go to Nashville and I get to play at some grotty working-men's club for a lot of cloth-eared drunken yobs who wouldn't know a good country song if it bit them in the ankle. Why him, anyway? He's just a copycat, an imitator, a Meon Valley would-be American. There's not an original bone in his body." At this point she seemed to run out of steam. She finally lowered her finger that had been pointing at Derek.

"You're right, Jessie," said Derek, sounding defeated. "That's all I am. Anyway, I don't think I'm going to be going to Nashville after all." He took the strap off his guitar and placed it in the pocket at the front of the case.

"What do you mean?" said Alan. "You've got your tickets and everything, haven't you? It's all fixed."

"The baby's ill," said Derek. "She's in hospital. She

might not make it. She might not pull through."

Pete moved over and put his hand on Derek's shoulder.

"I didn't like to bother you all with it," said Derek. "Chalky knows, of course, but I told him not to say nothing." He sat down on the nearest stool, feeling a little faint after finally telling them. "You've been so good to me, Pete, taking me to get the passport and visa and everything." His voice was quavering now and he felt embarrassed.

The silence that followed should have been the time for Jessie to apologise and retract her decision to quit, but she said nothing at all: just rolled her eyes as if this was something Derek had made up just to spite her. She picked up her discarded waistcoat and walked over to Alan. She held her hand out, palm up. Alan put her £5 earnings into her hand and she turned on the heel of her white knee-length books and went out of the dressing room.

"She'll be back," said Chalky.

"Not this time," said Alan. "I've had enough of her being a drama queen. What about the rest of you?"

"You're the boss," said Pete, picking up his bass guitar. "And you're a good one, in my opinion. So, let's get packed up, shall we?"

*

The next afternoon Derek and the children all sat around the kitchen table after tea. Sharon had wanted to go out with one of her friends but Derek had told her that this was a 'council of war' and she had to attend. Bobby thought it was great and looked expectantly from face to face, wondering if they were still sitting there because ice cream might be served. Georgie hummed a tune under his breath and moved the arms of his Action Man back and forth.

"I want to talk to you all about Lor," said Derek. "As you know, I've just got back from the hospital again and your mother is still staying there with her. We saw the doctor this time."

"What did he say?" asked Sharon, trying to distract Bobby from banging his hands on the table. "Is Lor coming home soon?"

"We don't know, love," said Derek. "She's still very poorly."

"Will she die?" asked Georgie, not looking up from his Action Man.

There was a silence. Derek cleared his throat. "We hope not, darling."

"OK – so can I go and play upstairs now?"

"Wait a minute. There's something else. If Lor … if Lor doesn't get better, then I can't go to Nashville."

Georgie looked up at last and saw his father's pale and serious face.

"You've got to go, Dad. We're all so proud of you winning that competition. I'm the oldest – I can look after everyone at home while you're away."

Sharon made a tutting noise.

"What? Why are you doing that?" said Georgie.

"You're not the oldest. You're just the oldest boy."

Bobby started to wail: it was clear there would be no ice-cream tonight.

Chapter Fourteen

Gerry's first run up to Covent Garden market was scheduled for Monday morning. He was happy to just wing it, but his father had given him a detailed briefing, together with a wad of banknotes that would choke a horse. He knew which wholesalers to avoid, which to butter up and how much he could drive down the prices without upsetting them. He'd be going three times a week: his start-time was 2am and the only downside was that he'd have to use his dad's van, a fractious motor that rolled worryingly on corners and didn't have enough suspension to cushion the driver's seat from bumps and potholes. On the days he wasn't making the run to London, he'd work on the stall with his parents. Gerry supposed his dad would insist on him buying one of those brown button-up overalls to wear on the stall.

Gerry ruffled through the wad of banknotes as if they were a deck of cards and, after a bit of consideration, decided to stash them at his own flat until Monday, rather than at Tina's. He tried to block from his mind the reason why this was the right course of action. In the meantime, he peeled off a couple of fivers and went off to treat himself to a couple of new shirts from Shirt King.

The first few trips to Covent Garden were a big learning-curve for Gerry. His dad had a litany of complaints every time he arrived back with his consignment of fruit and veg. They were the wrong kind of tomatoes, the pears weren't ripe enough, or the onions were too big; he'd paid too much for the potatoes and how on earth did he expect them to sell pineapples on the stall? Part of this, Gerry realised, was just two alpha males locking horns, trying to prove who was boss, and nothing to do with the produce itself. Once he'd settled down, he enjoyed bartering for the goods and chatting to the wholesalers. It was even pleasant driving to London in the middle of the night: the roads were empty and though the van didn't have an eight-track player, it had an old radio that Gerry tuned to an all-night station. He was back in Charlotte Street by 7am and over at Tina's in time to make sure Darren went to school. He even began to enjoy serving on the stall on his non-London days, bantering with the little old ladies and doing tricks with the coins he gave them as change to make them laugh. He still hadn't told his parents about Tina.

A couple of times, some of the cabbies from the Double-A came by the stall to buy. They were a bit guarded with Gerry, so he assumed that Big Bertha had been bad-mouthing him ever since he left. Lenny was more friendly – one day Gerry took a break and went round the corner with Lenny to Cox's Hotel, the nearest pub, for a pint and a gossip. Gerry broke the news that he was getting married again.

"By the way," Lenny said, after congratulating him, "are you still living in your flat in Copnor or have you moved in with your girlfriend? Only I had a pick-up from your block yesterday and there was a patrol car outside. Your car was there and while I was waiting for my customer, the copper came out of the block and went over to the car and peered through the windows."

"I've no idea what that could have been about," said Gerry, taking a large swig from his pint to cover his discomfort. "I take a van up to London, so that's why the car's left in the car park. Not still poking around about the death of that bloke …. what was his name … are they?"

"Paterson. I don't know, mate."

Gerry looked at his watch, exclaimed in false surprise and said: "Look at the time! Gotta go, Lenny. Duty calls!"

The first thing to do, thought Gerry, was to move out of his flat.

*

It was easy for Derek to find excuses not to go and visit his parents, what with minding the stall all week and gigging at weekends, but on his father's 70th birthday – with the stall rebuilding not finished – Chalky drove Derek and the children over. Wendy was at the hospital, staying with Lor, and urged Derek to go even if only to give the children a bit of an outing. Sharon fussed around getting Georgie and Bobby ready and wrapping up the presents. The children had bought their granddad a set of handkerchiefs, just as they did every Christmas and birthday he must have had drawers full of them, still in their presentation boxes. Derek had bought him a tooled leather belt and, of course, a copy of the band's EP.

As Chalky pulled into the potholed drive, which had once been tarmac but was now mostly packed earth due to a longstanding feud with the neighbours over shared responsibility for its upkeep, Derek couldn't help comparing it all with Pete's parents' house. The only thing he couldn't understand was why Pete's parents had so much old stuff when they surely could have afforded new. All those old rugs, going bare in places, and the worn leather of the armchairs. Even the pictures on the walls looked old. In his own parents' place, everything was brand spanking new.

The bungalow had a good spread of land around it with an adjacent field where they grew all the produce, some inside a twenty-foot long greenhouse. As the car drew up, the dogs came charging around the side of the house, barking continually, until a shout from Derek's father quietened them down.

Derek supposed that in normal families, hugs would be exchanged, but his own father had never been a demonstrative man, except with the strap when the children had been young. As it was, he gave Derek and Chalky a brief nod by way of greeting and said: "your mother's in the kitchen". The children and the dogs had already raced off towards the house, Sharon carrying Bobby, who was demanding to be put down. The three men walked slowly over to the bungalow, his father's limp a little more pronounced than when Derek had last seen him. His capacity for confrontation, however, was undiminished.

"So, you been making enemies, Derek, and costing me money."

"What do you mean?"

"The stall – what did you think I meant? Somebody with a grudge, was it? Someone you upset?"

"No," said Derek, rather less forcefully than he wanted to. Why did his father always seem to put him on the spot before he'd even got through the front door?

"One of your country-and-western nutters I expect." Derek's father had always made it clear that he thought his son was wasting his time being in a band. The same venom, for some reason, was never directed at Chalky but perhaps that was because drummers were always at the back of the stage and he felt that Derek, right at the front, was 'showing off'.

"Just vandals. Probably kids."

"Well they've cost me a bundle."

"I knows, dad, but I'm paying for the new stall … and it was hardly my fault anyway."

"Hah!" said his father, closing the subject.

Derek noticed that Chalky, ever eager to avoid any bickering, had walked ahead. Maybe this wasn't the time to mention Nashville, or even the EP, assuming that Chalky hadn't already told them. He decided to have a quiet word with his mother about it and allow her to tell his dad. His father hadn't even asked how Lor was doing in hospital. A lump came into Derek's throat and he was relieved when they reached the door to the kitchen and entered into its noisy, crowded space with its smell of freshly baked cakes. He saw through the window that the children had joined their cousins in the garden, screaming and running around to an improvised game of their own making. In the kitchen, his father took a beer out of the fridge and tossed one over to Derek.

"Thanks, Dad." He looked for a bottle opener and his mother passed one to him, squeezing his hand as she handed it over.

"How's Loretta?" she said, looking into his face.

Derek found tears springing into his eyes for the first time since Lor had become ill: until now, abject fear had been his only emotion.

"We don't know yet, mum. Still very poorly."

Henry walked into the kitchen before she could reply. He was the brother nearest in age to Derek: built like a wrestler, he worked on the docks in Southampton and earned an astronomic amount in wages. He still had a way with women, though had remained unmarried. He and Derek had been so close when they were in their teens, yet now Derek felt he hardly knew him. Henry helped himself to a beer and took the top off with his teeth, a something he'd been doing since he'd been old enough to drink – in his case, since he was fifteen.

"What's this about Loretta?" he asked, idly picking up a cake from a full tray on the kitchen table. His mother rolled her eyes but didn't say anything. Derek explained about the baby, but although Henry had asked the question he didn't seem much interested in the answer. He licked the icing off his finger then wandered off into the garden. Derek glanced at his watch: it was going to be a long afternoon.

*

Gerry gave up his old flat and moved his stuff – not that there was much to move – into Tina's. Darren seemed more settled and they ate as a family every evening, even if it was mostly take-aways. Tina was still thin as a rail. There had been a row about the pills, of course. A horrible row: Gerry tried not to dwell on it but the things they had both said kept going round and round in his mind. Of course, she'd found all the empty bottles that he'd forgotten he had put in the kitchen cupboard when that stupid social worker knocked the door. The pill bottles had been everywhere: in the back of the wardrobe, under the bed, in the toilet cistern and under the sink inside a box marked 'bleach'. He'd cleared them all out and flushed all the pills down the toilet. She hadn't been angry, exactly, though she'd screamed and shouted and pummeled her fists against Gerry's chest. No, it was more like sheer terror.

"You don't need them any more," he'd said, over and over again. "I'm here to look after you now."

Tina had been hysterical and Gerry was grateful that Darren had been on a sleepover with a friend from school. Eventually, worn out with sobbing, Tina had sat on the sofa with her head in Gerry's lap. Her hands were shaking.

"I'm sorry," she'd said.

"Don't be silly – you've nothing to be sorry about. I just want to see you getting better."

"I know, Gerry. Does this mean you don't want to marry me any more?"

"Now you're the one being silly. Of course I do." As he said it, he seemed to convince himself of it. He kissed the top of her head. "I've got to tell my parents and my kid, Joe, and after that we can set a date."

"Thank you, Gerry. You're so good to me. It's just that my head hurts so much without the pills."

"It'll pass, love," he said, not knowing whether that was true or not. "Just stay strong and trust me. If anyone comes knocking when I'm not here, just don't answer the door."

"All right, Gerry."

"We're going to be a proper family - you, me and Darren. OK? We're going to do boring things like going to the pictures, eating out, having holidays. Stuff that normal families do."

Tina gave a thin laugh and Gerry tried to quell the notion that he was only doing all this because of what he'd done to Daniel Paterson; what he'd not been punished for doing. Or not yet punished.

*

Carol's new house was in Solihull, the part of Birmingham that considered itself to be 'posh', on a small estate of houses that had been built within the last few years. It had a tile-hung frontage, a double garage, and a garden with a manicured lawn and gravel drive. Net curtains were hung at every window. Gerry tugged at his new denim shirt to remove the creases and quickly ran a comb through his hair.

Darren had begged to come to Birmingham with him, convinced that he and Joe could become friends. Gerry said no – that it was too early: he hadn't yet told Joe that he was getting married again. Darren sulked for a few minutes, then retired amiably enough to his bedroom to count all the racing cars on his wallpaper.

Carol opened the front door almost immediately and Gerry glanced at his watch in case he was late. No, it was smack-on 10am. He'd been on the road for over three hours and could have done with a cup of coffee, but he didn't think Carol would offer him one.

"Shoes!" said Carol by way of greeting as he stepped over the threshold. He wondered about pecking her on the cheek, but her aura of 'stay away' was palpable. He shucked off his Hush Puppies and padded across the hall in his socks (who on earth laid white carpet in a hall, he thought?), following her into the conservatory at the back, where Joe was waiting.

"Hello, Joe," said Gerry, looking across at Joe who was sitting on the arm of a wicker sofa with his hands in his pockets. He did not get up but just nodded at his father. He looked bored already with the idea of a day out.

"So ..." said Gerry in a hearty manner, about to call Joe 'son' then deciding against it. "What would you like to do today? I thought we might go to Sutton Park as the weather's good – hike round the lakes then try a bit of canoeing, maybe. You can rent canoes there."

"Joe doesn't like the water," interrupted Carol. "Anyway, he's not dressed for it."

Joe was wearing neatly pressed grey trousers, a purple shirt and the kind of shoes that Darren only wore for school. Gerry mentally noted the fact that Joe was allowed to wear his shoes inside the house.

"I was hoping we'd go to the airport," said Joe in a small voice. Gerry was convinced he was developing a Birmingham accent.

"A pleasure flight?" asked Gerry. "That'd be fun." He wondered if he had enough money on him, remembering that Carol said the boy had expensive tastes. Then he noticed that, on the sofa next to Joe was a small leather case with a strap attached to it.

"Plane-spotting," said Joe with something that might have passed for a smile, or at least an easing of what seemed to be his permanent petulant expression.

Gerry's heart sank at the picture of tedium this conjured up but he answered chirpily: "Good idea. I'm sure there'll be a caff or something at the terminal where we can grab some lunch."

He wondered when his boy had changed into the sort of kid whose idea of a good day out was to dress like he was visiting a maiden aunt for afternoon tea and write down plane numbers in a notebook. Gerry remembered when Joe was about five he was a real rough-and-tumble lad: they used to mock-wrestle and Joe would scream with delight when he put a hold on his dad. He supposed it was when Carol moved to Solihull and moved in with what's-his-name, of whom – he noted – there was no sign, sent the boy to a posh school and felt she was moving up in the world. She still looked good, though – he had to give her that. Her figure had always been curvy but trim and although her tan had probably come out of a bottle, she clearly took good care of herself. She seemed to have a ring on every finger and noticing this made Gerry think about Tina and her engagement ring. He'd have to tell Carol about Tina when he dropped Joe back at the end of the day.

"There's a Berni Inn on the road back," said Joe, evidently with his eye on a pricey steak.

"Sounds ideal," said Gerry. Carol looked across unbelievingly at him but Gerry maintained a bland smile.

When Joe stood up, Gerry realised the boy had grown a couple of inches since they'd last met – or was it just that he'd got used to Darren and Joe was always that bit taller? He'd filled out a bit too and Gerry could see he was a chip off the old block. Joe hadn't yet called him 'dad' – but maybe he called Carol's boyfriend 'dad' these days?

The day was every bit as tedious as Gerry had anticipated, and if Joe was beside himself with excitement at seeing all the planes taking off and landing, then he was doing a good job of disguising it. There was only one pair of binoculars so mostly what Gerry saw all day was just a series of grey shapes moving up and down the runway. They sat in the 'viewing area' and after half an hour, Gerry left him to go and get a coffee. He'd offered to bring over a Coke and a Kit-Kat, but Joe said he wasn't allowed to have fizzy drinks. The café was quiet and Gerry had a bit of banter with the staff, including the only woman under sixty, and she couldn't have been far short of her pension. Still, a bit of harmless flirtation didn't hurt and helped to pass the time.

The only good thing about sitting in the terminal hour after hour was that it would give Gerry chance to talk to Joe about getting married again. He wondered whether to mention Darren or not.

"How's school, then?" he said for openers.

"All right. I'm starting Latin this year."

"Fancy! I saw 'Up Pompeii' a couple of years ago," said Gerry, about to launch into a quote from the scene with Frankie Howerd in the Roman baths, then remembering that it might not be a suitable tale for an thirteen-year-old.

Joe gave him a withering look.

"We'll be doing Virgil, I expect." He noted something down in his book and put the binoculars to his eyes again.

The stop-start conversation continued in this vein for some time and eventually Gerry just blurted out: "I'm getting married again. I thought I ought to tell you."

He was gratified that Joe put down the binoculars and turned to face him, but the question Joe asked was not the one that Gerry had expected.

"Why?"

"Well … I've met this nice lady … and …"

Joe gave a sniff of distain.

"I meant why are you getting married again when you didn't like being married the first time?"

"That's actually a very good question, Joe. I think because when I married your mum we were both very young. I've done a lot of growing up since then."

"Mum says you've never grown up."

"Well, she's probably right ... at least about the time she knew me. I'm different now. I'm more settled and I've got a good job in the family firm. I'm not driving taxis any more." Gerry felt that if he kept saying the bit about having changed, he could convince even himself.

Joe returned to his binoculars and it wasn't until they were in the Berni Inn and the boy had started tackling his mixed grill, that Gerry felt able to raise the subject again.

"Tina – that's the name of the lady I'm marrying – has got a son your age."

Joe raised his head, a forkful of sausage halfway to his mouth.

"What's his name?"

"Darren."

"That's a common sort of name," said Joe, airily. "People from council estates have that sort of name."

"As a matter of fact, he does live on a council estate, but that's a very snobby attitude to have, Joe. Me and your mother lived in a council flat when we first got married."

"But now I live in Solihull and go to a private school."

Gerry felt the old anger surging up. He put down his knife and fork.

"That's because your mother is being bankrolled by someone with a lot of money, Joe. It doesn't make you better than other people and certainly not better than Darren."

"I bet Darren hasn't got any binoculars. I bet he doesn't go plane-spotting or learn Latin."

"No he bloody doesn't! Darren's idea of a good day out is to go to the beach and the amusement arcade, and eat fish and chips out of newspaper. He likes riding his bike and having a laugh. He's got mates that he hangs out with. I'm taking him on holiday soon – to Butlin's. I would have invited you along if your mum would have let me."

Joe crinkled his nose.

"Butlins? I don't think so." He looked across at Gerry's plate. "Are you going to eat those chips or can I have them?"

Gerry's rage lasted throughout the drive home. When he dropped Joe back at his mother's house, he didn't get out of the car. Joe would tell her soon enough about Gerry getting married again. He felt angry with Joe, for what a prissy little snob he'd become, but also angry with himself, for having felt ashamed of Darren, for thinking that he didn't measure up to Joe. Now he knew different. He remembered playing table football with Darren at Brighton and the innocent joy on Darren's face, his delight when he was able to choose his own wallpaper, how thrilled he had looked when Gerry had called him 'son'. When he stopped the car at some traffic lights in Warwick, he removed Joe's photograph from his wallet and threw it out of the window. He realised he was behaving exactly as Carol accused him of always behaving – not like a grown-up – but right now he didn't care.

He channeled his aggression into his driving, hogging the outer lane in the dual carriageway stretches and banging the steering wheel with frustration when he reached Winchester and there was a long tail-back due to an accident. He decided to go the country route, and turned off towards Twyford. The roads were clear and he was soon speeding along the stretch of road opposite the Bere Forest. In the layby on the right was a brand new stall, dazzlingly white, with a new sign over the top depicting a giant strawberry. Gerry was surprised that the stall would still be open in the early evening, especially since the strawberry season was surely over. Maybe they sold other stuff too. He slowed the car: the truth was he was itching to confront Derek again, to make sure he'd done enough to warn him off.

He pulled the car to a halt rather showily, with a spray of gravel. He knew Derek wouldn't immediately recognise the car because he'd taken the taxi signs off the roof and doors, but he pulled up slightly behind the stall and then walked around the other side, noticing the tubs of carnations.

"Two bunches of your best carnations, mate," he said, leaning on the counter and looking into the stall for the first time. But it wasn't Derek behind the counter: it was a young lad - he couldn't have been more than about nine. He had a thin face and a long fringe that he kept flicking out of his eyes.

The lad took two dripping bunches of flowers out of the bucket and wrapped them quickly and expertly in paper. He held his hand out for the money.

"All on your own, then?" asked Gerry.

"No – my Dad's just gone up to the pub to use the toilet. He'll be back in a minute." The lad counted out the change. "I knows you, don't I?" he said, looking up at Gerry. "You're the bloke who gave me 5p. You were with your son."

Gerry was baffled for a moment, especially as he had Joe on his mind, then remembered being in the hospital lobby with Darren, where the young lad was trying to buy a Kit-Kat from the machine. Now he realised why the boy had looked familiar in some way – he had Derek's dark hair, thin lips and narrow face.

"That's right, I did. Fancy you remembering that."

"Dad says I've got a good memory for faces. We was there with my baby sister."

"I remember now. Is your sister better?" asked Gerry, not really interested in the answer, especially as he saw out of the corner of his eye that Derek was approaching, though a twitch of anxiety ran through him at the phrase 'a good memory for faces'. He assumed that it was this boy who was with Derek in the forest that day.

"Dad says she's over the worse now. She's still in the hospital. I hate hospitals."

Reluctant to talk to Derek in front of the boy, Gerry nodded and walked off to intercept him.

"Nice new stall, I see, Hank. Doing well are you?"

"What do you want? Why were you talking to my son?" said Derek, his face angry and set.

"Just buying some flowers for my fiancée," said Gerry, waving the wrapped bunch. "Anyway, we've met before, me and your son. At the hospital. He's a bit of a singer, too, isn't he? A chip off the old block."

"You can't do this."

"Do what?"

"Follow me around. Harass me. I knows it was you who burned the stall out, so don't deny it."

"I don't know what you're talking about, Hank."

"Why have you taken the taxi signs off?" asked Derek, nodding towards the car. "Afraid someone will recognise it?"

Gerry smiled. "Changed my job, that's all. I don't drive taxis any more. As a matter of fact, I'm in the same business as you now."

Derek looked baffled.

"Not the music business," said Gerry. "The fruit and veg business."

Derek made a dismissive gesture, as if Gerry had just made this up to rile him or distract him.

"I'm going to the police."

"No you're not."

"I've still got the tape. Why shouldn't I?"

"You still don't get it, do you, Hank?" said Gerry. 'Do you need another little lesson?' He tapped Derek with his fingers in the middle of his chest.

Derek's expression did not change, nor did he drop his eyes from Gerry's gaze.

"Your threats don't frighten me, " said Derek, whose guts were beginning to churn in abject fear. "It's what's on the tape that should frighten you." He glanced beyond Gerry, to see with horror that Georgie had left the stall and was walking towards them. "I had to pay for the stall to be rebuilt – I've got no money anyways. I've got debts … the baby's ill …"

"Oh, for goodness sake," said Gerry in exasperation, taking out of his pocket a huge wodge of banknotes that he'd got ready for the next day's trip to Covent Garden. He peeled off a number of twenties and handed them to Derek. "Just take this and shut up about the tape, OK? Let's draw a line under all this."

"What's happening, Dad?" asked Georgie, taking his father's arm.

"Nothing at all, nipper. Just having a chat," said Derek, sliding the notes into his pocket.

Gerry held out his hand.

"All square?"

"All square," said Derek, shaking Gerry's hand briefly. "Come on, Georgie – let's get packed up."

Gerry walked back to the car, wondering whether he was turning soft. He'd stopped at the stall with the definite intention of giving Derek a bit of a frightener and, if he was honest, working off some of the frustrations of the day. Then he'd ended up feeling sorry for the guy and giving him a handout. What was happening to him? 'Growing up at last – and about time too' … he heard his dad's voice in his ear. Maybe so, maybe so.

*

The day Lor came home from hospital was a joyous one. Wendy had spent the previous night with her, while Derek looked after the other children at home, and in the morning Chalky arrived to drive him over to the hospital.

"It's really good of you to do this," said Derek as he put a bag of Lor's clothes and nappies in the boot of the car.

"I was owed some leave by the Mill," he said, "so it's no problem. Anyway, it will be good to see my baby niece looking fit and well again."

When they arrived, Lor didn't look particularly fit or well. Never a particularly plump baby, she had lost weight during her illness and her skin seemed lack-lustre, but when she saw Derek she stretched out her little arms towards him, her eyes open wide. He picked her up out of the cot and held her up in front of his face. She gurgled with pleasure.

"I've done all the discharge paperwork," said Wendy, "so we can just go straight home." She looked worn out, with deep shadows under her eyes.

"What did the doctor say yesterday?"

"That she's fine, but we have to take special care of her over the next few weeks, watching for any sign of a temperature. They've given us a better thermometer to use and some special formula milk."

"Come on then," said Chalky. "Let's reunite this little one with her brothers and sister."

When they got back, Derek picked up Bobby from the neighbour's and they all waited for Georgie and Sharon to get back from school, unable to take their eyes off Lor. Chalky, having had enough of the family for one day, headed back home.

"Just as well," said Wendy after he'd gone. "I was worrying there wasn't enough ice-cream for all of us."

At the mere mention of ice-cream, Bobby stopped grizzling and sat down abruptly on the carpet to await the treat.

Sharon and Georgie arrived together, Sharon surreptitiously rolling down the waistband of her skirt so that it was a length that would not cause a ticking off again from her dad. They both whirled Lor around the room, laughing and shrieking, until Wendy reminded them that she was still recovering. Guiltily, they put her back into her Moses basket. There was a silent interlude while they all relished the chocolate ice-cream.

Finally, Georgie said: "Does this mean you can go to Nashville now, dad?"

"Well, son, I don't …" Derek began.

"He is definitely going," said Wendy, firmly.

Chapter Fifteen

Derek went through the money he would have left over once he had paid off his debts. He calculated he still had enough to buy souvenirs for the family in Nashville and some left over, particularly as the band members were all getting extra cash each week now from sales of the EP. He looked again at the card in the Post Office window. It had a picture of a Gibson Les Paul-style semi-acoustic guitar, a price and a local phone number. He would soon have to give back the guitar that Alan had lent him – and he didn't really like a solid body electric: it felt too heavy and the sound was not mellow enough for his taste. How good it would be to have his own guitar to take to Nashville, he thought. He wrote down the phone number on the back of his hand with a pen he borrowed from the girl on the Post Office counter and went to find a phone-box.

At the next rehearsal, he didn't know who looked the more surprised when he paid back what he owed. He settled with Chalky first, mindful of what Wendy had said about there always being a price to pay if Chalky did you a favour. Chalky didn't ask where Derek had found the money – just put it in his pocket and muttered "thanks, nipper". Alan raised his eyebrows when Derek paid him not only the money he'd lent to cover Derek's contribution to the cost of cutting the EP, but had also taken off the guitar he'd borrowed and handed it back.

"You've bought yourself a new one already?"

"Well, not exactly new, but new to me," said Derek. "I picks it up on Thursday so you'll see it when we play the Bitterne Park gig. It's a beauty."

"Got it on the never-never, I guess," said Alan.

Derek made a non-committal noise.

Pete refused the loan payback outright.

"Look, keep it for Nashville. You're bound to need it."

"No," said Derek, "I don't want to be in debt to nobody."

"You won't be – I'm making it into a gift instead of a loan. Buy something nice for the kids from Music City Row."

"You know, Pete," he said, as they walked out to the car, "you're nothing like I expected you'd be, that day when you first turned up to the audition."

"What exactly did you expect me to be like?"

"I don't know." Derek laughed. "I guess it was all the hair … and the clothes. But you've fitted into the band real well. And you've been wonderful to me."

"It's nothing. When are you going to tell Wendy about learning to read?"

Derek thought for a moment. "When I gets back," he said. "That's when I'll tell her. She's going to be gobsmacked. She's been wondering why I've been doing all this 'harmony practice' with you, week after week. As for the money, I told her it was part of my prize and that we won't have debts no more."

"And nothing's worrying you now, is it?"

Derek grinned. "Everything's worrying me, mate. The airport, the plane, finding my way around Nashville, the time difference …"

"But at least you don't have to fret about the baby any more."

"No – Lor's fine."

"And that other matter?"

Derek thought about pretending he didn't understand what Pete meant, but there seemed little point in it. "That's settled too," he said, more confidently than he felt.

That night, he couldn't sleep, the same thoughts whirling round and round in his head. He had tried to justify taking the money from Gerry on the grounds that Gerry had burnt down the stall, so it was only right that he should pay. But who exactly was the criminal? Gerry, because clearly he had hit that man in the forest and the man had died. But then Derek had blackmailed him about it, so the money was blackmail money really, not payment for the stall at all. A charge of blackmail would be hard to prove because he had destroyed the evidence by getting rid of the cassette tape. Perhaps that was a crime too? And then there was the question of not coming forward to tell the police what he had seen and heard: wasn't that 'obstructing their enquiries' or even acting as an 'accessory'? Derek had never had any truck with the police: it was part of the culture of travelling families, who had reason to avoid the police as much as they could. 'Never tell them nothing,' his mother had said firmly when Derek was quite small and told her had seen another child stealing from a shop. He had gone on to do some petty thieving himself, but once he started going out with Wendy, he had tried to be a better person for her sake and because he feared that her parents would not allow her to go out with him, let alone marry him, if he didn't toe the line.

It wasn't just whether he might have committed a criminal offence that was keeping him awake. He knew that by not coming forward, Derek was allowing Gerry to get away with it. He gave up trying to sleep and padded downstairs to make a cup of tea. He had taken a sneaky look at Wendy's copy of the *Southern Evening Echo* on several occasions after the issue that had announced the 'suspicious death' of a man in the forest, but as far as he could see there had been only one small story, saying something about the man's clothes having been found miles away from the scene. He had struggled to read it, but could hardly ask Pete again without arousing his further suspicions. He sighed, finished his mug of tea, put it in the sink and went back upstairs to bed, spooning himself around the warmth of Wendy's back. She stirred slightly then went back to sleep.

*

The half-term holiday at Butlin's in Bognor was one of the best Gerry had ever had. He didn't spend a single minute thinking about Joe, or wondering if he'd done the right thing about Derek, or worrying about the police, or fretting over whether Little Jonno would send some of his 'heavies' round. He just lived for the moment. They stayed in one of the chalets, part of a large quadrangle of chalets that faced a grassed patch in the centre: the accommodation was fairly basic, with toilets in a block at the end. Gerry joked that it was more like Colditz than a holiday camp and he and Darren pretended they were prisoners of war plotting their escape. They swam, played table tennis, ate together in the canteen and were cajoled by the relentless enthusiasm of the Redcoats into entering into every competition, Darren being outraged when Gerry only came third in the knobbly knees contest. In the evenings, when Darren fell asleep exhausted, Gerry and Tina would go and watch the entertainment in the clubhouse, much of it fairly naff in Gerry's opinion – but that's what holiday camps were all about, he reckoned.

Tina had put a little weight on, and the dark circles under her eyes had started to fade. At the beginning of the week, Gerry was watching her closely, fearful of another hysterical outburst - he'd packed the suitcase for both of them, so knew there were no pills in it – but although she often claimed she had a headache, she did seem to relax and by the end of the holiday he felt able to raise the question of when they were going to get married.

"Can it be soon?" asked Tina.

"Of course," said Gerry. "Oh … I need to break the news to my parents before we fix a date, though. And introduce you and Darren, of course. Maybe we can all go out for a meal next week?"

"You still haven't told them?"

Gerry shifted uncomfortably.

"I've never quite found the right moment, to be honest. What about you? I don't know anything about your family."

"I don't really have one," said Tina. "My father left us when I was just a toddler. I had a baby brother, but he died."

"I'm sorry," said Gerry, taking her hand, and turning the engagement ring round and round. "And your mother? Will she come to the wedding?"

"Not spoken to her or seen her since I was sixteen and she kicked me out. She's never even seen Darren."

"She'd love him – she'd be proud he was her grandson."

"I hope they never meet. She's a poisonous old cow, always was and always will be. He's better off without her."

"Just a quiet wedding then," said Gerry, laughing.

*

Derek hovered at Wendy's shoulder while she packed his suitcase, trying to express his willingness to help but knowing that she would brook no interference. She folded his stage gear in tissue paper and placed it carefully on the top of his other clothes. Then they sat side by side on the bed while Wendy talked through his itinerary for the week. He could read some of it, but affected a blank look so that she would not guess.

"A car is going to pick you up at the airport and the driver will be holding up a sign with your name on it. You're OK with that, aren't you, love? Then he'll take you straight to your hotel – it's close to Music Row so you'll be right at the centre of everything. It's a four-star so it should be very posh." She looked up. "Do you think they'll have those little bottles of shampoo and bath oil in the room? Could you bring them back for me?"

Derek laughed. "I think I can do better than that for a present."

"Don't go spending all the prize money on us. Spend some on yourself too." She went through the rest of the itinerary, which included a champagne reception and award ceremony at the Country Music Association headquarters, a guided tour of the local sights, and of course the highlight of the week: a guest spot on the Grand Ole Opry.

"They've left you plenty of free time, so you'll be able to choose what live music venues you want to go to and where you want to eat. I've packed the camera and two rolls of film, so you can bring back lots of photos to show us."

"I wish you was coming with me, Wendy," he said, fiddling with the buckles on the suitcase. "What if I get lost? What if something goes wrong here and I'm thousands of miles away?"

She pointed to some numbers at the bottom of the itinerary.

"This is the number for the CMA. They said you can call them anytime during the week if you need help while you're there. And I've written Cheryl's number down too, for when you phone me on the Tuesday. Chalky's taking me over to Cheryl's, so I'll be waiting by the phone. Just try to remember the time difference!"

"I just can't get my head around that," said Derek. "I'll be having breakfast and you'll be getting the tea ready … or is it the other way around?"

*

Gerry had been proud of Tina and Darren on the evening when they'd gone out with his parents. He'd bought Tina a new dress and she'd been to the hairdresser's earlier in the day. Darren had seemed somewhat in awe of Gerry's parents, probably because he'd never had grandparents of his own, but soon was chatting away like his usual bubbly self and winning them over with his enthusiasm for everything from the prawn cocktail through to the knickerbocker glory. So Gerry had been taken by surprise when he'd gone up to the bar with his father and his dad had said: "are you sure you're doing the right thing?"

"What do you mean?"

"Marrying Tina. Do you love this girl or do you just want to rescue her?"

"I don't understand."

"I think you do, son." He picked up the tray of drinks and headed back to the table, leaving Gerry to trail in his wake, unsure whether to be angry about what his father had said, or whether anger would just be covering up some other feeling altogether.

The next week was a busy one, with three early-hours trips to Covent Garden and several shifts minding the stall, so Gerry saw little of Tina. He found that, unless he was there to encourage her to clean and tidy the flat and shop for food, that these things didn't get done and he'd come home in the afternoon to find her still in her dressing gown, curtains drawn, staring at the television, and Darren out God knows where after school. An idea struck him.

"I tell you what, love," he said one evening as they ate fish fingers and chips at the kitchen table. "How about coming to work with me on the stall a couple of days a week? I'm thinking of branching out, starting a second stall that will be our own business – yours and mine."

"I don't know – I don't think I'd be any good at it."

"Course you would. You must have had a Saturday job when you were younger, surely?"

"No, I never did. I was pregnant with Darren by the time I was sixteen, wasn't I?"

Gerry reached across the table and held her hand.

"Trust me, you'll like it – and it means we can spend more time together." He squeezed her fingers, then drew his hand away as if it had been scalded.

Tina quickly put her hand under the table but Gerry stood up and grabbed her arm, pulling her to her feet.

"Stop it, Gerry! You're hurting me!"

"Where's your engagement ring? Why aren't you wearing it?"

Tina started to cry and Gerry let go of her arm.

"I'm sorry but I lost it. Must have been this morning when I went to get my Giro. It was loose, you see … and I think it must have fallen off in the road. I thought if I looked and looked, I'd be able to find it and get it back before you noticed. But I couldn't find it. Please don't be angry with me."

Gerry forced himself to sit down and bite back what he was about to say.

"I'm sorry I grabbed you like that," he said stiffly. "It was the shock, that was all. Don't worry about the ring. You can report it to the police tomorrow – someone might turn it in."

"Can't you report it for me, Gerry?"

Gerry opened his mouth to say 'yes' then shut it again,

realising that the last thing he wanted to do right now was to walk into a police station.

"No, you'll need to do it yourself." He cleared the plates away and glanced at his watch. "When's Darren due back?"

"About eight o'clock. He's with his mate Tommo trying out his new Chopper bike."

"Tommo?" said Gerry. "At least it's not Jonno."

Tina gave him a strange, calculating look, then said she was going to put the TV on.

*

"Stand back behind the yellow line, sir!" The uniformed woman was stocky, with tightly permed hair. Her face, devoid of make-up, was stern and she tucked her thumbs into her webbing belt almost as if she was getting ready to withdraw a pistol. Derek stumbled back behind the painted line, clutching his guitar case and feeling his guts churning with anxiety. The flight had been uneventful, and once they had been airborne for an hour or so, Derek managed to put out of his mind the fact that 300 people were crammed into a cigar-tube 35,000 feet above the earth, drinking beer and eating something that might possibly have been chicken casserole. The air stewardesses had been delightful and had found a special place to stow Derek's guitar, where it would be spared the ordeal of other passengers piling their cases on top of it. But after the length flight his legs felt cramped and he longed for a brisk walk to stretch them.

The official behind the desk gestured him to come forward. He presented his passport.

"Hat," said the official.

Derek didn't know what he meant.

"Remove your hat, sir, so that I can see your face properly."

Derek took off the Stetson. The only reason he was wearing it was that he couldn't find a safe place to store it in his luggage without is getting crushed.

"The purpose of your visit?" asked the official, as he finished flipping through the blank pages of Derek's passport. "Business or pleasure?" he added when Derek seemed stumped for a reply.

"I think … pleasure. I won a competition and this trip was the prize."

"Enjoy your stay," said the official in a way that implied Derek was lucky to be let in at all. He stamped the passport and pushed it back across the counter.

Derek managed to navigate the baggage hall and retrieve his suitcase with the help of a young woman who saw his bewilderment. She seemed astonished to hear his accent.

"You're from London?" she asked. "I saw the hat and the guitar and assumed you were from the US."

"South of London," said Derek, realising that Americans saw 100 miles as being like on the next corner.

"Are you famous?" she said. "Will I have heard of you?" Her voice had that Southern drawl that Derek was familiar with from country-and-western records. She had called his guitar a 'gee-tar'.

"No, I'm not famous – just in a small band in my … er … hometown."

She pulled a notebook from her handbag. It had a glittery cover and a loop to hold a pen.

"Well, can I have your autograph, just in case you hit the bigtime?"

He laughed and felt some of the tension of the flight draining away.

"Are y'all playing while you're over here?"

"I've got a guest-slot at the Grand Ole Opry – but it's just for one number, so it's all of three minutes."

"That's awesome …" She looked down at his signature. "… Hank. Good to meet you. Have a nice day now!" They shook hands and he watched her sashay away, her tight blue jeans calling attention to her pert buttocks. He looked away but couldn't resist a small smile.

That smile was quickly wiped off his face when he got to the Customs desk. After asking him whether he was bringing in any contraband goods or harboured anti-American feeling, they went through his suitcase.

"What's this?" they said, holding up an apple as if it

were a grenade.

"I didn't know that was there," said Derek. "One of my children must have slipped it into my case."

"We'll be confiscating this," said the older of the two customs men. Derek almost laughed but then realised they were serious. "You cannot import fruit into the United States of America without a licence."

"Open the music case, sir," said the younger one, who had a narrow foxy face and improbably wide shoulders.

Derek unsnapped the clasps and opened the lid. The guitar that nestled on the velvety lining was a semi-acoustic Gibson copy with a sunburst finish and twin pick-ups. The action was much lower than on his old Hofner and the whole body had a deep lustre. Even the strings shone in the harsh overhead fluorescent lights. He sighed just to see it.

"Well, well," said the foxy-faced one. "A nice piece of kit you got here."

"Thank you, sir," said Derek, wondering if the guitar would be snatched away from him like the apple.

"Alright with you if I take it out?"

Derek's heart lurched. They'd probably break it over the edge of the metal table just to make sure there was no 'contraband' hidden inside. But Foxy-Face picked up the guitar and started to play a blues lick, bending the strings and making them cry.

"Lawd, that's good!" he said, putting it back gently in its case. "Happy jamming."

"Thank you," said Derek. The older customs man made as if to strangle his younger colleague and they both laughed. Foxy-face even high-fived Derek as he sent him on his way.

*

Gerry was convinced that Tina had sold the ring, especially when she told him that her Giro had been stopped because social services had found out that Gerry had moved in. He thought he'd managed to slip off the radar, by not driving for the Double-A any more but being paid cash-in-hand by his father, and by moving out of his flat … but clearly that snooping old bag from the Council had twigged that he was not just the painter and decorator. They'd probably been spying on him for weeks. He knew that if Tina had sold the ring, then it was for one purpose only – because he took care of all the bills now and bought her stuff when she wanted it. Hadn't he just bought her a new dress? He made sure she wanted for nothing … except, of course, what she really wanted. What she couldn't do without. The words his father had used kept echoing around his brain: 'or do you just want to rescue her?'

A further search of the flat revealed nothing. Gerry was careful to put things back exactly where he found them, so that when Tina got back from the shops she would not know he'd been looking. Maybe she hadn't bought the pills yet? But in that case, where was the cash she'd got for the ring? He gave up searching the flat and went down to Fratton High Street, where there were a number of shops selling secondhand jewelry, but could not spot the distinctive ring among those in the window. He decided what he needed to do was to get Tina out of the flat for the day – and then lie in wait for her dealer. He called up Barry, an old mate who'd struck lucky (or, as Barry put it, worked his socks off) and now owned a rather spiffy beauty salon and spa on the front at Hayling Island.

When he heard the sound of the key in the lock, Gerry fixed a big grin on his face.

"Tina!" he said, hugging her. "I've got just the thing to cheer you up after losing the engagement ring."

"What?" said Tina suspiciously, still holding two Fine Fare carrier bags.

"A day at a spa on Hayling Island. Massages, beauty treatments, manicure and all that. The height of luxury. I've fixed for you to go tomorrow – I'll drive you over there in the morning. I've arranged with my dad to get to the stall a bit later, so I'll have time. It's all paid for and I know the chap who runs it, so I got a good discount." He was aware that he was gabbling on, but didn't want to give Tina a chance to find an excuse not to go.

"Tomorrow? I don't know, Gerry. I've got things to do here."

"Like what? I'll be here when Darren gets home from school, and I can bring him with me when I pick you up."

"Are you sure you can afford all this? We've only just had the Butlin's holiday, then the dinner with your parents. And then there's the ring ..."

"I'm quids in, love, so don't worry. I just want you to have a good time."

"I think I'd rather stay here. Anyway, I don't want to go on my own. Don't you want to come too?"

"Don't be silly," said Gerry, now convinced that the next day was when her dealer was due to bring the pills. "Not exactly a bloke's day out, is it? Don't you have a girlfriend who could go with you? My treat, of course – and I'm sure Barry won't mind an extra lady turning up."

"I don't have anyone, really," said Tina, dolefully.

"You'll be fine on your own. Anyway, you deserve a day of pampering and I won't take no for an answer."

*

All bloody morning he waited in. After an hour, he was bored. After three hours, he was feeling stir-crazy. He couldn't even risk going out to the corner shop, in case he missed the bloke. Tina had still been reluctant to go to the spa and Gerry had had to chivvy her along. They dropped Darren off at school rather early and drove to Hayling Island, with Tina still ticking on about how she'd rather be at home, but when she saw the place, with its marble floors and fake pillars – not to mention the Swedish-looking blond masseur who greeted her at the door – she changed her mind and gave Gerry a distracted wave to say goodbye.

He prowled around the flat, double-checking boxes he'd checked the day before, running his hand along the bottom of the drawers in the chest, and looking in the gap between the back of the wardrobe and the wall. Nothing. He'd gone through her handbag the previous night, while she was asleep. So, where could she have put it?

At lunchtime, the phone rang. He couldn't recall Tina getting a phone call before – the phone was mostly there so he could talk to her during the day in a break from the stall, to reassure himself that she was OK. Most of the time she sounded as if she had just woken up, even though it was usually early afternoon when he rang. He debated not answering, but after ten rings he picked it up. He didn't say anything; just held the receiver to his ear. After all, he didn't know who else she might have given the number to.

"Gerry?" She sounded distraught.

"What's up, love?"

"Can you come and get me?"

He checked his watch.

"I thought you were there until five o'clock."

"I can't do it, Gerry. I need to come home. Please."

Part of him wanted to tell her to get the bloody bus, but then she started to cry.

"OK, I'm on my way. Just sit down and try to relax until I get there. Is someone with you?"

"I'm in Reception – they let me use the phone. Please hurry, Gerry."

When he put the phone down, he felt sick. Was she in this state because she hadn't had her pills … or because she had?

*

Night after night, Gerry had the same dream. He was there in the forest, getting the baseball bat out of the car boot and turning to face Daniel, who was stark naked and wailing incoherently. Gerry swung the bat back like he was going to hit a ball clean out of the stadium and then swept it round in a perfect arc, hitting Daniel on the back of his head as he tried to turn away. Daniel went down like a felled tree and Gerry laughed and wiped Daniel's blood off the bat with Daniel's discarded paisley shirt. In the dream, he could see and hear everything in perfect detail: the sound of the leaves rustling in the trees, the play of light on the forest floor, the 'swish' of the bat as he swung it, and the crumpling sound of Daniel's skull as it was broken. Every time he had the dream he woke up sweating and with his heart beating wildly. Tina tried to get him to tell her what the nightmare had been, but each time he refused to say. There seemed to be so much that they could not tell each other.

Chapter Sixteen

Derek was surprised to hear that the Grand Ole Opry would soon be moving from its home at the old Ryman Auditorium into a big new steel-and-glass theatre, and that the President of the US, Richard Nixon, was scheduled to be at the opening. Derek was glad he'd caught the Ryman just in time. These boards had been trodden by all his heroes: backstage were plaques to all those Opry 'members' (the elite group of performers who were permanent Opry stars) – a kind of country music hall of fame. They were all there – Patsy Cline, Tex Ritter, Hank Lochlin … and George Jones of course. Derek was pleased and proud to be able to decipher most of the names. Wayne, the man showing him around, had told him so much about the history that Derek was finding it hard to take it all in – he just wanted to soak up the atmosphere. Wayne was stocky with slicked-back hair, well-worn Wranglers, crocodile boots and a shirt with pearl buttons that strained around his belly. He took Derek out onto the empty stage so he could see exactly what it would be like to look out at the audience. The stage was smaller than he had imagined and the auditorium with its red seats, looked like the inside of a womb.

"Now," said Wayne, consulting a clipboard. "You'll be introduced as the BCMA vocal award winner all the way from England – Hank Wesson. Is that right?"

Derek nodded.

"That's a mighty American-sounding name for an Englishman," said Wayne with a grin.

Derek shuffled nervously. "Just a stage name," he said.

Wayne clapped him on the back. "Now, Hank, the band will already be on stage and they'll cue you. They know the correct key, so don't worry about that. You'll walk on stage with your guitar already strapped on. It won't be plugged in because the band has a rhythm player, and so yours will be there just for show. There will be two microphones at the front of the stage – just move to the nearest one. Merle Haggard is on before your guest spot, so the audience will be having a good time."

Merle Haggard? Derek could hardly believe it. Merle had been one of his idols ever since *Branded Man* was released in 1967. He was 'proper' country, pure country.

"Then," Wayne continued, "as you start singing, George will walk on from stage right and join you in the chorus. He'll do harmony throughout, so you just need to keep on singing the melody."

"George?" said Derek.

"George Jones," said Wayne. "Did you not realise you were duetting with him? He's top-of-the-bill so he'll do the duet, you'll walk off stage left, and then he'll do his spot."

Derek felt like his legs might give way.

*

Back in his hotel room, which was slightly bigger than his entire house and had a bed at least seven feet wide, Derek placed a phone call to Wendy's sister in Botley. Cheryl had a phone and Wendy had arranged to get a lift over there to take the call. When Derek was put through, slightly nervous about how much this was going to cost, there was a delay on the line which made conversation difficult. They found themselves interrupting each other or leaving long pauses. Wendy assured him that they were all fine and well and he told her he'd picked up some souvenirs for the children in a tourist shop on Music Row.

"You wouldn't believe it, love," he said. "The whole street is full of recording studios, record labels, live music venues and radio stations. I went into Ernest Tubb's Record Shop just to look around – they've got everything and outside, the sign is a big light-up guitar."

"You should drop off a copy of the EP at some of those

big record label places," said Wendy.

"Nah. That wouldn't be right. I'll just concentrate on the performance at the Opry. I've got some big news to tell you about that. You won't believe it!"

"I've got to go, Derek – I brought Lor with me but she's woken up and she's crying her head off. Sorry. Tell me how it all went when you phone me on Friday. Good luck, love."

Derek felt deflated after he hung up the phone. He imagined what Georgie's face would have looked like when Wendy told him the news. He'd always shared everything with Wendy so not being able to tell her was hurtful. He thought about that for a second then realised it actually wasn't true. He hadn't shared everything – not about what he'd seen and heard in the forest, not about the burning of the stall being arson, not about the money. Not even about Pete teaching him to read.

He put on his hat and headed out of the hotel in search of a burger joint and maybe a beer.

*

Setting up his own stall at Charlotte Street had been easier than Gerry had anticipated. It was difficult for outsiders to get a pitch, but everyone knew that Gerry was Alf's son and they helped him through the application. His pitch would be right at the other end of the market from his dad's stall and Gerry was going to specialise in produce that his dad did not sell.

"I suppose this means pineapples?" said Alf.

"It certainly does," said Gerry, laughing. "And pink grapefruit. And uglis."

"Uglies? Never heard of them."

"You will soon, dad."

Alf put him in touch with a stallholder who had recently retired, and Gerry was able to buy his old stall – a proper one with big wooden wheels, a striped canopy and a fake-grass cloth for the display – at a bargain price. He enlisted Darren to help with repainting it in a glossy maroon colour; a signwriter added gold trim and the name in fancy lettering: Gerry Chandler and Family.

"That's me, isn't it?" said Darren, pointing to the word 'family'.

"It certainly is," said Gerry. "When you turn fourteen, you can work here on Saturdays if you want – it'll mean more pocket money."

"Yes please."

Gerry laughed.

"What's so funny?"

"Nothing – it's just that when I was your age I hated working on the stall. You're so enthusiastic about everything, Darren – I really love that about you."

Darren grinned delightedly.

"What about mum?"

"She'll be here with me three days a week, starting next Wednesday."

The schedule was going to be gruelling, with Gerry still doing his Covent Garden runs and then working a full day on the stall afterwards – but they needed the money and they needed to build the business.

Before that, however, was the knock on the door by the police. It came late on the Friday afternoon, when Gerry and Tina were sitting on the sofa watching TV with their feet up on the coffee table. Darren was in the kitchen, allegedly doing his homework.

"I'll go!" he shouted and had opened the door before Gerry had chance to get up. Gerry heard the unmistakable tones of the Old Bill. He went to the door.

"That's OK, Darren – I'll talk to the officer," he said, turning Darren back in the direction of the kitchen. He put his foot firmly on the edge of the front door in order to block the policeman's way into the flat.

"Gerald Frederick Chandler?" said the burly copper, the same one who had interviewed him at the Double-A, the one with a bit of an attitude.

"That's me." Gerry stood very still, waiting for the next phrase, the one about 'I am arresting you on suspicion of ….' He could sense Darren behind him, peeping through the gap in the kitchen door.

"Formerly of 406 Copnor Road?"

"Yes."

"I'm here in connection with the abduction and death of one Daniel Paterson. You'll recall that we interviewed you about this at the time?" Gerry nodded, wondering what Tina was making of all this. "A witness has come forward and we'd like you to take part in an identity parade of Double-A taxi drivers tomorrow morning down at the station. It's just routine – nothing to worry about."

Nothing to worry about? Gerry was already feeling his legs buckling under him. He cleared his throat and looked the copper in the eye.

"I'm no longer working for the Double-A," he said, in the faint hope that this might get him out of it.

"I'm aware of that, Mr Chandler, but we still need you in the identity parade for the purposes of elimination. Please be there by 9.15am."

"I'm actually due to be in London tomorrow morning, for work."

The copper just stared at him until he said: "but I'm sure I can rearrange things."

After they'd gone, Gerry stood for a moment at the door, his hand on the yale lock, to compose himself and to put the right expression on his face when he turned back into the sitting room.

"Gerry?" said Tina in a worried tone, getting up from the sofa.

"It's nothing, love. They're asking all the Double-A drivers to take part in a line-up, that's all."

"I thought he said something about 'abduction and death'."

Darren emerged from the kitchen and sat down on the arm of the sofa. Tina put her hand on his shoulder.

"I told you about it – some bloke died out in the Bere Forest and a witness says he was picked up in a Double-A cab. I've been questioned about it already."

"I don't think you did tell me. In fact I'm sure you didn't. And did you know anything about it?"

"Of course not," said Gerry, fiddling with the pile of

magazines on the table next to the sofa and not meeting Tina's eye. "Probably wasn't even one of our cabs."

"And it wasn't anything to do with that thing you asked Darren to do?"

"What thing?"

"Getting the registration number of that man who was taking the cab firm's business."

"No – that all came to nothing in the end. I passed the number on to Big Bertha, but I think the guy got bored with doing it." He shot a quick glance at Darren, but the boy was picking at a thread in the arm of the sofa and not looking at him. He was glad that Darren didn't ever see the *Portsmouth Evening News* or he might have recognised Daniel's photograph as the man in the taxi that picked him up. Darren hated the TV news too, and always walked out of the room if it came on.

"Only ..." Tina paused.

"What?"

"Darren – go and finish your homework in the kitchen," said Tina. "You can't possibly have done it all by now."

"Oh, mum! I have!"

"Well go and look over it again and then we'll get the tea."

Darren slouched reluctantly off to the kitchen and Tina pushed the door closed with her foot.

"You've been shouting out in your sleep these past few weeks, Gerry."

He laughed.

"Nah! Been sleeping like a log."

"Thrashing around, pulling the bedclothes about. Crying, too, sometimes."

"What have I been shouting then?" He tried to sound jokey. "Hope I wasn't calling out another bird's name!" He didn't really want to know what he'd been shouting but it would have looked odd if he hadn't asked.

"The words are all muddled – I can't understand them. It just sounds like you're frightened, like something's after you."

"A monster maybe! It's probably just the worry about

changing jobs, starting the new business. Getting married –
now that would frighten any man!"

"Get away with you, Gerry," she said, laughing. "You're
sure there's nothing else worrying you?"

"Not a thing, my love," he said, kissing her.
"Everything's coming up roses. Let's get the tea and feed
that hungry monster in the kitchen. Then I want to talk to
you about our wedding reception – I've booked this really
great band. They're called Smith & Wesson. You'll love
them."

*

Because of the show the following evening, Derek was
determined to have an early night. Sleeping had been hard;
the unaccustomed hum of the air conditioning unit had kept
him awake – that and what he supposed was jet-lag.

He went for a beer in a tavern that was so dimly lit that
he could barely see where the bar was. There were stools
around the horse-shoe shaped bar and he fumbled his way
onto one of them. He could just about make out booths
around the edge of the room and a tiny stage in the corner,
with PA, drums and instruments already set up. He lit a
cigarette and wondered what beer to try. They all seemed
too gassy. Eventually he ordered a Pabst Blue Ribbon. He
took off his hat and placed it on the bar. Almost everyone in
town seemed to wear a Stetson and he knew enough about
cowboy etiquette – or maybe wannabe cowboy etiquette –
to place the hat crown-down.

"You here on a visit?" asked the man on the next
barstool. He was in his fifties and had a rugged face with a
graying moustache. Maybe the cowboy trick with the hat
hadn't worked after all, as he was immediately pegged as a
tourist.

"Yes, I'm over here from England," said Derek.

"England? I don't suppose you know my cousin, do ya?
Name's Curt Stevens and he works in London somewhere."

This wasn't the first time someone had asked Derek this
kind of question, as if England was so tiny that it was
natural to assume everyone would know everyone else.

"No, sorry – I'm from a small village south of London." He took a sip of the ice-cold beer: it wasn't bad. Emboldened, he added: "I'm here to do a guest spot on the Grand Ole Opry tomorrow night."

The man shook his hand and insisted on buying him a whiskey chaser.

"What kind of music do you play?"

"Pure country. Always have and always will."

"You don't like the new country?" asked the man, downing his whiskey in one and gesturing to Derek to do the same. "You wanna stick around for an hour – there's gonna be some country-rock types on this very stage." He nodded towards the small circle of parquet flooring in the corner of the room. "Just might change your mind."

Derek nodded just to be agreeable, and bought another beer for the man.

"You in the business too?" he asked.

"Nah, I work in real estate, selling ranches and places like that all over Tennessee. But I like to come to downtown Music City whenever I can to catch the up-and-coming acts. Look – they're coming on stage now."

Derek turned to see four men with hair down to their waist and wearing the kind of flared trousers that Pete always wore – 'loons' they were called, apparently. He remembered the postcard that he'd sent to Pete the day before. He'd printed the address carefully, though it straggled over the card and was more like something a five-year-old would do. Instead of writing a message, Derek had drawn a little stickman picture in biro of himself with his guitar on and his mouth open as if singing, and had just written 'Derek' underneath it. He'd probably be back in England well before the card was delivered He couldn't send a card to anyone else because that would give away his secret about learning to read and write.

His attention was drawn back to the stage as the drummer hit a rim shot and then made an adjustment to the snare. They didn't look like country musicians but they did have a fiddle player. He decided to listen to the first two numbers then call it a night.

At first he couldn't understand why this was called country-rock. If anything it was more like a traditional bluegrass sound, but it had an edge and a rawness that made it different. It wasn't smooth-surfaced like the stuff Nashville had been pumping out for years: it sounded more truthful somehow. Derek listened carefully when they introduced each song: they played numbers by some artistes he'd already heard of – Waylon Jennings and Willie Nelson – and some by people he had never heard of: the Flying Burrito Brothers, Emmylou Harris, the Ozark Mountain Daredevils … and a few others that he didn't quite catch. There was also a song called *Backslider's Wine* that he liked. He asked the man on the next barstool to write down some the names for him. After a dozen or so songs, the band took a break and Derek got up, rather reluctantly, said goodbye to the man and left the tavern, feeling thoughtful.

*

Gerry did his best to look bored at the police station as he was shown into a large room, empty apart from a row of metal filing cabinets along one wall. All six of the Double-A drivers were already there, plus a couple of blokes he didn't recognise. The fluorescent lights were blazing overhead, giving everyone dark shadows under their eyes and a uniform pallor. The cabbies greeted him warmly enough, and he asked Lenny who the strangers were.

"New recruits?"

"No. Policemen, I think. They always add a couple into the mix, apparently, just to confuse the witness."

Gerry noted that both men were the same height and build as him, and both had sandy-coloured hair. As he looked around the group of drivers, he began to feel nervous. They were a varied lot in terms of their physical appearance: tall, short, fat, thin, middle-aged, young … but none had Gerry's build. He fretted again about who the witness could be. He'd been turning it over in his mind all night. Surely not Hank? He was pretty sure he'd bought Hank's silence, what with the burning of the stall, then giving him money, then – the final irony – booking his band for the wedding reception. It must be someone who had seen him in the street, when he'd confronted Daniel and done that stupid swaggering walk up the middle of the road. He felt a twitch begin in the corner of his right eye.

The copper who'd come to the house entered the room, organised the men into a line and told them what the procedure was. They were to look straight ahead and not speak to the witness unless asked to do so. The witness would be permitted, if they choose, ask each man to repeat a phrase or sentence. They can also ask the men to turn sideways so that they can be viewed in profile.

He handed out numbered cards to each man: Gerry got number five.

"My lucky number," he said, grinning round at the other drivers.

"Shut up, Gerry," said Lenny, who – Gerry noted – was holding his number card upside-down.

"Just one other point," said the copper, looking sour-faced at Gerry. "The usual way we do these things is to have identity parades with men who are of similar age, build and appearance. In this case, the fact that the witness says in her statement that the man was driving a Double-A taxi, it made more sense to bring you all in."

The men muttered their agreement but Gerry was not so sure. If that was the reasoning, he thought, then why was it that the two stooges looked rather like him … and unlike anyone else in the room? He fidgeted, scuffing the toe of his shoe on the concrete floor. His eye was twitching again and he rubbed it. Had anyone else noticed it? He'd felt a certain easing of tension, however, when the policeman had referred to the witness as 'she'. Probably some half-blind old duck who'd been peering through her net curtains.

The copper finally went out the door to fetch the witness.

"It's a done deal anyway," said young Dave, the cabbie with shoulder-length hair and a figure like a rake.

"What do you mean?" asked one of the drivers.

"The fuzz already know who did it – they just go

through this rigmarole to confirm it."

Gerry gestured with his head at the two stooges in the line-up and Dave shut up.

"That's rubbish, Dave, because it wasn't none of us that abducted that geezer – we know that, don't we?" said Lenny, finally turning his card the right way up. "Must have been some other firm. No-one in the Double-A would do anything like that."

One of the other drivers sighed.

"You know that for sure, do you Lenny? How do we know it wasn't YOU?"

"Shut up, the lot of you," said Gerry.

After a couple of minutes of uncomfortable silence, during which Gerry tried to work out how best to stand so as not to replicate his usual stance, the copper ushered in the witness. All the men's heads lifted up at the sight of the young, trim-figured brunette who had walked through the door. She was wearing knee-high white boots, a navy blue mini skirt and a matching jumper. She had a round face and large blue eyes, enhanced with a generous amount of mascara. So much for the half-blind old duck, thought Gerry. This one was only about 20. She looked nervous, and although all the men were staring straight at her, she did not meet their eye, but looked at the policeman for guidance. Lenny elbowed Gerry in the ribs and smirked. Gerry ignored him.

The woman walked slowly along the line, stopping in front of each man and gazing seriously into his face before moving onto the next. When she reached Gerry, he felt the blood draining away and worried that he would faint. Instead, he concentrating on not drawing attention to himself by any body-movement or change of facial expression, keeping his gaze fixed firmly just above the young woman's head. It wasn't until she moved on that he realised he had been holding his breath.

When she reached the end of the line, she had a whispered conversation with the policeman, who told them all to turn to the left, so she could see them in profile. They went through the same process again, and once again a whispered conversation ensued.

"Listen up, gentlemen," said the policeman. Gerry thought he'd only added the word 'gentlemen' because of the presence of the young woman. "In turn, I want you to say the words that are written on this card that I will hold in front of you. Just say the words naturally, in your usual speaking voice." He laboriously wrote something in capitals onto a piece of card then walked over to number one in the line. The young woman stayed where she was.

When Gerry heard the words, he felt panic rising up in his chest.

"You're a bastard who steals other people's business," said the first driver in the line, in an expressionless and almost robotic voice.

If that's what the witness had overheard, then the police had more of a motive to work on – and the motive led straight back to the Double-A. Gerry wondered how much, if anything, Big Bertha had told the police about the vandalising of the cabs, Lenny's mugging, and the attempts to intercept and steal fares. He wondered what they had found in Daniel's car – a fake taxi sign? A meter? Certainly there would have been a radio that Daniel had used to listen in to Ginny's despatch calls. He remembered Big Bertha telling him to 'stay away from it' and he wished he'd heeded that.

They'd now got as far as Lenny, who read out the words on the card with some dramatic emphasis. Gerry almost felt like applauding. Then it was his turn. He cleared his throat, out of nervousness contemplated putting on a comic Scottish accent, but then read the words in a flat tone that was just slightly lower than his normal speaking voice. If anyone asked, he could say he had a sore throat. As he read, he glanced quickly over at the witness, who was staring intently at him. Then it was time for the two stooges to read: they both seemed blasé about the whole thing, presumably because they'd done this routine so many times before. They rattled through the words at high speed, and the witness asked one of them to do it again, only more slowly this time.

Finally, it was over and the card was put away. The copper went into a whispered exchange with the witness, and then nodded.

"Please could you confirm your identification by touching the shoulder of the man who you believe you saw that day arguing with, and then abducting, Daniel Paterson?" he said out loud.

The young woman approached the line. Gerry half closed his eyes, waiting for the moment that would signal the end of his new job, his engagement, his relationship with Daniel, his only-recently-repaired relationship with his parents. There was a gasp and Gerry opened his eyes fully.

Next to him stood the young woman, reaching out her hand to touch number 4 in the identity parade on the shoulder: Lenny. It was a brief touch, and as if it had burnt her hand she withdrew quickly and the policeman ushered her through the door, where a WPC was waiting for her.

"Thank you, everyone. You can all go home now," said the copper, and moved to stand directly in front of Lenny, so close that Lenny must have been able to feel the copper's breath on his face. "Leonard Jason Thompson, I am arresting you on suspicion of the abduction and manslaughter of Daniel Paterson."

As he began to read Lenny his rights, he took out a pair of handcuffs that were hanging from his belt. Another policemen arrived to escort the others quickly out of the room. Gerry glanced back and saw Lenny's panicked face. He was shaking his head.

"It wasn't me, it wasn't me," he was saying, then he looked beyond the policeman to Gerry and some expression came into his eyes that Gerry didn't know how to interpret. Almost a knowing look. Gerry went quickly through the door and, ignoring the other drivers, walked straight through the double doors onto the street.

He felt relief wash over him, but it only lasted a second or two, and was followed by a flush of guilt that seemed to permeate his whole body. He went straight into the nearest pub, sank onto a barstool and asked for a double Scotch. After downing it in one, he felt instantly sick. Lenny had been his mate: how could he let Lenny be arrested for something he hadn't done? On the other hand, how could he walk back into the station and make a confession? Anyway, it just wasn't fair – he hadn't even touched Daniel Paterson: he'd only meant to give him a scare, but the police would never believe that if he told them – he'd go down for manslaughter and how many years was that? He drank a second Scotch, rebuffed rather rudely the overtures of the friendly barmaid, and went out to the Gents, where he filled a basin with cold water and dunked his whole face into it. He dried it on the grubby looking roller towel and slicked back his hair with his hand.

The thing to do was to tell Tina everything. After all, they were getting married in four weeks' time – he couldn't carry on keeping secrets from her. Not secrets like this. And maybe she could tell him what he should do. He thought again about Lenny: that time they'd gone to A&E when Lenny got mugged; their many late-night chats at Pat's burger van; Lenny's pride in his son getting into technical college; his infernal whistling all the time. No, he couldn't see Lenny go down for this. He went out to find his car and started to think about how to tell Tina, where to begin. The sick feeling began to ebb away.

*

When he opened the door of the flat, the curtains in the kitchen were still drawn, but Tina often preferred to keep them drawn when Gerry wasn't there. He called out to her, but there was no reply. As he put down his car keys on the kitchen table, he noticed Darren's cereal bowl was still there alongside a green plastic robot figure out of the cereal packet. There was a half-drunk mug of coffee on the worktop, the mug that Gerry had bought Tina at Butlin's that had a big red heart printed on both sides. He touched the mug: it was cold. She must have gone back to bed after he'd left for the police station. He steeled himself for what he needed to tell her about Daniel Paterson – he'd practised how to get started on it and what tone of voice to use. Maybe she would open up too, about the pills, something he both wanted and dreaded. But then it would be a clean slate – they could start again.

He went through into the sitting room, where the radio was on with the sound turned down low. He could hear Jimmy Young's voice, relentlessly chirpy and upbeat. The door to the bedroom was open and he caught a glimpse of Tina lying on her side in bed, the eiderdown pulled up to her chin. He knelt down and planted a kiss on her forehead. She did not stir.

"Sweetheart – I'm back," he said, stroking her hair. "Everything went fine."

A strange cold feeling came over him and he grabbed at her shoulders, hauling her up from a prone position. She hung limply in his arms. He felt for a pulse in her wrist, in his panic grabbing at her roughly. There was nothing. He tried over and over before placing her gently back onto the pillow, pulling up the eiderdown again and stumbling out into the hall to call 999.

Chapter Seventeen

It was beyond a dream for Derek to stand in the wings of the Ryman Auditorium to watch Merle Haggard's set. The band was tight, Haggard was on form and the audience were loving it. Best of all, when Haggard came off stage, he squeezed Derek's arm as he passed by and wished him good luck.

Derek took a sip from the glass of water provided for him by the crew, adjusted the angle of his Stetson and got ready to walk onto that fabled stage. The announcer did a great job of building him up and all the jitters had had felt whilst waiting evaporated the second he strode from the wings like he owned the place. Allowing his 'Hank' persona to take over was what made it possible.

He stepped up to the first microphone and the band counted in the song. It was great to hear the pedal steel cut in and he decided there and then that his own band needed to recruit a permanent steel player, even if it meant a slight drop in money for each of them.

Because of the theatre lighting, he couldn't see the audience at all, but the applause washed over him as they welcomed him onto the stage.

By the time he reached the line about 'at least you thought you wanted it' he risked a glance at the far side of the stage. Surely George should have started his walk on by now? But the wings looked empty. As they went into the chorus, the lead guitarist supplied the harmony and Derek – fraught with anxiety – willed himself to concentrate and to smile. The rest of the song went by in a blur – there was still no sign of George but somehow, despite feeling hollowed out inside – Derek had got through it. He raised his hat to the audience at the end to acknowledge their applause, and strode off the stage, a sour taste in his mouth.

Wayne was waiting in the wings.

"Well done, Hank," he said. "I'm sorry about No Show George. Don't take it personal."

Derek took off his guitar.

"No Show George?" he asked. "You mean he's done this before?"

"Over and over," said Wayne. "Here's here but he refuses to come out of his dressing-room."

Derek was surprised that someone who had been on the Opry since 1956 would still have stage fright. It made George seem more human somehow.

"You sang real good, Hank, and we got some good photos of you that I'll mail to you when you're back home in England."

"Thanks, Wayne," said Derek, shaking his hand. He still felt the bitter taste of disappointment but tried to shrug it off as he walked back down the corridor to the dressing room.

As he walked he heard someone shouting.

"Get away from me, you son of a bitch. And take your fucking contract and stuff it up your ass, you hear me?" The yelling was coming from Dressing Room No 1. The door burst open as Derek went by and a young man emerged white-faced and angry, carrying a folder under his arm. As the door swung to behind him, there was a loud splintering noise and a whole panel of the door was split open, the toe of a boot poking through into the corridor.

"Goddamn it to Hell!"

Derek realised with revulsion that the voice belonged to George Jones. At that moment, the man himself burst through the door. He was red-faced, his hair was mussed and his shirt button up wrong. Derek froze, unable to look away and unable to take in what was only too obvious: George Jones was as drunk as a skunk.

"What y'all looking at?" yelled George when he saw Derek. "You that Britisher?" His voice was slurred on the word 'Britisher'.

"Yes, sir," said Derek.

"Get in here right now and have a drink with me."

Derek gripped his guitar case handle more tightly.

"Thanks, but I won't, sir."

"Wassa matta with y'all? Wanna sound like me but don't wanna drink with me – is that it? Y'all the same. Take Merle, for instance …"

Derek didn't want to hear what George was going to say about Merle Haggard. He walked briskly away down the steps and out through the stage door, his whole body shaking with shock.

*

The weeks after Tina's death passed by in a blur. Gerry felt like there was a thick glass plate between him and the rest of the world. Everything seemed to be happening at a distance, sounds and images slightly muffled. Only Darren was real: Darren who seemed inconsolable and whose grief forced Gerry to reach out and try to assuage it, though he was at a loss as to how to do this. At Portchester crematorium there were only four of them in the chapel: Gerry, Darren and Gerry's parents. He had not been able to trace any relatives and Tina hadn't seemed to have had any friends. The minister, though well-meaning, was hampered by the fact that he had never known Tina, so did his best with platitudes, which made Gerry unaccountably angry. The place always gave him the creeps anyway, and he was glad to get away after the short service and go to the pub on the corner. After a couple of pints, his dad kept putting his arm around Gerry, obviously preparing to say something 'meaningful', but Gerry shook him off. Darren had been impassive and white-faced throughout the service. In the week following his mother's death, he had asked Gerry over and over again whether it was his fault; whether it was something he had done. Again and again Gerry reassured him that it had just been an accidental overdose and that his mother had loved him very much.

"Is she in heaven now?" asked Darren.

Gerry looked into the boy's face, expecting to see a

slight smirk, as if he might be challenging or baiting him, but Darren's expression was open and earnest. He didn't really know how to reply, not ever having had much truck with notions of God and all that.

"Of course she is, son," he said. "She's watching over us both and always will be." Despite what he thought was his obvious insincerity, he felt choked and tears formed in his eyes for the first time since her death. He hugged Darren's thin frame, so the boy wouldn't see he was crying.

The new stall stood under a tarpaulin in the corner of the market. At first Gerry wanted to remove the words 'and family' because the thought of them gave him so much pain, but then he remembered Darren and left them. Darren would soon turn 14 and be able to work on the stall on Saturdays, if he chose to. Gerry still went up and down to Covent Garden: the need to earn money never went away, particularly since the Council, in their usual caring way, had issued an eviction notice on the flat, but the new stall would have to wait.

A friend of Gerry's dad rented them a little terraced bay-and-forecourt house in a back-street in Fratton. It wasn't much, but it had a small garden, and at £12 a week, it was affordable. When Darren saw what would be his bedroom, he showed real animation after weeks of passivity.

Gerry borrowed his dad's van for the day to move their stuff. While he was manhandling the double divan out of the front door of the flats, he was astonished to see Lenny draw up in his cab. Lenny didn't toot the horn or wave: he just sat there, looking out at Gerry.

Gerry leant the bed against the side of the van and walked over to the driver's window of the taxi. He gestured to Lenny to wind the window down.

"I'm on a job. Customer will be out in a second," said Lenny, unsmiling.

"Lenny, mate – I'm so pleased to see you. What happened about the arrest?"

Lenny looked as if he were weighing up whether to tell Gerry anything or not. He fiddled with the ventilation grilles on the dashboard before finally speaking.

"They released me. No evidence - just what the witness said, that's all. Not enough to bring the case."

"Well that's marvelous. It was obvious it couldn't possibly be you. They got anyone else for it?" Gerry looked over at the van at this point, unwilling to meet Lenny's eye.

"Not yet. They reckon the bloke who got done in had been the one sabotaging the Double-A's business. They found some fake taxi stuff in his car, apparently. So it was someone taking revenge." He looked straight at Gerry.

"Big Bertha in that case," said Gerry, laughing loudly. "I wouldn't want to come across *her* at night in a dark alley."

Lenny started the engine as a tall skinny man emerged from the block of flats carrying a holdall.

"You moving again already, Gerry?."

"Yeah. This is my fiancee's flat. Or at least it was."

"She walk out on you, did she? Piss her off, did you?"

"Something like that, Lenny," said Gerry, turning and walking back to the van. His heart was thumping.

*

With so much else on his mind, Gerry almost forgot to cancel the booking for Smith & Wesson to play at the wedding reception. As he was within spitting distance of the strawberry stall one afternoon, he thought he'd swing by and tell Derek in person. As he drew up, he saw that it was the nipper in the stall – Georgie ... that was his name. Derek was probably in the pub, spending the day's takings, though he didn't look much of a drinker.

"Is your dad here? he asked.

"No, he's in Nashville," said Georgie, a hint of pride in his voice.

"Nashville? You're kidding me."

"He won a competition – with his record."

"I've got his record," said Gerry. Georgie looked disbelieving, so Gerry warbled a bit of *A Good Year For the Roses*. He'd played it so many times since Tina died that he knew every note, every little guitar trill, every slide on the pedal steel. Night after night, when Darren had gone to bed, he'd sit there crying over it and berating himself for being so maudlin. He cleared his throat. "Could you give him a message?"

"Yeah, OK."

"I booked the band to play for my wedding, but there isn't going to be a wedding any more, so I need to cancel."

"Oh," said Georgie.

"You see, the girl I was going to marry – well, she died." He leaned with his elbows on the serving hatch of the stall. Georgie didn't say anything and together they listened to the swish of passing traffic and some loud birdsong from the trees behind the layby. "What about your baby sister?" asked Gerry, suddenly remembering.

"She's better. Dad thought he wouldn't be able to go to Nashville, but she got better."

"I'm glad about that. Have you had a slow day today?"

"Yeah, it's been really boring. It's the end of the season and I've hardly sold a thing all day. Chalky won't be pleased."

"Who's Chalky?"

"My uncle. He's picking me up later."

"Bit of a stickler, is he?"

"Yeah," said George, ruefully.

"How much for all the flowers you've got left?" Georgie looked incredulous as Gerry took out his wallet and removed a twenty-pound note from it, handing it to the boy. "I don't want any change."

"Thanks, mister," he said, "thanks a lot," scooping up bunch after bunch of flowers, all dripping with water. "Here – take one of the buckets to put them in."

"Tell your dad …"

"Tell him what?"

"Nothing. I'm glad your baby sister is OK." Gerry picked up the blue plastic bucket and put it into the seat-well behind the driver's seat.

*

When Derek emerged into the Arrivals hall at Heathrow, feeling exhausted but happy to be back on home turf, he didn't spot Pete straight away among the sea of faces and Pete had to wave to get his attention.

"What happened to all that hair?" said Derek, looking at Pete's neatly trimmed and shaped locks.

"Thought it was time for a more grown-up look," said Pete, laughing. "So, how was the trip?"

"Amazing. Being in America is like being in a film."

"And the Opry?"

Derek hesitated, not yet ready to talk about No Show George, even to Pete.

"It went really well. Great backing band, too. You know, we really ought to get a permanent steel player." He stopped as they crossed the airport concourse as a thought occurred to him. "Did Jessie come back?"

"No. She did change her mind but Alan refused to have her back in the band. He's not quite what he seems under that laid-back exterior, is he?"

"So, we can afford a steel player in that case."

"Will they have to be called 'Smith'?" said Pete, laughing.

"I never thought of that."

"Don't worry – Alan's already changed the name to the Hank Wesson Band. Since that article came out in Country Music World the phone has been ringing off the hook. We've got an agent now too, so Alan won't have to do all the bookings himself any more."

"A lot's happened in a week!" said Derek. He put his suitcase and guitar case into the book of Pete's car, then said: "Wait a minute – I got something for you." He reached into the front pocket of the suitcase and withdrew a bag marked 'Ernest Tubb's Record Store'. "I think you just might like this."

Inside the bag were three cassette tapes: *The Gilded Palace of Sin* by the Flying Burrito Brothers, *Geronimo's Cadillac* by Michael Murphey, and *A Good Feelin' to Know* by Poco. Judging by Pete's expression, he hadn't heard of any of them.

"It's country, but not like we plays it," said Derek. "Or not yet anyway."

Pete gave him a shrewd look and Derek could almost hear him filing away that bit of information to think about later.

"Did you pick these out yourself?"

"Well, I had a bit of help at the shop," he confessed.

"Thanks, Derek. I really appreciate this."

On the drive back they sat in companionable silence for a while. Derek wondered again whether to tell Pete about George Jones and just as he was working out what to say, Pete cleared his throat.

"I've got another bit of news, Derek."

"Oh?"

"I've met someone."

Into Derek's mind came the image of the schoolgirl who had been brought round to Pete's house by her father.

"Well, I've known her for ages. She works for the Council but in a different department. I asked her out a couple of weeks ago and we've seen each other almost every night since. I know it's early days yet, but I think she might be 'the one', Derek."

Derek was relieved that this one was clearly old enough to be at work.

"What's her name?"

"Joy. She's coming to the next gig, so you'll meet her."

"Now I know the reason for the new hairstyle," said Derek with a grin.

*

The problem with cremation, thought Gerry, was that the person just vanished. There was no grave, no headstone, where you could go and talk to them. Somehow, in his mind's eye, he had envisaged crouching down by Tina's grave, arranging the flowers and telling her about Daniel and the guilt he felt; all the things he had planned to tell her that day after the police identity parade. Reassuring her about Darren – how he would always look after him. Maybe he was remembering a scene from some film, but with the memorial gardens at the crematorium, there was nothing like that. No plaque, nothing personal. In the end he put all the flowers down under a tree, muttered something that might have been a prayer and hurried off, hunched against the wind.

Back in the car, he fretted again about Darren. Social services had already been round twice with a long list of questions: they made it clear they thought that Darren should be taken into care or farmed out to a foster family but Gerry insisted that Darren should stay with him. In the end, he hired a solicitor to be the go-between with the Council – his dad had advised him that was the best course of action, and would let life with Darren continue as normal while the case was thrashed out away from the boy. Gerry's biggest fear was that Darren's real father would suddenly pop out of the woodwork and claim him.

He started the engine. Time to get back to work.

*

Derek was close to tears to see Wendy and all the children standing in the front garden ready to welcome him home. Wendy was wearing that blue-and-white gingham blouse that he liked so much and was lifting up the baby so he could see her healthy little face, noticeably plumper than when he went away. Georgie and Sharon were each holding the end of a banner they had made and Bobby was ducking back and forth underneath it, knowing something exciting was happening but unsure what.

Georgie pointed to the crayoned message. "It says 'welcome home, Nashvil star' he told his father with a serious expression.

Derek gave a secret smile and ruffled Georgie's hair.

"Is that right, son?" he said. 'Well, that's really good."

"What have you bought us?" asked Sharon before being shushed by her mother.

"Don't worry – I've got presents for you all," said Derek, walking past them into the hallway.

That night, Derek found it hard to sleep, despite Wendy's comforting presence next to him in the bed. He looked at the alarm clock: 3am. The encounter with George Jones kept going round and round in his head, squeezing out all the good things that had happened on the trip. How could someone with a voice like his be an obnoxious, violent drunk? When George sang Derek believed it was the sound of truth, so pure and full of emotion was George's voice. But it was just a sham. He got out of bed and tiptoed downstairs to the sitting room. His LP collection was arranged on a shelf in the corner, above the record player. The albums were in no particular order but Derek knew exactly where each one was. He pulled out all the George Jones ones, pausing to look at the picture on the front. The man looked so sincere – those deep brown eyes that gazed straight into the camera, the benign expression.

Quickly, Derek slid the records out of their sleeves and piled them on the floor. He wanted to break them in half, but feared the noise would wake the entire household, so he put them into a carrier bag ready to take out to the dustbin. The coloured sleeves made him more angry the more he looked at them and he started tearing them in half. The glossy cardboard was hard to rip and he felt like crying with frustration. At that moment Wendy appeared, her slight figure silhouetted in the doorway.

"What's going on, love?" she whispered, looking at the pile of torn covers.

Derek threw his arms around her and began to sob. She steered him over to the settee and waited until his ragged breathing had returned to normal.

"Shall I make us a cup of tea?"

"No," he said, "The sound of the kettle will wake the children up."

"They're sound out. Nothing will wake them until the morning." She went out to the kitchen.

Derek wrapped his hands around the hot mug of tea – strong enough to stand a spoon up in it, which was just the way he liked it – and began to tell Wendy what had happened. She listened without interrupting.

"The thing is," he said as he finished up, "I've built my whole life around that man. I've tried so hard to sound just like him and all this time it's been a lie."

"No, it hasn't, love. George Jones has a beautiful voice and so do you. How he behaves is nothing to do with that – it doesn't take nothing away from it just because he's not a saint."

"Well it does for me," said Derek, sitting up straighter on the settee. "I'm done with George Jones." He nudged the pile of torn album covers with his foot. "From now on I'm going to have my own voice. There's something else too, but I want to tell the whole family when we're all together."

Wendy touched his hand tentatively.

"You're not leaving us, are you?"

He turned to look at her, to look at the face he loved most in the world.

"No, don't be silly. It's a good thing, what I want to tell you all, so don't go worrying about it."

*

At the next band rehearsal – their first without Jessie – Derek told them all about the Nashville trip but made no mention of George Jones. Instead he said that he was keen to take the band in a new direction.

"Have you got those cassettes with you, Pete?" he asked.

Pete, already primed on what Derek was going to do, took them out of his bag.

"There's some exciting 'new country' on the scene," said Pete. "It's been coming through for a few years now, while we've still been concentrating on the mainstream Nashville sound. Derek brought these back with him and I've been listening to them. I think this is the kind of sound we ought to be aiming for, especially the Flying Burrito Brothers."

Chalky made a face when he saw the photographs of the long-haired lads on the cassette cover.

"Hippy music? That's not what our audience want – they want to hear Hank Williams, Buck Owens, Patsy Cline,

Loretta Lynn, Jim Reeves."

"We can still play that stuff alongside the 'new country' sound," said Derek. "But we needs to give it a twist, to make us sound different."

"No, it's not for me," said Chalky buttoning his jacket as if he was about to leave. Given that Chalky still looked and behaved as if he was still in the 1950s, his reaction did not surprise the rest of the band.

"Wait a minute," said Derek. "You've not even heard any of it yet."

"I just know I won't like it, nipper."

Derek sighed. "The other thing …" he glanced across at Alan, hoping that Alan was going to support him "… is that I think we should be doing our own original material too."

"Good idea," said Alan at the same time as Chalky said "no way!"

"But who's going to write it?" asked Pete.

"I've made a start already," said Derek. "On the plane on the way back. I've only worked out the first verse and chorus so far. It's a ballad and it's called 'A New Way to be Me'."

"Go on, then," said Pete. "Let's hear it."

Derek picked up the guitar and struck a G chord.

"It's only four chords so you can join in if you want," he said. Alan and Pete picked up their guitars as Derek began to sing:

> Starting down a new road
> Don't know where it may lead
> The path that I've been on
> Has turned out to be wrong
> I need a different song.

"Now we build up to the chorus," he said. Alan and Pete were playing along by this time, Pete nodding his head to the beat as he always did.

> So hold me in your arms
> Tell me I can make it.

I'm not too blind to see
That what I really need
Is a new way to be me.

"That's as far as I've got," he said, feeling a bit embarrassed. "There'll be a key-change after the chorus, then another verse and a middle eight." No-one said anything and Derek felt a lurch of fear that the song was rubbish and that they were trying to find a diplomatic way of saying it.

"It's beautiful," said Alan. "I love it. And what it really cries out for is a nice pedal steel."

"Ah," said Derek. "I was going to ask you about that."

*

On Darren's fourteenth birthday, he had a party for a dozen or so schoolfriends at the house, including a couple of girls. Gerry had fixed up decorations, bought paper plates, and his mother had provided food and a large chocolate cake with 'Happy Birthday Darren' iced on it. Gerry was in charge of the record player and all the boys were soon leaping around to Gary Glitter, Slade and the Sweet. The girls, clearly superior beings, stayed seated in the corner, twirling their hair around their fingers and watching the primitive antics of the boys. Darren's main present from Gerry had been the record player and a stack of 45s, but after the party guests had all gone home, he told Darren he had something special for him that he had saved until last. From behind the settee he withdrew a large flat package wrapped in Star Trek paper. Darren pulled off the wrapping and looked puzzled at the contents.

"What is it?"

"It's your brown overall. Look at the pocket on the front."

"It says 'Gerry Chandler and Family'," said Darren, reading the embroidery. He then suddenly realised what it meant and a beaming smile lit up his face.

"You start work on the new stall next Saturday. You're

now officially a partner in the business," said Gerry, laughing at Darren's expression. "We're a team, you and me."

*

With Darren's help, Gerry pulled off the tarpaulin that covered the market stall and carefully dusted off the paintwork. The gold gleamed in the dimness of the warehouse. Darren ran his hand along the lettering on the side. He had already put his overall on, ready for business. Together, they wheeled the stall outside and into position and Gerry went to the van with a sack-truck to start bringing over all the produce. There were pineapples, just like he'd told his father there would be, but also mangoes, kiwi fruit, pink grapefruit, sweet potatoes and a host of other produce that Charlotte Street had never seen before.

"No call for it," had been the response of the other fruit & veg traders, but Gerry felt he knew better. Darren proved adept at displaying the merchandise, his small hands making minute adjustments to the stacking of the fruit, turning them so their best side faced the front. When they were ready for business, Darren went to get a cup of tea, carrying back two mugs of dark brown liquid, each with three spoons of sugar - 'builders' tea' as Gerry liked to describe it.

"This is great, Gerry," he said, as he took his place behind the stall and set up the stack of brown paper bags next to the scales. "I just wish mum was here to see it."

"I know. She would be so proud of you – you know that, don't you?" Gerry gave him a hug. "There's something else I need to tell you. I only just got the news."

"What?"

"I'm now your legal guardian. That means that, if they trace your real father and he doesn't want to claim you, I can apply to adopt you. You'll be my son - forever."

"So I can call you 'dad' now?"

"If you want." He glanced up to see a cluster of women surrounding the stall. "First off, you've got to serve these customers."

Darren grinned and Gerry felt a weight lift from his chest for the first time in months.

*

Wendy and Sharon sat side by side on the settee, Sharon holding Bobby. Lor had already been put in her cot and so far was sleeping peacefully. Georgie perched on the arm of a chair – he was wearing the purple Music Row T-shirt that his father had bought him in Nashville. They were all looking fixedly at Derek, who as standing, feet apart, clutching something in his hands, his jeans neatly pressed and his boots newly polished.

"You all know I've been spending quite a bit of time with Pete, our bass player. Pete's been very good to me over the last few months."

"Helping with the harmonies," said Georgie, "except you're not going to be doing those songs no more."

"Well, that's no strictly true, son. It's just that I'm not going to try and imitate George Jones any more. I want to find my own voice and write my own songs."

"Is that why you put his records in the dustbin?"

"In a way," said Derek, feeling that he was losing control of the situation and that the discussion was not going in the direction he had planned. "Anyway, that's not what we're here to talk about. The truth is, I wasn't practising harmonies with Pete. I was doing something else."

"Something secret?" asked Sharon, always keen for a bit of gossip, especially if it was about Pete.

"Yes," he said, lifting up the object in his hands. "This is a book about Johnny Cash. It's called 'Winners Got Scars Too'." He opened it. "And now I'm going to read you a bit from the first chapter."

Sharon laughed out loud and elbowed her mother in the ribs.

"Yeah, right Dad," she said. "A party trick is it?"

Derek cleared his throat and began to read, hesitant at first and stumbling over some of the longer words. His hands felt sweaty holding the book but he kept going until he had read the whole of the first page.

He looked up, expectant, and was baffled to see they were all laughing at him.

"Very clever, Dad," said Georgie. "How long did it take you to memorise all that?"

"Neat," said Sharon. "No excuses not to do mum's shopping now – she'll just read out the list and you can memorise the whole thing … just like that." She moved her hands like Tommy Cooper performing a magic trick.

Derek felt his face flush.

"No, you don't understand. I was really reading it. Pete has been teaching me to read. That was the secret."

They all laughed again, then Wendy shushed them when she saw Derek's face. She picked up the *Southern Evening Echo* from the table and handed it to him.

"Go on then, love. Read a little bit from the paper."

"I might not be able to."

"Just give it a try."

He opened up the paper at random and picked the shortest article on the page. Even then he was convinced he would fail and would never be rid of the shame he had felt all his life. This little performance in front of his family had seemed a good idea only an hour ago; now he wished it had been a memory trick after all. His memory had always been good – it had been his survival technique. He tried to concentrate on the newspaper. The headline was easy enough: 'Man falls from ladder.' He then read out the first two sentences, just focussing on one word at a time. At the beginning of the third sentence he hesitated as there was a long word that he couldn't make sense of.

"The man …" he began, and faltered.

Wendy was on her feet straight away, moving to stand alongside Derek and prompting him gently, her arm around his waist.

"Sustained," she whispered.

"Sustained," repeated Derek, "only minor cuts and …"

"And bruises," said Wendy.

He looked into her face, that dear face he'd first seen all

those years ago in the sweet shop when she was fifteen. Tears were coursing down her cheeks, but she was smiling. She held out her other arm to beckon the children over.

"We're all so proud of you, Hank Wesson," she said as Sharon, Georgie and Bobby ran over to embrace him.

*****

A Good Year for the Roses

I can hardly bear the sight of lipstick
On the cigarettes there in the ashtray
Lying cold the way you left them
At least your lips caressed them while you packed
And a lip print on a half filled cup of coffee
That you poured and didn't drink
But at least you thought you wanted it
And that's so much more than I can say for me

It's been a good year for the roses
Many blooms still linger there
The lawn could stand another mowing
Funny, I don't even care
And when you turned to walk away
As the door behind you closes
The only thing I know to say
It's been a good year for the roses

After three full years of marriage
It's the first time that you haven't made the bed
I guess the reason we're not talking
There's so little left to say, we haven't said
While a million thoughts go racing through my mind
I find I haven't spoke a word
And from the bedroom the familiar sound
Of our one baby's cryin' goes unheard

Words and music by Jerry Chesnut
Copyright Sony/ATV Music Publishing LLP
First recorded by George Jones on the Musicor label, 1970